C000319421

**Edgar Wallace** was born illegitimatel
adopted by George Freeman, a porter
eleven, Wallace sold newspapers at Lu
school took a job with a printer. He enlisted in the Royal West Kent
Regiment, later transferring to the Medical Staff Corps and was sent
to South Africa. In 1898 he published a collection of poems called
*The Mission that Failed*, left the army and became a correspondent
for Reuters.

Wallace became the South African war correspondent for *The
Daily Mail*. His articles were later published as *Unofficial Dispatches* and
his outspokenness infuriated Kitchener, who banned him as a war
correspondent until the First World War. He edited the *Rand Daily
Mail*, but gambled disastrously on the South African Stock Market,
returning to England to report on crimes and hanging trials. He
became editor of *The Evening News*, then in 1905 founded the Tallis
Press, publishing *Smith*, a collection of soldier stories, and *Four Just
Men*. At various times he worked on *The Standard*, *The Star*, *The Week-
End Racing Supplement* and *The Story Journal*.

In 1917 he became a Special Constable at Lincoln's Inn and also
a special interrogator for the War Office. His first marriage to Ivy
Caldecott, daughter of a missionary, had ended in divorce and he
married his much younger secretary, Violet King.

*The Daily Mail* sent Wallace to investigate atrocities in the Belgian
Congo, a trip that provided material for his *Sanders of the River* books.
In 1923 he became Chairman of the Press Club and in 1931 stood as
a Liberal candidate at Blackpool. On being offered a scriptwriting
contract at RKO, Wallace went to Hollywood. He died in 1932, on
his way to work on the screenplay for *King Kong*.

# When the Gangs came to London

HOUSE OF
STRATUS

This edition published in 2001 by House of Stratus, an imprint of Stratus Holdings plc, 24c Old Burlington Street, London, W1X 1RL, UK.

www.houseofstratus.com

Typeset, printed and bound by House of Stratus.

A catalogue record for this book is available from the British Library.

ISBN 1-84232-711-9

We would like to thank the Edgar Wallace Society for all the support they have given House of Stratus. Enquiries on how to join the Edgar Wallace Society should be addressed to: The Edgar Wallace Society, c/o Penny Wyrd, 84 Rigefield Road, Oxford, OX4 3DA. Email: info@edgarwallace.org Web: http://www.edgarwallace.org/

For two weeks London experienced gang warfare at its most brutal – then came a lull, until a shot echoing through the House of Commons signalled an outbreak of terror more violent than ever before.

# 1

All this began on the day in '29 when 'Kerky' Smith met his backer in the Beach View Café and put up a proposition. This was at the time when Big Bill was lording it in Chicago, and everything was wide open and the safe-deposit boxes were bursting with grands. But to cut into the history of these remarkable happenings the historian would probably choose the adventures of a lady in search of a job.

The girl who walked up the two steps of 147 Berkeley Square and rang the bell with such assurance and decision was difficult to place. She was straight of back, so well proportioned that one did not notice how much taller she was than the average. She was at that stage of development when, if you looked to find a woman, you discovered a child, or, if prepared for a child, found a woman.

One of the assistants at Clark & Gibbs called her a bathing suit girl, and meant this coarsely, but his description was not extravagant. You saw and admired her shape, yet were conscious of no part of it: there was a harmony here not usually found in the attractive. Her feet were small, her hands delicately made, her head finely poised. Her face had an arresting quality which was not beauty in its hackneyed sense. Grey eyes, rather tired looking, red mouth, larger than perfect. Behind the eyes, a hint of a mind outside the ordinary.

The door opened and a footman looked at her inquiringly, yet his manner was faintly deferential, for she might just as easily have been a grand duchess as one of the many girls who had called that day in answer to Mr Decadon's advertisement.

'Is it about the position, miss?' he dared to ask.

'About the advertisement, yes.'

The footman looked dubious.

'There have been a lot of young ladies here today.'

'The situation is filled, then?'

'Oh no, miss,' he said hastily.

It was a dreadful thought that he should take such a responsibility.

'Will you come in?'

She was ushered into a large, cold room, rather like the waiting room of a West End doctor. The footman came back after five minutes and opened the door.

'Will you come this way, miss?'

She was shown into a library which was something more than an honorary title for a smoke-room, for the walls were lined with books, and one table was completely covered by new volumes still in their paper jackets. The gaunt old man behind the big writing table looked up over his glasses.

'Sit down,' he said. 'What's your name?'

'Leslie Ranger.'

'The daughter of a retired Indian colonel or something equally aristocratic?' He snapped the inquiry.

'The daughter of a clerk who worked himself to death to support his wife and child decently,' she answered, and saw a gleam in the old man's eye.

'You left your last employment because the hours were too long?' He scowled at her.

'I left my last employment because the manager made love to me, and he was the last man in the world I wanted to be made love to by.'

'Splendid,' he said sarcastically. 'You write shorthand at an incredible speed, and your typewriting has been approved by Chambers of Commerce. There's a typewriter.' He pointed a skinny forefinger. 'Sit down there and type at my dictation. You'll find paper on the table. You needn't be frightened of me.'

'I'm not frightened of you.'

'And you needn't be nervous,' he boomed angrily.

'I'm not even nervous,' she smiled.

She fitted the paper into the machine, turned the platen and waited. He began to dictate with extraordinary rapidity, and the keys rattled under her fingers.

'You're going too fast for me,' she said at last.

'Of course I am. All right; come back here.' He pointed dictatorially to the chair on the other side of the desk. 'What salary do you require?'

'Five pounds a week,' she said.

'I've never paid anybody more than three: I'll pay you four.'

She got up and gathered her bag.

'I'm sorry.'

'Four ten,' he said. 'All right five. How many modern languages do you speak?'

'I speak French and I can read German,' she said, 'but I'm not a linguist.'

He pouted his long lips, and looked even more repulsive than ever.

'Five pounds is a lot of money,' he said.

'French and German are a lot of languages,' said Leslie.

'Is there anything you want to know?'

She shook her head.

'Nothing about the conditions of service?'

'No. I take it that I am not resident.'

'You don't want to know what the hours are – no? You disappoint me. If you had asked me what the hours were I should have told you to go to the devil! As it is, you're engaged. Here's your office.'

He got up, walked to the end of the big room and opened a recessed door. There was a small apartment here, very comfortably furnished, with a large walnut writing desk and, by its side, a typewriter on a pedestal. In the angle of two walls was a big safe.

'You'll start tomorrow morning at ten. Your job is not to allow any person to get through to me on the telephone, not to bother me with silly questions, to post letters promptly, and to tell my nephew none of my business.'

He waved his hand to the door.

3

She went, walking on air, had turned the handle and was halfway into the hall when he shouted for her to come back.

'Have you got a young man – engaged or anything?'

She shook her head.

'Is it necessary?'

'Most unnecessary,' he said emphatically.

In this way Fate brought Leslie Ranger into a circle which was to have vast influence on her own life, bring her to the very verge of hideous death, and satisfy all the unformed desires of her heart.

The next morning she was to meet Mr Edwin Tanner, the nephew whom Mr Decadon had warned her. He was a singularly inoffensive, indeed very pleasant person. He was thirty five, with a broad forehead, pleasant, clean shaven face and very easily smiling eyes that were usually hidden by his gold-rimmed spectacles.

He came into her room with a broad beam soon after her arrival.

'I've got to introduce myself, Miss Ranger. I'm Mr Decadon's nephew.'

She was a little amazed that he spoke with an American accent, and apparently he was prepared for her surprise.

'I'm an American. My mother was Mr Decadon's sister. I suppose he's warned you not to give me any information about his affairs? He always does that, but as there is no information which isn't everybody's property, you needn't take that very seriously. I don't suppose you'll want me, but if you do my house phone number is six. I have a little suite on the top floor, and it will be part of your duty to collect every Saturday morning the rent my uncle charges for the use of his beautiful home – he is no philanthropist, but there is a lot about him that is very likeable.'

So Leslie was to discover in the course of the next few months.

Mr Decadon very rarely mentioned his nephew. Only once had she seen them together. She often wondered why Tanner lived in the house at all. He was obviously a man with some private income of his own, and could have afforded a suite in a good London hotel.

Mr Decadon expressed the wonder himself, but his innate frugality prevented his getting rid of a man for whom he had no very deep affection. He was suspicious of Edwin Tanner, who apparently visited England once every year and invariably lived with his uncle.

'Only relation I've got in the world,' growled old Decadon one day. 'If he had any sense he'd keep away from me!'

'He seems very inoffensive,' said the girl.

'How can he be inoffensive when he offends me?' snapped the old man.

He liked her, had liked her from the first. Mr Tanner neither liked nor disliked her. Edwin Tanner gave her the impression of a picture painted by a man who had no imagination. His personality did not live. He was invariably pleasant, but there was something about him that she could not reduce to a formula. Old Decadon once referred to him as a gambler, but explained the term at no length. It was strange that he should employ that term, for he himself was a gambler, had built his fortune on speculations which had, when they were made, the appearance of being hazardous.

It was a strange household, unreal, a little inhuman. Leslie never ceased to be thankful that she had decided to live away from the house, and in comfort, as it happened, for most unexpectedly Mr Decadon doubled her salary the second week of her service.

She had some odd experiences. Mr Decadon had a trick of losing things – valuable books, important leases. And when he lost things he sent for the police. And invariably before the police arrive they were found. This alarming eccentricity of his was unknown to the girl. The first time it happened she was genuinely terrified. A rare manuscript was missing. It was worth £2,000. Mr Decadon rang up Scotland Yard whilst the girl searched frantically. There arrived a very young and good looking chief inspector whose name was Terry Weston – the manuscript was found in the big safe in Leslie's room before he arrived.

'Really, Mr Decadon,' said Terry gently, 'this little habit of yours is costing the public quite a lot of money.'

'What are the police for?' demanded the old man.

'Not,' said Terry, 'to run around looking for things you've left in your other suit.'

Mr Decadon snorted and sent up to his room, where he sulked for the rest of the day.

'You're new to this, aren't you?'

'Yes, Mr—'

'Chief Inspector Weston – Terry Weston. I won't ask you to call me Terry.'

She did not smile readily, but she smiled now. There was an air of gaiety about him which she had never associated with the police.

For his part he found a quality in her which was very rare in women. If she had told him that she was Mr Decadon's granddaughter he would not have been surprised. Curiously enough, her undoubted loveliness did not strike him at first. It was later that this haunting characteristic brought him unease.

He met her again. She lunched in a shop off Bond Street. He came there one day and sat with her. It was not an accidental meeting so far as he was concerned. No accident was more laboriously designed. Once he met her when she was on her way home. But he never asked her to go to a theatre or gave her the impression that he wished to know more of her. If he had, he might not have seen her at all, and he knew this.

'Why do you work for that old grump?' he asked her once.

'He's not really a grump,' she defended her employer a little half-heartedly – it was the end of a trying day.

'Is Eddie Tanner a grump?'

She shot a swift look at him.

'You mustn't cross examine me.'

'Was I? I'm sorry. You get that way in my job. I'm not really interested.'

Nor was he – then.

Leslie had little to do: a few letters to write, a few books to read and references to examine. The old man was a great lover of books and spent most of his time reading.

The second unusual incident that occurred in that household took place when she had been there about four months. She had been out to register some letters, and was going up the steps to the house, when a man she had noticed as she passed called her. He was a little man with a large, grotesque bowler hat. His collar was turned up to his chin – it was raining, so there was an excuse for that – and when he spoke it was with a distinctly American accent.

'Say, missie, will you give this to Ed?'

He jerked a letter out of his pocket.

'To Mr Tanner?'

'Ed Tanner,' nodded the man. 'Tell him it's from the Big Boy.'

She smiled at this odd description, but when she went up in the little elevator to the top floor where Edwin Tanner had his suite, and gave it to him, he neither smiled nor displayed any emotion.

'The Big Boy, eh?' he said thoughtfully. 'Who gave it to you – a little man, about so high?'

He seemed particularly anxious to have a description of the messenger. Then she remembered the extraordinary derby hat he wore, and described it.'

'Is that so?' said Mr Tanner thoughtfully. 'Thank you very much, Miss Ranger.'

He was always polite to her; never invited her into his suite; was scrupulously careful never to earn the least rebuff.

Events were moving rather rapidly to a climax, but there was no indication of this. When it came with dramatic suddenness, Leslie was to think that the world had gone mad, and she was not alone in that view.

7

# 2

'There are two supreme and dominating factors in life: the first is the love of women, and the second the fear of death – get that?'

Captain Jiggs Allerman, of the Chicago Detective Bureau, sat back in his chair and sent a ring of cigarette smoke whirling upward to the ceiling. He was tall and spare. His face was almost as brown as an Indian's from his native Nevada.

Terry Weston grinned: Jiggs was a joy to him.

'You're a chief inspector or sump'n,' Jiggs went on. 'Maybe they're takin' children for chief inspectors nowadays. First time I saw you I said to myself, "Gee, that's a kid for a detective," and when they told me you were chief inspector I just thought Scotland Yard had gone plumb crazy. How old are you now, Terry?'

'Thirty five.'

Jiggs' nose concertina'd.

'That's a lie! If you're more'n twenty three I don't know anything.'

Terry chuckled.

'Every year you come to Scotland Yard you pull that crack – and it isn't even getting stale. You were telling me about the dominating factors of life.'

'Sure – Women and death.' Jiggs nodded violently. 'The first have been a racket for years, but up to now only doctors an' funeral parlours have exploited the second. But that racket's on the jig, Terry – I'm telling you!'

'I'd hate to believe it,' said Terry Weston, 'and, I'll be interested to know just why you say that.'

Jiggs shifted his lank form into a more comfortable position.

'I've got nothing to go on: it's just instinct,' he said. 'The only thing I can tell you is that rackets are profitable. They're easy money. In the United States of America, my dear native land, umpteen billions a year are spent by the citizens for protection. What's a good racket in the United States must be a good racket in England, or in France, Germany – anywhere you like.'

Terry Watson shook his head.

'I don't know how to put it to you – ' he began.

'Fire away, if you have anything to say about law enforcement.'

'I was thinking of prohibition for the moment,' said Terry.

Jiggs sniffed.

'Bit tough that we can't enforce prohibition, ain't it? I suppose it couldn't happen in this country – that there'd be a law that the police couldn't enforce?'

'I don't think it's possible,' said Terry, and Jiggs Allerman laughed silently.

'Ever heard of the Street Betting Act?'

Terry winced.

'There's a law, isn't there? Maybe it's not called that, but it's against the law to bet on the streets, and if a fellow's pinched he's fined and maybe goes to prison. And a thousand million dollars changes hands every year – on the streets. And when you're talking about prohibition, turn your brilliant intellect in that direction, will you? No, Terry, where human nature is human nature, the thing that goes for one goes for all. I can tell you, they've been prospecting in England, some of the big boys in Chicago and New York, and when those guys get busy they go in with both feet. Your little crooks think in tenners, your big men think in thousands and don't often get at 'em. But the crowd I've been dealing with work to eight figures in dollars. Last year they opened a new territory and spent two million dollars seeding it down. No crops came up, so they sold the farm – I'm speaking metaphorically. I mean they cut their losses. That makes you stare. And here's London, England. They could take out a hundred million dollars every year and you'd hardly know they were gone.'

It was Jiggs Allerman's favourite argument. He had used it before, and Terry had combated it glibly, though this peculiar type of crime would have fallen within his province, for at the time he controlled that department of Scotland Yard which dealt exclusively with specialised felony.

He went out to lunch with his visitor, and a lunch with Jiggs Allerman was an additional stripe to his education.

It was in the Carlton Grill that he saw Mr Elijah Decadon and pointed him out.

'That's the meanest millionaire in the world.'

'I could match him,' said Jiggs. 'Who's the dark fellow with him? He seems kind of familiar to me.'

'That's his nephew. You might know him; he lived in Chicago. Not on the records by any chance?' he asked sarcastically.

Jiggs shook his head.

'No, sir. None of the best crooks are. That surprises you, that the big fellers behind the rackets have never seen the inside of a police station? I've got him! Tanner – that's his name, Ed Tanner, playboy, and a regular fellow.'

'Does that mean he's good or bad?'

'It means he's just what he is,' said Jiggs. 'I often wondered where he got his money. His uncle's a millionaire, eh?'

'He didn't get it from him,' said Terry grimly.

Jiggs shook his head.

'You never know.'

Mr Decadon, that severe old man, sat bolt upright in his chair, his frugal lunch before him, his eyes fixed malignantly upon his sister's son. Elijah Decadon was an unusually tall man, powerfully built, and, for his age, remarkably well preserved. His straight, ugly mouth, his big, powerful nose, his shaggy grey eyebrows, were familiar to every London restaurateur. The threepence he left behind for the waiter was as much a part of him as his inevitable dispute over the bill. The bill was not bothering him now.

'You understand, Mr Edwin Tanner, that the money I have I keep. I want none of your wildcat American schemes for making quick money.'

'There's no reason why you should go in for it Uncle Elijah,' said the other good humouredly, 'but I had private advice about his oil field, and it looks to be good to me. It doesn't benefit me a penny whether you go in or whether you stay out. I thought you were a gambler.'

'I'm not your kind of gambler,' growled Elijah Decadon.

The two men sitting at the other side of the room saw him leave, and thought there had been a quarrel.

'I wonder what those two guys had a talk about. No, I don't know Decadon – I know Ed. He's the biggest psychologist in the United States, believe me, and – Suffering snakes! Here's the Big Boy himself!'

A man had come into the dining room. He was very thin, of middle height, and perfectly tailored in a large-pattern grey check. His hair was close-cropped; his long, emaciated face, seamed and lined from eye to jaw, was not pleasant to look upon, and the two scars that ran diagonally down the left side of his face did not add to his attractiveness.

Jiggs whistled. He was sitting bolt upright, his eyes bright and eager.

'The Big Boy himself! Now what in the name of heck...'

'Who is he?' asked Terry.

'You ought to know him. He'll be over here in a minute.'

'He didn't see you – ' began Terry.

'I was the first man in the room he saw, believe me! That guy sees all the pins on the floor. Never heard of him? "Kerky" Smith – or Albuquerque Smith – or Alfred J Smith, just according whether you know him or read about him.'

Mr Kerky Smith strolled aimlessly along the room, and suddenly, with an exaggerated lift of his eyebrows, caught Mr Tanner's eye. Ed Tanner was smiling.

Kerky was leaning on the table, looking down at his fellow customer. On his thin lips was a peculiarly knowing smile.

'Heard you were in the bread line. Caught in the market for two million, someone told me. Staying long?'

Ed leaned back in his chair. He was chewing a toothpick.

'Just about as long as I darn well please,' he said pleasantly. 'Jiggs is having an eyeful.'

Kerky Smith nodded.

'Yeah. I seen him – damn rat! Who's the guy he's talking to?'

'A Scotland Yard fellow.'

Kerky Smith drew himself up and laid his long, slim paw on Ed's shoulder.

'You're going to be a good boy, ain't you – stand in or get out. You'll want a lot of money for this racket, Ed – more money than you've got, boy.'

A friendly pat, and he was strolling over to where Allerman sat.

'Why, Jiggs!'

He hastened forward, his face beaming. Jiggs Allerman kicked out a chair.

'Sit down, you yellow thief,' he said calmly. 'What are you doing in London? The British Government issue visas pretty carelessly, I guess.'

Kerky smiled. He had a beautiful set of teeth, many of which were gold-plated.

'Wouldn't you say a thing like that! You might introduce me to your boyfriend.'

'He knows all about you. Meet Chief Inspector Terry Weston. If you stay long enough he'll know you by your fingerprints. What's the racket, Kerky?'

'Lo, Kerky,' he said. 'When did you get in? Well, who would have expected to see you?'

He held out his hand. Kerky shook it limply.

'Will you sit down?'

'Staying long?' asked Kerky, ignoring the invitation.

'I come over here every two years. My uncle lives here.'

'Is that so?' Kerky Smith's voice was almost sympathetic. 'Left Chicago in a hurry, didn't you, Ed?'

'Not so,' said the other coolly.

Kerky shrugged his thin shoulders.

'Listen, chief, would I be here on a racket? This is my vacation, and I'm just over looking around for likely propositions. I've been bearing the market, and how! I make my money that way. I'm not like you Chicago coppers – taking a cut from the racketeer and pretending you're chasing him.'

Into Jiggs Allerman's eye came a look that was half stone and half fire.

'Some day I'll be grilling you, Big Boy, up at police headquarters, and I'll remember what you say.'

Kerky Smith flashed a golden smile.

'Listen, chief, you take me all wrong. Can't you stand a joke! I'm all for law and order. Why, I saved your life once. Some of them North Side hoodlums was going to give you the works, and I got in touch with a pal who stopped it.'

He had a trick of dropping his hand casually on shoulders. He did so now as he rose.

'You don't know your best friend, kid.'

'My best friend is a forty-five,' said Jiggs with suppressed malignity, 'and the day he puts you on the slab I'm going to put diamonds all round his muzzle.'

Kerky laughed.

'Ain't you the boy!' he said, and strolled off with a cheery wave of his hand.

Jiggs watched him sit down at a table, where he was joined by a very pretty blonde girl.

'That's the kind you don't know in England – killers without mercy, without pity, without anything human to 'em! And never had a conviction, Terry. He's always been in Michigan when something happened in Illinois, or floatin' around Indiana when there was a killing in Brooklyn. You don't know the cold-bloodedness of 'em – I hope you never will. Hear him talking about saving my life! I'll tell you sump'n. Four of his guns have made four different attempts to get me. One of his aides, Dago Pete, followed me two thousand miles and missed me by that.' He snapped his fingers. 'Got him? Of course I got him! He was eight days dying, and every day was a Fourth of July to me.'

Terry was hardened, but he shivered at the brutality of it; and yet he realised that only Jiggs and his kind knew just what they were up against.

'Thank the Lord we haven't got that type here – ' he began.

'Wait,' said Jiggs ominously.

# 3

Terry had hardly got to his office the next morning, when the Deputy Commissioner phoned through to him.

'Go down to Berkeley Square and see old Decadon,' he said.

'What's he lost, sir?' asked Terry, almost offensively.

'It isn't a loss, it's a much bigger thing…the girl phoned through, and she asked whether you would go.'

Terry jumped into a cab and drove round to Berkeley Square. Leslie must have been watching for him, for she opened the door herself.

'Lost something?' he asked.

'No, it's something rather serious, or else it's a very bad joke. It's a letter he received this morning. He's upstairs in his room, and he asked me to tell you all about it. As a matter of fact I can tell you as much as he can.'

She led the way into her own little office, unlocked a drawer and took out a printed blank on which certain words had been inserted in handwriting. Terry took it and read.

### MUTUAL PROTECTION

These are dangerous days for folks with property and money, and they need protection. The Citizens' Welfare Society offers this to Mr ..............................................................................

Here the name of Mr Elijah Decadon was filled in in ink.

They undertake to protect his life and his property, to prevent any illegal interference with his liberty, and they demand in return the sum of £50,000. If Mr ...........................................

Again the name of Elijah Decadon was filled in in ink.

will agree, he will put an announcement in *The Times* of Wednesday the letters 'WS' and the word 'Agree,' followed by the initials of the person advertising.

Here followed in heavy black type this announcement:

If you do not comply with our request within thirty days, or if you call in the police, or consult them, directly or indirectly, you will be killed.

There was no signature printed or otherwise.

Terry read it again until he had memorised it, then he folded it and put it in his pocket.

'Have you the envelope in which this came?'

She had this. The address was typewritten on an LC Smith machine; the type was new; the postmark was EC1; the envelope itself was of an ordinary commercial type.

Leslie was looking at him anxiously.

'Is it a joke?' she asked.

'I don't know.' Terry was doubtful. 'It came by the early morning post. Does anybody else know about this being received? Mr Eddie Tanner, for example – does he know anything about it?'

'Nobody except Mr Decadon and myself,' said the girl. 'Mr Decadon is terribly upset. What had we better do, Mr Weston?'

'You can call me Terry, unless you feel very bad about it. Of course, no money will be sent, and you did the right thing when you sent for the police.'

She shook her head.

'I'm not sure about that,' she said, to his surprise. 'I'm willing to confess that I tried to persuade Mr Decadon not to phone you.'

'That's not like a law-abiding citizen,' he smiled. 'No, you did the right thing. It's probably a bluff, and anyway we'll see that no harm comes to Elijah Decadon. I'd better have a talk with him.'

He went upstairs, and after considerable delay Mr Decadon unlocked the door of his bedroom and admitted him. The old man was more than perturbed, he was in a state of panic.

Terry telephoned to Scotland Yard, and three officers were detailed to guard the premises.

'I've asked Mr Decadon not to go out, but if he does, the two men on duty in the front of the house are not to let him out of their sight.'

He put through a second call to Jiggs Allerman's hotel, asking the American to meet him at Scotland Yard. When he got to headquarters Jiggs had already found the most comfortable chair in the room.

'Here's something for your big brain to work on,' said Terry.

He handed the printed letter to the visitor. Jiggs read it, his brows knit.

'When did this come?'

'This morning,' said Terry. 'Now what is it? Something serious or a little joke?'

Jiggs shook his head.

'No, sir, that's no joke. That's the pay-and-live racket. It's been worked before, and it's been pretty successful. So that's the game!'

'Do you think there's any real danger to Decadon?'

'Yes, sir.' Jiggs Allerman was emphatic. 'And I'll tell you why. This racket doesn't really start working till somebody's killed. You've got to have a couple of dead people to prove they mean business. Maybe a lot of others have had this notification, and they'll be coming in all day, but it's just as likely that only one has been sent out and Decadon is the bad example.'

He took the paper again, held it up to the light, but found no watermark.

'I've never seen it done this way before – a printed blank – but it's got its reason. Anyway, it's an intimation to everybody that these birds mean business.'

Terry got an interview with the Chief Commissioner and took Jiggs along with him. The Chief was interested but a little sceptical.

'We don't expect this sort of thing to happen in our country, Captain Allerman,' he said.

'Why shouldn't it?' demanded Jiggs. 'Say, Commissioner, get this idea out of your head about England being a little country surrounded by water, and that it's difficult for people to leave once they're known. This isn't an ordinary felony. When the shooting starts it'll start good and plenty, and all the theories about this sort of thing not being done in England will go skyways!'

# 4

Usually Leslie left about five o'clock in the afternoon. Decadon had been very nervous and morose all the afternoon, and she was so sorry for him that, when he suggested she might stay late, she readily agreed. She had plenty of work to do.

Ed Tanner saw her coming back from her tea and was surprised.

'Why, what's keeping you so late tonight, Miss Ranger? Is the old gentleman busy?'

She made some explanation, which did not seem convincing even to herself.

Tanner had not been told: the old man had been very insistent about this.

At about seven o'clock that evening she heard Tanner's voice in the library, and she wondered whether Mr Decadon had told him. They were talking for quite a long time. After a while she heard the squeak of the elevator as it went up to Eddie Tanner's suite. A little later the bell rang, and she went into the library.

The old man was writing rapidly. He always used sheets of foolscap, and wrote in a very neat and legible hand for one so old. He had half covered the sheet when she came in.

'Get Danes,' he said, naming one of the footmen. 'Ring for him, my girl,' he went on impatiently. 'Ring for him!'

She pressed the bell and Danes came in.

'Put your name, your occupation, and your address here, Danes.'

He pointed to the bottom of the paper, and Danes signed.

'You know what you're signing, you fool, don't you? You're witnessing my signature, and you haven't seen my signature,' stormed the irritable old gentleman. 'Watch this, Miss What's-your-name.'

He invariably addressed Leslie by this strange title, for he could not remember names.

He took up the pen and signed it with a flourish, and Danes obediently put his name, address and occupation by the side of the signature.

'That will do, Danes.'

The man was going, when Leslie said quietly:

'If this is a will I think you will find that both signatures must be attested together and in the presence of one another.'

He glared at her.

'How do you know it's a will?' he demanded.

He had covered the writing over with one big hand.

'I'm guessing it's a will,' she smiled. 'I can't imagine any other kind of document – '

'That will do – don't talk about it,' he grumbled. 'Sign it here.'

He watched her as she wrote.

' "Ranger" – that's it,' he muttered. 'Never can remember it. Thank you.'

He blotted the sheet, dismissed the footman with a wave of his hand and thrust the document into a drawer of his desk.

Presently he frowned at her.

'I've left you a thousand pounds,' he said, and she laughed softly. 'What the devil are you laughing at?'

'I'm laughing because I shan't get the thousand pounds. The fact that I have witnessed your will invalidates that bequest.'

He blinked at her. 'I hate people who know so much about the law,' he complained.

After Leslie was dismissed he rang the bell himself, had Danes up again and the cook, and procured a new witness. She did not know this till afterwards.

At half-past eight she was tidying up her desk when she heard a faint click, and looked up. It seemed to be in the room. She had put on her hat, when she heard the click again, and this time she heard the sound of the old man's voice, raised in anger. He was expostulating with somebody. She could not hear who it was.

And then she heard a piercing cry of fear, and two shots fired in rapid succession. For a moment she stood paralysed; then she ran to the door which led to the library and tried to open it. It was locked. She ran to the passage door; that was locked too. She flew to the wall, pressed the bell, heard a running of feet, and Danes hammered on the door.

'What is it, miss?'

''The door's locked. The key's on the outside,' she cried.

In another second it turned.

'Go into the library and see what's happened.'

Danes and the second footman ran along, and returned with the report that the library door was locked and that the key was missing. It was an eccentricity of Mr Decadon that he kept keys in all locks, usually on the outside of doors. With trembling hands she took that which had opened her own door, and, kneeling down, looked through the keyhole into the library. Carefully she thrust in her own key and pushed. That which was on the inside of the door had by chance been left so that the thrust pushed it out. As it dropped on the floor she unlocked the door with a heart that was quaking and flew into the room. She took three paces and stopped, paralysed with fear.

Old Mr Decadon lay across the desk in a pool of blood, and she knew before she touched him that he was dead.

# 5

Terry had arranged to go that night with Jiggs to see a musical comedy, and he was just leaving the house when the urgent call came through. Fortunately Jiggs, who was collecting him, drove up at that moment, and the two men went as fast as the taxicab could carry them to Berkeley Square.

There was a crowd outside the house already. Somehow the news had got around. Terry pushed his way to the steps and was instantly admitted.

The two plain clothes officers who had been on duty outside the house were in the passage, and their report was a simple one. Nobody had entered or left within half an hour of the shooting.

Terry went in and saw the body. The old man had been shot at close quarters by a heavy-calibre revolver, which lay on the floor within a few feet of the desk. It had not been moved.

He sent for a pair of sugar-tongs, and, after marking the position of the revolver with a piece of chalk, he lifted the weapon on to a small table and turned on a powerful reading lamp. It was a heavy, rather old-fashioned Colt revolver. As far as he could see, there were still four unused cartridges. What was more important, there were distinct fingerprints on the shiny steel plate between the butt and the chambers.

There was something more than this – a set of fingerprints on a sheet of foolscap paper. They were visible even before they were dusted. There was a third set on the polished mahogany edge of the desk, as though somebody had been resting their fingers on it.

Terry went into the girl's room and interviewed her. She was as pale as death, but very calm, and told him all she knew.

'Has Tanner been told?'

She nodded.

'Yes, he came down and saw...poor Mr Decadon, and then went up to his room again. He said nothing had to be touched, but by this time of course the police were in the house. Mr Tanner did not know that they had been outside watching.'

He sent one of the servants for him. Ed Tanner came down, a very grave man. He went without hesitation into the library.

'It's dreadful...simply shocking,' he said. 'I can't believe it.'

'Have you seen this revolver before?'

Terry pointed to the gun on the table. To his amazement, Tanner nodded.

'Yes,' he said quietly, 'that is my revolver. I am pretty certain of it. I did not touch it when I came into the room, but I could almost swear to it. A month ago a suitcase of mine was stolen at the railway station, and it contained this revolver. I notified the police of my loss and gave them the number of the missing weapon.'

Terry remembered the incident because the theft of firearms came within his department, and he had a distinct recollection of the loss being reported.

'You haven't seen the pistol since?'

'No, sir.'

'Mr Tanner,' said Terry quietly, 'on that revolver and on the desk there are certain fingerprints. In a few moments the fingerprint department will be here with their apparatus. Have you any objections to giving the police a set of your fingerprints in order that they may be compared with those found on the revolver?'

Eddie Tanner shook his head with a smile.

'I haven't the least objection, Inspector,' he said.

Almost as he said the words the fingerprint men came in, carrying their mystery box, and Terry, taking the sergeant in charge aside, explained what he wanted. In a few minutes Tanner's fingerprints were on a plain sheet of paper, and the sergeant set to work with his camera men making the record of the other prints which had been found. The easiest to do were those on the sheet of foolscap. A dusting with powder brought them out clearly. The sergeant examined them, and Terry saw a look of wonder in his face.

'Why, these are the same as that gentleman's.'

'What?' said Terry.

He took up the revolver, made a dusting, and again examined it.

'These also.'

Terry looked at the imperturbable Mr Tanner. He was smiling slightly.

'I was in this room at seven o'clock, but I didn't touch the paper or the desk or any article in the room,' he said. 'I hope you will realise, Mr Weston' – he turned to Terry – 'that the fact that I *was* here at seven o'clock could be offered as a very simple explanation of those fingerprints – apart, of course, from those on the revolver. But I could not possibly have made them, because I was wearing gloves. In fact, I intended going out, and changed my mind after interviewing my uncle.'

'What was the interview about?' asked Terry.

There was a little pause.

'It concerned his will. He called me down to tell me that he intended making a will for the first time in his life.'

'Did he tell you how he was disposing of his property?'

Tanner shook his head.

'No.'

Terry went out in search of the girl, and learned to his surprise that the will had been made and witnessed. She had not seen the contents, and knew nothing about it except that it was a document which she had witnessed, and in which she had been left a thousand pounds.

'I told him the fact I had witnessed the will invalidated it, as I was a beneficiary,' she said.

'Have you any idea where he put it?'

She could answer this readily.

'In the top left hand drawer of his desk.'

Terry went back to the chamber of death. The divisional surgeon had arrived and was examining the body.

'Do you know how your uncle was leaving his money in the will?'

'No, I don't,' repeated Tanner. 'He told me nothing.'

Terry went round the desk and pulled open the top left hand drawer. It was empty!

He went back to Tanner.

'You realise how serious this is, Mr Tanner? If what you say is true, and your uncle never made a will, you, as his only relative, are the sole legatee. If, on the other hand, your uncle made a will, as he undoubtedly did, it is quite possible that you were disinherited, and the destruction of the will, as well as the killing of your uncle, are circumstances which suggest a very important motive.'

Tanner nodded.

'Does that mean – '

'It merely means that I shall ask you to go with an officer to Scotland Yard, and to wait there until I come. It doesn't mean you're under arrest.'

Tanner thought for a moment.

'Can I see my attorney?'

Terry shook his head.

'That is not customary in this country. When any definite charge is made you may have a lawyer, but it's by no means certain that any charge will be made. The circumstances are suspicious. You agree that the revolver is yours, and the sergeant says that the fingerprints resemble yours; though of course that will be subject to more careful scrutiny, and I am afraid there is no other course than that which I am now taking.'

'That I understand,' said Tanner, and went off with one of the officers.

Jiggs Allerman had been a silent witness to the proceedings, so silent that Terry had forgotten his presence. Now he went across to where the American was standing watching the photographing of the body.

'Is this a gang killing or just plain interested murder? I can't decide.'

Jiggs shook his head.

'The only thing that strikes me as queer are those fingerprints on the foolscap paper. Do you notice how coarse they are?'

The fingerprint sergeant looked round.

'That struck me too, Mr Weston. The lines are curiously blurred; you'd think the impressions had been purposely made, and that whoever put them there laid his hand down deliberately, intending to make them.'

'That's just what I was going to say,' said Jiggs. 'And the gun on the floor – whoever heard of a gangster leaving his gun behind? He'd as soon think of leaving his visiting-card.'

Terry's own sergeant had come on the scene, and to him he delegated the task of making a careful search of the house.

'I particularly want Tanner's room gone through with a comb,' he said. 'Look for cartridges or any evidence that may connect him with the crime. I am particularly anxious to find a will made by Decadon this evening, so you'll make a search of fireplaces or any other place where such a will might have been destroyed.'

After the body had been removed and the grosser traces of the crime had been obliterated he called in Leslie. She was feeling the reaction: her face was white, her lips were inclined to tremble.

'You go home, young lady. I'll send an officer with you – and God knows I envy him! – and be here tomorrow morning at your usual hour. There'll be a whole lot of questions asked you, but you'll have to endure that.'

'Poor Mr Decadon!' her voice quivered.

'I know, I know,' he said soothingly, and dared put his arm about her shoulder.

She did not resent this, and his familiarity gave him the one happy moment of his day.

'You've got to forget all about it tonight, and tomorrow we'll look facts more squarely in the face. The only thing I want to know is, did you hear Tanner talking in the library, and at what time?'

She could place this exactly, and it corresponded with the story Tanner had told.

'And you heard voices just before the shooting?'

'Mr Decadon's,' she said, 'not the other's.'

'You heard the click as the key was turned, both on the library door and on your own?'

She nodded.

'The first click was on your own door?' he went on. 'That is to say the corridor door. The last click was the door into the library. So we may suppose that somebody walked along the corridor, locked your door first, went into the library, and then, either known or unknown to Mr Decadon, locked the communicating door between library and office.'

She nodded again.

'I suppose so,' she said wearily.

He took her by the arm.

'That's enough for tonight,' he said. 'You go home, go to bed and dream of anybody you like, preferably me.'

She tried to smile, but it was a miserable failure. When she had gone:

'What do you make of that, Jiggs?'

'Very much what you make of it, old pal,' said Jiggs. 'The murderer came from the back of the house – '

'It might have been Tanner,' suggested Terry, and Jiggs nodded.

'Sure. It might also have been one of the servants. Let's take a peek at these premises.'

They went along the corridor to the far end. The elevator was here on the left. On the right was a flight of stairs leading down to the kitchen. Under the stairs was a large locker, containing overcoats, waterproofs, umbrellas and rubber over-shoes. Jiggs opened the door of the elevator, switched on the light, and the two men got in. Closing the door, he pressed the button and the lift shot up to the top floor, where it stopped. Apparently there were no intermediate stations, and no other floor was served by this conveyance.

They got out on a small landing. On the left was a half-glass door marked 'Fire.' Terry tried this and it opened readily. As far as he could see, a narrow flight of iron stairs zig-zagged to a small courtyard. Terry

27

came in, closing the door, went on to Tanner's apartment, which was being searched by the sergeant and an assistant.

'Nothing here that I can find, sir,' reported the officer, 'except these, and I can't make them out.'

He pointed to a chair on which were placed a pair of muddy and broken shoes. They were the most dilapidated examples of footwear that Terry remembered seeing.

'No, they weren't on the chair when I found them: they were under it. I put them up to examine them more closely.'

They were in Tanner's bedroom, and the sergeant drew attention to the fact that a little secretaire was open and that a number of papers were on the floor. Several pigeon-holes must have been emptied in some haste.

'It looks as if the room has been carefully searched, or else that Tanner has been in a hurry to find something.'

Terry looked at the boots again and shook his head.

'Did you find any burnt paper in the grate?'

'No, sir,' said the sergeant. 'No smell of burnt paper either.'

'Listen, Terry,' said Jiggs suddenly. 'You've had a couple of coppers outside since when?'

'Since about half-past ten this morning.'

'Any at the back of the premises?'

'One,' said Terry.

'It's easier to get past one than two,' said Jiggs. 'Let's go down the fire escape and see if anybody could have got in that way. You notice all the windows are open in this room? It's a bit chilly, too.'

Terry had noticed that fact.

'I don't think the idea of the fire escape is a bad one,' he said, and the two men went out to investigate.

Terry left his companion outside the elevator door whilst he went down to borrow an electric torch from one of the policemen. When he came back the fire escape door was open and Jiggs had disappeared. He flashed his lamp down and saw the American on the second landing below.

'That's better than matches,' he said. 'Look at this, Terry.'

Terry ran down the stairs to where his companion was standing. Jiggs had something in his hand – a rubber over-shoe.

'You call 'em galoshes, don't you?'

In the light of the lamp Terry made a quick examination. The shoe was an old one, and subsequently proved to be one of the unfortunate Decadon's.

'What's it doing here?' asked Jiggs.

They went down the next two flights, but found nothing. At the bottom the stairs turned abruptly into the courtyard. Jiggs was walking ahead, Terry behind with a light showing him the way.

'There's a door in that wall. Where does it lead to – a mews?' asked Jiggs. 'That's what you call it – '

Suddenly he stopped.

'For God's sake!' he said softly. 'Look at that!'

Almost at their feet was a huddled heap. It was a man, ill-clad, his trousers almost in rags. On one foot was a rubber over-shoe, on the other a slipper. His hat had fallen some distance from him.

Terry moved the light; he saw the back of the head and the crimson pool that lay beyond.

'Here's our second dead man,' said Terry. 'Who is he?'

# 6

Jiggs leaped over the body and reached for the lamp. His examination was a careful one.

'If he isn't a tramp he looks like one. Shot at close range through the back of the head. A small-calibre pistol...dead half an hour. Can you beat that?'

Terry found a door which opened into the kitchen and sent one of the horrified servants in search of the police surgeon, whom he had left writing his report at Leslie's desk. Whilst he awaited his coming he scrutinised the dead man's feet.

He wore soft leather slippers, which were a little too small for him, and over these had evidently drawn the galoshes.

A detective came running out, and Terry sent him back to bring the fingerprint outfit. He then began a careful search of the dead man's clothes. In the left hand pocket of the shabby overcoat he found a small steel box, rather like a child's money box. It was black-japanned and fastened with a small patent lock. Terry tried to open it, but failed.

'It wouldn't have been much use as an indicator of fingerprints,' he said. 'It's been in his pocket. Did you find anything else, Jiggs?'

Allerman had taken up the search where Terry left off. The Inspector heard the jingle of coins, and Jiggs held out his hand.

'That's an unusual phenomenon in England,' he said, and Terry gasped.

There were about ten or twelve English sovereigns.

'In the waistcoat pocket, wrapped up in a piece of paper, and this man is a hobo or nothing.'

They left the body to the care of the surgeon and drove back to Scotland Yard in a squad car. Tanner was waiting in Terry's room. He was smoking a cigarette and reading a newspaper, which he put down as they entered.

'Did you find the will?' he asked.

'No, but we found one or two other things,' said Terry. 'When were you in your bedroom last?'

Tanner's eyebrows rose.

'Do you mean in Berkeley Square? I haven't been there since morning.'

Terry eyed him keenly.

'Are you sure?'

The man nodded.

'Have you been to your desk for anything?'

'Desk? Oh, you mean the little secretaire. No.'

'Was there anything valuable there?'

Eddie Tanner considered.

'Yes, there were twelve pounds in gold. It has been amusing me to collect English sovereigns since your people came off the gold standard. As for me going into my bedroom, I have just remembered that when I tried to get into the room this afternoon is was locked. I thought the housekeeper had locked it, but I didn't bother to send for her. She does lock up sometimes. Mr Decadon had a servant who stole things a few months ago – I wasn't in the house at the time, but I've heard about it – and apparently there was quite an epidemic of caution. Has the money gone?'

'I have it in my pocket, as a matter of fact,' said Terry grimly, 'but I can't give it to you yet.'

He took from his pocket the little iron box, went to his desk, took out a collection of keys and tried them on the lock. Presently he found one that fitted, and the box opened. One side fell down; behind it was a small linen pad. When he pushed back the lid he saw the contents.

'A rubber stamp outfit!' he said in surprise.

Jiggs, looking over his shoulder, picked out one of the three wooden-backed stamps and examined it in amazement.

'Well, I'll go to – !'

They were the rubber impressions of fingerprints, and their surface still bore a thin film of moisture.

'That's where the fingerprints came from,' said Terry slowly. 'The man who killed Decadon stopped to fix the blame on somebody.'

He looked at Eddie Tanner.

'You must have some pretty powerful enemies, Mr Tanner.'

Tanner smiled.

'I've got one,' he said softly, 'and he's got a whole lot of friends.'

He looked up and caught Jiggs' questioning eye, and smiled again.

# 7

At three o'clock in the morning there was a conference of all heads of Scotland Yard, and it was a delicate compliment to Jiggs Allerman's prescience and popularity that he was admitted.

The fingerprint officer on duty brought one or two interesting facts.

'The tramp has been identified,' he said. 'His name is William Board, alias William Crane, alias Walter Cork. He has seven convictions for vagrancy and five for petty larceny.'

'He is a tramp, then?' said Terry.

'That's all we know about him,' said the fingerprint man.

Jiggs shook his head vigorously.

'He committed no murder,' he said. 'I never met a hobo who was quick enough for that kind of crime. He may have put the prints on. How did he get into the yard?'

The Chief Constable, wise in the ways of criminals, had a logical explanation to give.

'The man who killed Mr Decadon also killed Board. He was used as a tool and destroyed because he would have made a dangerous witness. He was shot with a powerful air-pistol at close range, according to the doctor. You've released Tanner?'

Terry nodded.

'Yes, we couldn't very well keep him after we found the stamps. The only tenable theory is that Board broke into the house earlier in the day, before the police came on the scene, and concealed himself in Tanner's bedroom. He was wearing Tanner's slippers and a pair of galoshes which were admittedly in the bedroom. What I can't understand is why he should take that risk. Tanner was in and out of the suite all day.'

'Suppose Tanner had him there?' said Jiggs.

They looked at him.

'Why should Tanner have him there?' asked Terry scornfully. 'To manufacture evidence against himself?'

'That sounds illogical, doesn't it?' said Jiggs with strange gentleness. 'Maybe at this late hour I have got a little tired and foolish. One thing is certain gentlemen: the first shot in the campaign has been fired. Tomorrow morning's newspapers are going to carry the story of the demand for fifty thousand pounds – old man Decadon is the awful example that will start the ball rolling. The point is, will it start both balls rolling? I rather think it will.'

The Chief Constable laughed.

'You're being mysterious, Jiggs.'

'Ain't I just!' said Jiggs.

Terry went back to his office, and sat down in the quietude of that hour and worked out the puzzle of the day. It was not going to be an easy one to solve, and he had a depressed feeling that Jiggs' pessimistic prophecy might be fulfilled.

He was sitting with his head on his hands, near to being asleep, when the telephone bell rang and jerked him awake. The Scotland Yard operator spoke to him.

'There's a woman on the phone who wishes to speak to you, sir. I think she's talking from a street booth.'

'Who is she?' asked Terry.

'She didn't give her name – oh yes, she did: Mrs Something. But I don't think you know her. Shall I put you through?'

Terry heard a click, and then an anxious voice hailed him.

'Is that Mr Terry, of Scotland Yard, the detective?'

It was rather a common voice.

'Yes, I'm Mr Terry Weston.'

'Excuse me for bothering you, sir, but is Miss Ranger coming home soon? I'm getting a little anxious.'

'Miss Ranger?' Terry sat up. 'What do you mean – is she coming home soon? She went home a long time ago.'

'Yes, sir, but she was called out again by a Scotland Yard gentleman – an American gentleman. They told her you wanted to see her.'

'What time was this?' asked Terry, a little breathlessly.

She thought it was about ten, but was vague on the subject.

'She'd only just got in, and was having a bite of supper, which I made her have, sir – '

'How long after she came in did she go out?'

The woman thought it was a quarter of an hour.

'Where do you live?'

She told him. It was little street in Bloomsbury.

'I'll be there in five minutes,' said Terry. 'Just wait for me, will you?'

He rang for a car, and went down the stairs two at a time. In less than five minutes he was in the neat parlour of the landlady. She could only tell him substantially the story she had already told.

There had been a knock at the door and she had answered it. A man was standing there, and by the kerb was a car and another man. He said he was from Scotland Yard and spoke distinctly with an American accent. He said Mr Terry Weston wished the young lady to go to the Yard immediately. She remembered now that he did say 'Weston'.

'Would you recognise him again?' asked Terry, his heart sinking.

She did not think so. It was a very dark night and she had not taken much notice of him. The young lady had gone almost at once. She had been particularly impressed by the fact that the two men had raised their hats to her as she came out of the house. She thought it was nice to see detectives being polite to a lady.

'They drove off towards Bloomsbury Square,' she said.

She had stood at the door and watched the car go.

'Did you notice the number of the car?' he said quickly.

'The car was numbered XYD 7000.'

The landlady had a weakness for counting up numbers on numberplates. She had, she said, a faith, and a very complete faith, that if the numbers added up to four and she saw two fours in succession, she was going to have a lucky day. She betted on races, she added unnecessarily.

Terry went round to the booth whence she had telephoned, got through to the Yard and handed in the number.

'Find out who owns this, and ask the Flying Squad to supply me with a unit.'

By the time he reached the Yard the information was available. The car was owned by the Bloomsbury and Holborn Motor Car Hire, but it was impossible to discover from their garage to whom it was hired at the moment. All inquiries in this direction were suddenly blocked when a report came up that a car bearing this number, and genuinely hired to a doctor, had been stolen that night in Bloomsbury Park.

'That's that!' groaned Terry. 'Warn all stations to look for it and arrest the driver and its occupants.'

Then began a feverish search which was almost without parallel in the annals of the Flying Squad. Crew after crew were brought in on urgent summons, and shot off east, west, north and south.

In the morning, as day was breaking, a cyclist patrol saw a car abandoned in a field by the side of the Colnbrook bypass. He went forward to investigate, and instantly recognised the number for which the whole of the Metropolitan police had been searching, and, jumping off his cycle, he ran forward. The blinds were drawn. He pulled open the door and saw a girl lying in one corner of the car. She was fast asleep. It was Leslie Ranger.

# 8

Leslie had had no idea that anything was wrong till the speed of the car increased and one of the two 'detectives' who were sitting with her leaned forward and began to pull down the blinds.

'Don't do that,' she said.

'You just sit quiet, missie, and don't talk,' said the man, 'and if you just sit quiet and don't talk you ain't going to be hurt – see?'

She nearly fainted when she realised that she had been the victim of a trick.

'Where are we going?' she asked, but they did not answer. In fact, neither of the men spoke.

They must have travelled for the better part of an hour, when the car swerved suddenly round a sharp corner, followed a bumpy road, turned again to the left and stopped. One of the men took a scarf from his pocket and blindfolded her, and she submitted meekly. She was assisted from the car, walked along a paved pathway and into a house.

It must have been a small house, because the two men had to walk behind her, one of them guiding her by her elbows. She turned sharp left again, and guessed that she was in a room where there were several men. She could smell the pungent odour of cigar smoke.

'Tell her to sit down,' said somebody in a whisper, and, when she had obeyed: 'Now, missie, perhaps you'll tell us what happened at old man Decadon's house. You'll tell us the truth and you'll answer any questions that are put to you, and nothing's going to happen to you.'

The man who said all this spoke in a sort of harsh, high whisper. He was obviously disguising his voice.

She was terribly frightened, but felt that there was nothing to be gained by refusing to speak or by suppressing anything she knew; so she told them very frankly and freely, and answered their questions without hesitation.

They seemed most interested and insistent in their inquiries about Eddie Tanner. Where had he been? Was she sure they were his fingerprints? When she told about the revolver on the floor somebody laughed, and the questioner snarled an angry admonition, after which there was silence.

This inquisition lasted two hours. They brought her hot coffee, for which she was grateful, and eventually:

'All right, kid. You can tell the police all about this – there's no reason why you shouldn't. But don't tell more'n the truth, or ever try to line me up by my voice.'

They had taken her back to the car and made her comfortable, and that was all she remembered, except that another car was following them all the time. She fell asleep whilst the machine was still in motion, and knew nothing until the cyclist policeman woke her up.

Terry expected something big in the morning Press, but he was hardly prepared for the importance which the newspapers gave to me two murders. 'Is this the beginning of a new era of lawlessness?' asked the *Megaphone* blackly.

Fleet Street seemed to recognise instantly the significance of the two crimes which shocked London that morning. 'The Beginning of the Rackets' was a headline in one journal. Fleet Street, living on print, was impressed by print. That notice which had been sent to Mr Decadon, neatly printed in blue ink, spelt organisation on a large scale.

And yet Scotland Yard received no intimation that any other rich or prominent man had had a similar warning. From one end of England to the other the newspapers were shocked and wrathful, and their leading articles revealed an energy to combat the new peril which impressed even Jiggs Allerman.

The tramp's antecedents had been quickly traced. He had been living in a lodging-house, but had not been to his room for two nights prior to the murder. He was a fairly reticent man, and had not discussed his business with anybody.

During the night the Assistant Commissioner had been on the transatlantic telephone to Chicago, and had secured permission to attach Jiggs Allerman to the Scotland Yard staff as a temporary measure. Jiggs, with his new authority, had spent all the morning at the house in Berkeley Square. He came back to the Yard to find Terry reading the newspaper.

'Did you find anything?' asked Terry.

'Yeah.' Jiggs nodded. 'The old man had fitted up a kitchenette for Tanner. There's a gas stove there.'

He took out of his pocket an envelope, opened it carefully and picked out a strand of thin wire six inches in length.

'Found this wound around one of the burners, and outside the top landing of the fire escape there's a hook fixed into the wall, and fixed recently.'

'What do you make of that?' asked Terry.

Jiggs scratched his chin.

'Why, I make a lot of that,' he said. 'What was the direction of the wind last night?'

Terry took up a newspaper and turned the pages till he came to the weather report.

'Moderate north-west,' he read.

'Grand,' said Jiggs. 'What's been puzzling me more than anything else has been the disappearance of the air-pistol. That had to be got rid of pretty quick, and the tramp Board wasn't the kind of man to think quick, and, anyway, he didn't get rid of it! But he helped.'

Terry frowned at him.

'You're being a little mysterious, Jiggs.'

'I know I am,' admitted Jiggs. 'That's my speciality.'

He leaned down over the table and spoke emphatically.

'There was only one possible way that gun could be got rid of, and I knew just how it had happened when one of the servants in the next house said somebody had smashed the window of her bedroom a few minutes after the murder was committed – I'm talking about the murder of the tramp, and the time we've got to guess at.'

He took a pencil from his pocket and made a rough plan.

'There's the courtyard. One side of it's made up of the back premises of the next door house. The servant slept on the fourth floor; she had gone to bed early because she had to be up at six. She was just going off to sleep, when her window was smashed in by somebody on the outside. When I say "somebody" I mean "something." Now the fourth floor of that house is one floor higher – roughly fifteen feet – than the top floor in Decadon's house, and when I heard about that window being smashed and found the wire on the gas burner and the hook on the wall, I got your people to phone every balloon maker in London and find out who sold a toy balloon that could lift a couple of pounds when it was filled with coalgas.'

Terry stared at him.

'I've heard of that being done once.'

'Now you've heard of it being done twice,' Jiggs finished for him. 'The bag was filled in the kitchenette; the end of it was tied round the burner – the gas pressure is pretty high in that neighbourhood. Just before the murder the mouth was tied, the balloon was taken out on to the fire escape and fastened with a string or wire to the hook. The hook was upside down – that is to say, the point of it was downward. After Board was killed the murderer tied the gun to the balloon and let it go. The wind must have been fresh then, and as it went upwards the pistol smashed the window of the housemaid's room. You know my methods, Weston,' he added sardonically.

Terry figured this out for a few minutes. Then:

'But if your theory is correct, the murderer must have come up the fire escape after he had killed Board.'

Jiggs nodded slowly.

'You've said it, kid,' he said.

'Do you still believe that Tanner was the murderer?'

Jiggs smiled.

'It's no question of believing, it's knowing. Sure he was the murderer!'

'And that he deliberately left evidence to incriminate himself?'

'Well, he's free, isn't he?' demanded Jiggs. 'And clear of suspicion. You haven't a case to go to the Grand Jury, have you? Those stamps with his fingerprints on let him out. You couldn't get a conviction. And in a way you've taken all suspicion from him, made him a victim instead of a murderer. He's free – that's the answer. I've told you, he's the greatest psychologist I have met. Suppose you hadn't found fingerprints or a gun, where would suspicion have pointed – at Ed! There's the will gone, and Ed's the old man's legatee at law. What he did was to bring suspicion upon himself at once, and destroy it at once. How far is the sea from here?'

'About fifty miles,' said Terry.

Jiggs whistled softly to himself.

'Ed never made a mistake. The gasbag he used would stay up two hours, so you'll never see that pistol again. It'll drop in the sea somewhere.'

'We've had no further complaints from people about these demands,' said Terry.

'You'll get 'em,' said the other, with a grim smile. 'Give 'em time to let it soak in.'

He looked at his watch.

'I'm going along to the American bar at the Cecilia,' he said. 'I've got quite an idea I'll hear a lot of interesting news.'

The Cecilia bar is the rendezvous of most Americans visiting London. The gorgeous Egyptian room, dedicated to the cocktail, was filled by the time Jiggs got there. He found a little table and a chair that was vacant, and sat down patiently for the arrival of his man. It was nearing noon when Kerky Smith came leisurely into the bar, the bony chin lifted, the thin, set smile on his face. He looked round, apparently did not see Jiggs, and strolled to the door. Jiggs finished his cocktail deliberately, beckoned the waiter and put his hand in his pocket. He had no intention of leaving, but it would require such a gesture as this to bring the Big Boy to him.

'Why, Jiggs!'

Kerky Smith came forward with a flashing smile, his ring-laden hands extended. He took Jiggs' hand in both of his and pressed it affectionately.

'Not going, are you? Say, I wanted to talk to you.'

He looked round, found a chair and dragged it to the table.

'Isn't it too bad about that old guy? I'll bet Ed is just prostrate with grief!'

'Where did you get that international expression from – "prostrated with grief"?'

'Saw it in a book somewhere,' said Kerky shamelessly. 'Funny how you can get all kinds of swell expressions if you keep your eyes open. Left him all his money, ain't he? Well, he needed it. He was short of a million to carry out all the big ideas he has.'

'It will be months before he can touch a cent,' said Jiggs.

The thin eyebrows of Kerky Smith rose.

'Is that so? I guess you can borrow money on wills, can't you? Ed was down at a moneylender's this morning.'

Jiggs was politely interested.

'What kind of a racket was he in when he was running round Chi?' he asked.

Kerky shook his head slowly. There was in his face a hint of disapproval.

'I hardly know the man,' he said. 'And what's all this about rackets? I read about 'em in the newspapers, but I don't know any of these birds.'

He said this with a perfectly straight face. Jiggs would have been surprised if he had not.

'Seems to be some kind of racket starting here,' he went on. 'Has anybody asked Ed to pay? He's a rich guy now.'

'What was his racket in Chicago' repeated Jiggs, without any hope of being satisfied, for gangland does not talk scandal even of its worst enemies.

'He was just a playboy, I guess. I used to see him around Arlington, and he lived at the Blackstone. That's the kind of bird he was.'

Jiggs leaned across the table and lowered his voice.

'Kerky, you remember the shooting of Big Sam Polini? The choppers got him as he came out of mass one morning – a friend of yours, wasn't he?'

There was a hard look in Kerky's eyes, but he was still smiling.

'I knew the man,' he said simply.

'One of your crowd, wasn't he? Who got him?'

Kerky's smile broadened.

'Why, if I knew I'd tell the police,' he said. 'Joe Polini was a swell fellow. Too bad he was shot up.'

'Did Ed know anything about it?'

Kerky wagged his head wearily.

'Now what's the use of asking fool questions like that, Jiggs? I've told you before I don't know anything about him. He seems a nice feller to me, and I wouldn't say a word against him. Especially now, when he's in mourning.'

Jiggs saw the sly, quick, sidelong glance that the other shot at him, and supplied his own interpretation.

'I'm going off to Paris one day this week,' said Kerky. 'If they start any racket here I want to be out of it. London's the last place you'd expect gunplay. So you're at Scotland Yard now, ain't you?'

'Who told you that?'

Kerky shrugged his thin shoulders.

'Sort of story going round that you've been loaned.' He bent over and laid his hand on Jiggs' shoulder. 'I kinda like you Jiggs. You're a swell guy. I wouldn't stay around here if I were you – no, sir! Of course, you could stay and make it pay. A friend of mine wants some detective work done, and he'd pay a hundred thousand dollars to the right kind of guy. All he'd have to do would be just to sit around and be dumb when anything was happening. You might be very useful to my friend.'

'Is your friend seeking a divorce or just salvation from the gallows?' asked Jiggs bluntly.

Kerky got up from the table.

'You make me tired, Jiggs,' he said, 'Some of you fellers are swell, but you can't think with your heads.'

'I can think better with my head than with my pocket, Kerky. Tell your friends there's nothing doing, and, if they try another way of making me drunk, that I'm packing two guns, and they've got to do their shooting pretty quick.'

Kerky shook his head and sighed.

'You're talking like one of them gang pictures which are so popular in Hollywood,' he said.

He called the waiter to him and paid him, beamed on his guest, and, with a little wave of his hand, sauntered across the room to the bar.

Jiggs went out, all his senses alert. There was a little dark faced man, elaborately dressed, sitting in the vestibule of the hotel, gazing vacantly at the wall opposite. He wore a gold and diamond ring on the little finger of his left hand. Jiggs watched him as he passed; he so manoeuvred himself that his back was never towards the idler, who apparently was taking no notice of him, and did not even turn his head.

By the door leading out to the courtyard of the hotel was another little man, blue chinned, dark eyed, quite unconscious, apparently, of Jiggs' presence. Captain Allerman avoided him, but he did not take his eyes off him until there were half a dozen people between them.

There would be quite an exciting time in town before the end of the week, he decided, as a cab took him back to his hotel, and he wondered if the English people in general, and the English police in particular, quite knew what was going to happen.

When he went in to lunch he met some men he knew. They were talking about the Decadon murder. None of them apparently saw anything in the threatening note that in any way menaced their own security.

He was called from lunch by a telephone message from Terry.

'I'll come along and join you,' said Terry. 'There's been a development. Can we go up to your room?'

'Sure,' said Jiggs.

He was waiting for the inspector when he arrived, and they went up in the lift together to Jiggs' suite.

'Here's a new one.'

Terry took from his pocket a leather case and extracted a folded note. It was exactly the same size as the warning which old Decadon had received, but it was printed in green ink and differently worded.

DEAR FRIEND (it began),

We are out to ensure your comfort and security. We are a band of men who will offer you protection against your enemies and even against your friends. You need not worry about burglars or hold-up men if you trust us. If you agree to employ us, put a lighted wax candle in the window of your dining room between 8 and half-past 8 tonight. We are offering you, for the sum of £1,000, payable within the next three days, the protection that only our organisation can give you. If you decline our services you will, we fear, be killed. If you take this note to the police or consult them in any way, nothing can save you. Have a thousand pounds in American or French currency in an envelope, and after you have put the candle in your window you will receive a telephone message explaining how this money is to be paid.

It was signed 'Safety and Welfare Corporation.'

'Printed in green ink, eh? Well, we've got 'em both working now, the green and the blue. Who had this?'

'A very rich young man called Salaman. He lives in Brook Street, and had it this morning by the first post. We've got no evidence that anybody else has had the warning. Salaman sent it to us at once, and we've put a guard on his house.'

'He didn't come to Scotland Yard?'

'No, we avoided that. He telephoned first and sent the letter by special messenger.'

Jiggs pursed his lips.

'They'll know all about it. What have you advised him to do?'

'To put a candle in his window, and we'll get a man into the house tonight who will take the message.'

Jiggs was not impressed.

'I'm telling you that they know he's been to the police. What sort of man is he?'

Terry made a little grimace.

'Not the highest type of citizen. Plenty of money and a few odd tastes. He's a bachelor, a member of the smartest set in town – which doesn't necessarily mean the best set. I've got an idea that he's rather on the decadent side.'

Jiggs nodded.

'He'll be very lucky if he's not on the dead side,' he said ominously.

# 9

Leslie went to her work rather late that morning, and with a sense of growing desolation. The tragedy of old Elijah Decadon's death was sufficiently depressing, and she had not yet recovered from the terrifying experience of the previous night.

The situation, so far as she was concerned, was reducible to bread-and-butter dimensions. She had lost her job, or would lose it when she had finished the week. For a second or two she thought of Terry Weston and the possibility of his using his influence to find her another situation, but this was hardly thought of before the idea was dismissed.

The police were still in occupation of the house. They had made a methodical search of the study, and the contents of the desk had been gone over by two men practised in this kind of search. There was plenty of work for her to do: arranging, sorting and extracting papers. For two hours she was with the police sergeant who was in charge of the work, explaining the importance of various documents.

Danes brought her some tea. He had had an exciting morning.

'About that will, miss, that we signed. The police have been trying to get me to say what was in it.'

'Well, you didn't know, Danes,' she smiled, 'so you couldn't very well tell them.'

Danes was doubtful whether he might not have offered more information than he had.

'It's a funny thing, miss, that Mr Decadon locked the drawer when he put the will away – you remember? He sent for us again because he'd left you some money in it and it wasn't legal. Well, we got the cook to come up and witness his signature. He didn't exactly sign, but he ran a pen over your name and said that legally that was the same thing. He locked the drawer and put the key in his pocket, yet when that detective started searching the drawer was unlocked. That's a mystery to me.'

'It isn't much of a mystery, Danes,' she said good humouredly. 'Poor Mr Decadon may have taken the will out of the drawer and put it somewhere else.'

'That's what I told Mr Tanner, miss,' said Danes. 'He's been asking me a lot of questions too – he just telephoned down to ask if you were in, and – '

The door opened at that moment: it was Eddie Tanner. He greeted the girl with his quiet little smile and waited till the footman had left.

'You had a very unpleasant experience last night, they tell me,' he said. 'I'm sorry. I wonder if you would mind telling me what happened?'

She told her story, which seemed less exciting to her than it had sounded when Terry Weston was her audience.

'Well, nothing happened to you – that's good,' he said.

She thought he was not particularly enthusiastic about her own safety.

'About this will, Miss Ranger – the one you signed. I suppose you didn't see anything that was in it…or to whom the money was left?'

She shook her head.

'It may have been left to you.'

His lips curled for a second.

'I shouldn't think that was very likely,' he said. 'My uncle really didn't like me – and I didn't really like my uncle. Have you see Captain Allerman?'

The name seemed familiar, but she could not recall ever having met that officer.

'He's an American policeman – Chicago,' he said. 'A very brilliant man, but occasionally he indulges in fantastic theories. One of his theories is that I killed Mr Decadon.'

He opened the door leading into the library, saw the men engaged and closed the door again.

'They're doing some high class searching. I wonder if they'll find the will? I suppose it was a will. It might have been some other document?' he said inquiringly.

He went to the door and stood there, leaning his head against the broad edge of it.

'By the way, I shall want you to stay on and deal with my uncle's papers and books – they will require cataloguing. The job will last six months, and at the end of that time I will find something for you.'

He looked at her for a long time without speaking, and then he said slowly:

'If you find that missing document will you oblige me by not reading it, and handing it to me – not to the police? I will give you fifty thousand pounds if you do this.' He smiled. 'A lot of money, isn't it? And it would be quite honestly earned.'

She gasped.

'But, Mr Tanner…' she stammered.

'I'm serious. And may I ask you not to repeat this to Mr Terry Weston? You are now in my employ – I hope you won't object to my reminding you – and I'm sure I can count on your loyalty.'

He went out, pulling the door to noiselessly.

She sat for a long time, looking at the door blankly. He had meant it…fifty thousand pounds! Then suddenly she remembered something; it was extraordinary that she had not thought of this before. She rang the bell and Danes came in.

'What time did you clear the postbox last night?' she asked.

'About half-past seven, miss.'

There was only one postbox, a large mahogany receptacle that stood on a table just inside the library. All letters except those sent by Eddie Tanner were placed in that box before they were despatched. Even the letters of the servants were supposed to be lodged in the old man's study – a practice that went back to the days when he found a luckless housemaid stealing his stamps. Thence onwards the stamps were perforated with his initial, and he was able to tell at a glance whether he was being victimised. In point of fact, none of the staff ever availed themselves of this method of posting.

'Mr Decadon rang for me – he just pointed to the box and I took the letters out.'

'How many were there?' she asked.

He was not sure; he thought about six. She went over in her mind quickly the correspondence for which she had been responsible.

'There was one large envelope, and the rest were just ordinary – '

'One long envelope?' she said quickly. 'Was it in handwriting or typewritten?'

'In handwriting, miss. It was in Mr Decadon's hand. I know because the ink was still wet and I smudged it a bit with my thumb.'

'Do you remember the address to which it was sent?'

Danes put his hand to his forehead and thought hard.

'It was written on the top, miss: "Personal attention of Mr Jerrington. Private and confidential." That's right, miss. I don't remember the address, though.'

The mystery was a mystery no longer.

'Will you ask Mr Tanner to come to me if he is in the house?' she said.

Ed Tanner was with her in a minute.

'Well?' he asked. 'Is it about the will?'

For the first time since she had known him he displayed some kind of emotion.

'Yes, I think I know what happened to it. Mr Decadon must have posted it himself.'

'Posted it?'

'The box was cleared at half-past seven, and Danes said he saw a long envelope which had recently been addressed in Mr Decadon's writing. It was marked: "For Mr Jerrington" – of Jerrington, Sanders & Graves, Mr Decadon's lawyers.'

'Oh, yes?'

He stood for a few seconds fingering his chin, his eyes downcast.

'Mr Jerrington. I know him, naturally. Thank you, Miss Ranger.'

She wondered afterwards whether she should not have informed the police, in spite of his warning, and she called up Scotland Yard, but Terry Weston was out.

# 10

Mr George Jerrington, the eminent head of a famous legal firm, was often described by his associates as being a little inhuman. He was sufficiently human, however, to develop a peculiar appendix, and a week before the murder he had gone into a nursing home and had parted with that troublesome and unnecessary thing, with the assistance of the most expensive surgeon in London.

That day he was near enough to convalescence to deal with his personal correspondence, and a telephone message was sent to Lincoln's Inn Fields, to his head clerk, requesting that the most urgent of the letters should be sent to him.

'You'd better take them yourself,' said Mr Jerrington's partner to the clerk. 'Who was that in your office half an hour ago?'

'Mr Decadon's nephew, sir – Mr Edwin Tanner.'

'Oh, yes,' said the partner. 'A fortunate young man. Decadon died intestate, I understand?'

'I believe so, sir.'

'What did he want – Mr Tanner?'

'I think it was in connection with the estate. I asked him if he'd see you, but when I told him that Mr Jerrington was ill he said he would wait. He said he had sent Mr Jerrington an urgent personal letter, and I told him Mr Jerrington would probably attend to that today. I have several such letters to take to him.'

The nursing home was at Putney. The clerk, whose name was Smethwick Gould, travelled by bus to the foot of Putney Hill and walked the rest of the way. It was nearly six o'clock and ordinarily it

52

would have been quite light, but heavy clouds were coming up from the south-west and there was a smell of rain in the air. Most of the cars which passed him had their headlamps alight.

He had reached the top of the hill and was turning left towards the houses which face Putney Common, when a car came abreast of him and a man jumped out.

'Are you from Jerrington's?' he said.

Smethwick Gould said that the man spoke with a slightly foreign accent. He wore a big, yellow waterproof coat, the high collar of which reached above the tip of his nose.

'Yes, I'm from Jerrington's,' said the clerk.

'Then I'll take that bag from you.'

And then Mr Smethwick Gould saw that in the man's hand was an automatic pistol. He stated afterwards that he made a desperate struggle, but the balance of probability is that he handed over the bag without protest. The man in the macintosh jumped into the car and it drove off. With great presence of mind, Mr Smethwick Gould realised that he had forgotten to note the number of the car. He realised this the moment the number was invisible, but in all probability he would not have been greatly assisted, for a car was afterwards found abandoned on Barnes Common which was proved to have been stolen from Grosvenor Square.

The report of the loss went straight through to Scotland Yard, but did not come to Terry. He was just going out to superintend the Salaman case, and to coach that young man in his conduct, when Leslie phoned through to him and told him what had happened that afternoon.

'I've got a guilty feeling that I should have rung you before.'

'My gosh! That's news!' said Terry. 'I'll ring through to Jerrington's right away.'

But Messrs Jerrington were precise people who closed their offices at five o'clock, and he had no satisfaction from them. It was not until he had smuggled himself into Salaman's handsome house that the report of the robbery reached him. He was not particularly interested until he learned that the victim was Mr Jerrington's head clerk, and then he swore softly to himself, realising what had happened.

'Tell me quickly, what were the circumstances?'

'I've got the report here, sir,' said the officer at the other end of the wire. 'Mr Jerrington has been in a nursing home. He's been operated on for appendicitis, and has seen none of his personal correspondence. As they knew he was making satisfactory progress, letters weren't opened but were kept for him until he was ready to deal with them. This morning they telephoned through from the nursing home asking somebody to take out the personal letters, and Mr Smethwick Gould went out with them. He carried them in a portfolio – '

'And he was held up and robbed on the way,' said Terry. 'Quick work! All right. Have all the facts ready for me when I get back to the Yard, and tell this Smethwick person that I would like to see him.'

He was hardly off the wire before the phone bell rang again. They were in Salaman's beautiful drawing-room. The ceiling was black, the curtains purple, the carpet a dead white. There were green candles in old gold sconces, and large divans. Even the telephone had been specially designed to match the apartment.

Terry did not like the house and he did not like the slim, sallow owner, and liked less the faint scent of incense which hung about the room.

He motioned to Salaman, who took up the phone and lisped an inquiry. Terry waited, listening.

'Yes, I have put the candle in the drawing-room window. You saw it. Where am I to meet you?'

By arrangement, he was repeating every word of the man who was phoning.

'At the top of Park Lane, on the park side. Twenty five paces from the Marble Arch corner. Yes, I understand. A man will come along wearing a red flower, and I am to give him the package. Certainly...not at all.'

He hung up the phone and smiled fatuously.

'We've got him!' he said.

Terry did not echo his enthusiasm.

The police had gone when Leslie reached Berkeley Square the next morning, and she was a little relieved. She was very uncomfortable, working under their eyes, never knowing at what moment they would come in and fire off some question which, if not embarrassing, was at least difficult to answer.

All the papers that had been taken from the old man's desk had to be filed or destroyed. She had been working half an hour, when Eddie came in, his cool and imperturbable self.

'No luck, I suppose?'

'I'm sure it went to Mr Jerrington, if you're talking about the will,' she said. 'Did you get on to him?'

He nodded.

'Yes, I called, but Mr Jerrington is in a nursing home with appendicitis. Apparently all his private papers were stolen yesterday by some hold-up man who robbed his clerk in broad daylight. I read it in the newspaper.'

She was staggered.

'That's terribly unfortunate,' she said.

'Isn't it?' said he, with that inscrutable smile of his. 'This country is becoming so lawless, so unlike the old England I used to know.'

He looked round.

'I think that is a mutual friend of ours, Mr Terry Weston.'

His sharp ears had heard the bell, and he went to the door, intercepting Danes.

'If that is Mr Weston, show him in here, please. He phoned to say he was coming,' he told the girl. 'I hope he isn't being infected with Captain Allerman's suspicion! Good morning, Inspector.'

'Good morning.'

Terry was bright, but it was a hard brightness, and Leslie was not quite sure that she liked him that way. He was kindly enough to her, and offered her his hand in greeting – a formality he had omitted in dealing with Eddie Tanner.

'We were just discussing the robbery of Mr Jerrington's private papers,' said Eddie.

'I wanted to discuss that too.' Terry looked at him keenly. 'Rather an extraordinary happening, in all the circumstances.'

Eddie Tanner ran his hand over his bald forehead and frowned.

'I don't perhaps know all the circumstances, but in any circumstances it was unfortunate.'

'You called at the office in the afternoon?'

Mr Tanner nodded.

'Naturally. Mr Jerrington is my lawyer – or, at least, he acted for my uncle. There are several matters which have to be straightened up, the most urgent being some interest he has in an oilfield in a town called Tacan, which I believe is in Oklahoma.' He looked at the girl. 'Have you heard about that?'

'No, Mr Tanner, but I knew very little about Mr Decadon's private investments.'

'The point is' – he frowned deeply, and this seemed to absorb his attention more than the theft of Mr Smethwick Gould's papers – 'Tacan – is there such a place?'

'That is not very important at the moment,' began Terry.

Then he saw the real Eddie Tanner. Two cold eyes stared at him. They held neither resentment nor anger, but there was in them a deadly cold that he had never seen in the eyes of man.

'It is important to me.'

Leslie was growing uncomfortable in the presence of this unspoken antagonism.

'I can easily tell you where Tacan is, Mr Tanner,' she said. 'We have a very good gazetteer.'

She went into the library, ran her fingers along the shelves and pulled out a big book. As she opened it a paper dropped to the floor. She stooped and picked it up, and uttered a little scream. In another second she came flying in to them.

'Look!' she said. 'The will!'

Terry snatched it from her hand.

'Where did you find it?' he asked.

'In a book – in the gazetteer I was looking at.'

Terry read quickly. There were half a dozen lines.

*I, Elijah John Decadon, being of sound mind, declare this to be my last will and testament. I leave all of which I die possessed without reservation to Edwin Carl Tanner, the son of my sister, born Elizabeth Decadon, and I hope he will make a good use of his new possessions, a better use than I fear he will make.*

It was signed in his own sprawling hand, and by the side were the names, addresses, and occupations of the three witnesses, one of which signatures was her own, and this had been crossed out and initialled by old Decadon.

Terry folded the paper slowly, his eyes still upon Eddie Tanner.

'Rather a coincidence Miss Ranger was looking in that identical gazetteer at this identical moment,' he said slowly. 'This, I presume, you will want to send to your lawyers – I don't think you will lose it.'

He handed the paper to Eddie.

'I congratulate you, Mr Tanner – so it wasn't necessary to destroy this document after all. It must have been a great surprise to you.'

Tanner did not reply. Danes, who saw him come out of the room, thought he was amused.

# 11

There was a consultation that afternoon at Scotland Yard, and everybody was wrong except Jiggs Allerman. He had interjected comments from time to time as the discussion proceeded, and when at the end the Chief Constable had asked him for an opinion:

'You don't want an opinion, you want approval,' he growled. 'I tell you, you people are just crazy. You don't realise what you're up against. If you imagine that this crowd is going to be caught tonight, you've got another guess coming. If they send anybody to collect this envelope, it'll be a pigeon anyway, and if it only ends with the pinching of a man who is earning a dollar for taking a risk he doesn't understand, I'll be glad, and so will you.'

There was one man on that board who did not like Jiggs. Detective Inspector Tetley was not particularly popular with anybody, least of all with his peers. He was a man with a remarkably small head and a remarkably generous appreciation of what was in it. Jiggs disliked him the first time he saw him. He hated his little waxed moustache; he disliked his pomaded hair, and loathed his lack of intelligence.

'What's your solution?' asked Tetley. 'I know you American police are clever fellows, and, personally speaking, I'd like to have the benefit of your advice, especially as I'm in charge of the show tonight.'

'My solution is a fairly simple one,' said Jiggs shortly. 'Take this boy Salaman and put him in prison – in a cell – anywhere these fellows can't get him. If you do that you'll break the jinx. They depend entirely upon quick results. If you can hold 'em off Salaman for two or three weeks, they're sunk!'

'You're talking as though this fellow's going to be killed!' said Tetley scornfully. 'I'll have twenty officers round him.'

'Tell 'em not to get too close,' said Jiggs.

Tetley had been given charge of the local arrangements. The trap had been staged in his division, and as the hour approached quite a respectable number of loafers began to appear on the sidewalk. They were working men, city clerks, white aproned tradespeople.

'Artistically they're wonderful,' said Terry, who inspected them in the station yard before they went out. 'But you men have got to realise you may be in a pretty tight corner. You've been chosen because you understand the use of firearms, and because you're single men. Whatever happens, you're not to lose your heads. The moment this man approaches Salaman you're to close on him. There'll be a squad car waiting, with four officers in attendance, and you will just turn him over to them and your work will be finished. If there's any shooting you'll shoot to kill – this is no wrist slapping expedition.'

He waited on the opposite corner of Park Lane. At three minutes before the hour Salaman drove up in his limousine and stepped down on to the sidewalk. Except for the detectives, there were very few people about, for the point chosen was well away from the bus stop.

Standing reading a newspaper on the kerb, Terry watched.

'Here comes the stool,' said Jiggs suddenly.

A middle-aged man, wearing a flaming flower in his buttonhole, was walking from the direction of Piccadilly. Terry saw him stop and look at his watch and then go on. He walked a little way past the spot where he had to meet Salaman, then he turned back and came to a halt within a foot of the position which had been described over the telephone. Salaman had seen him and strolled down to meet him. They saw the man touch his hat and ask Salaman a question, and the young man took an envelope from his pocket and handed it to the messenger. As he did so, the detectives closed. They were within a foot of their terrified prisoner, when the staccato crash of a machine-gun came from somewhere overhead. The little man with the flower in his coat and Salaman went down together. A detective drooped and sank by the railings, and a second doubled up and fell with his head in the roadway.

'In that block of flats!' yelled Jiggs.

The entrance to the flats was behind them. The elevator door was open.

'Upstairs, quick! We're police officers.'

The lift shot up, and even in the brief space of time it took to go from the ground floor to the fourth Terry learned the names of the occupants.

'One empty flat, eh? That's the place. Have you got a pass key.'

By the greatest good fortune he had. But there was no need for a key: the door of the flat was wide open, and even as the men ran into the room they could smell the acrid scent of exploded cordite.

Jiggs ran into the front room. The window was wide open and the room was empty, except for a chair drawn up near the windowsill and for the small machine-gun that lay on the floor.

'First blood to green,' said Jiggs between his teeth. 'I wonder how many of those poor coppers are killed. It doesn't matter about Salaman. I just don't like people who have black ceilings.'

Terry went for the liftman, who was also the assistant caretaker. He had admitted nobody to the empty flat, and was quite ignorant of the fact that there was anybody in the building. It was easy, he said, to get an order to view, and in the course of the last two or three days there had been several parties who had made an inspection of the apartment.

There was the usual fire escape; it was at the end of a short passage leading from the main corridor.

'That's the way they went,' said Terry, looking down.

Looking from the window of the flat, he saw a huge crowd surrounding the dead and the dying men, and as he looked an ambulance came up, followed immediately by another. Police whistles were blowing and men in uniform were coming from all directions, while from nowhere had appeared two mounted policemen who were peeling the edge of the crowd.

He sent a man in search of Tetley, and the inspector came, white of face and shaking.

'That young man's killed, and so is the fellow with the flower, and one of my best sergeants. I had a narrow escape myself.'

'You had a narrow escape,' said Jiggs, 'because you weren't on that side of the road. What made you stay over our side?'

Tetley shot a malevolent look at him.

'I was just going over –' he began.

'About two minutes too late,' said Jiggs. 'What made you stay over on our side? I'd like to know that, Mr Tetley.'

The man turned on him in a fury which was half panic.

'Perhaps if you ask the Commissioner tomorrow he'll tell you!' he shouted.

The last of the ambulances had moved away before Terry had sent for the inspector. The crowd was being skilfully dispersed, and already roadsweepers were working at the mess that the shooting had left on the sidewalk.

'This is going to put the cat amongst the pigeons,' said Jiggs. 'Incidentally, it's going to make London sit up and take notice, and I'm rather wondering how they'll take it.'

Terry was silent as they drove back to Scotland Yard in a service car. He was feeling bitterly his own responsibility, though it was not entirely due to his advice or judgement that Salaman had been allowed to walk blindly into a trap that had been set probably since the early morning.

The machine-gun yielded no clue. It was an American make, and of the type which, Jiggs said, was most frequently used by the gangsters of his city.

'That's one to the green,' said Jiggs again, 'and now it will be the blue's turn. The only hope is that these two bands of brigands won't be satisfied to sit quietly and share the loot.'

'By "the green" you mean the last set of notices, the one Salaman had: there are two gangs working – you are sure of that?'

'Absolutely sure,' said Jiggs. 'The blue caught old Decadon. The green are the smarter crowd, I think. It's going to be very interesting to see how it all works out.' He paused for a moment. 'And I hope we'll live to see it!'

# 12

A more exhaustive examination of the officials connected with the building brought no result. The empty flat was in the hands of two or three agents. It was the property of a stockbroker who had moved to other premises and had let his apartment to a group of estate firms. None of these had given the key to a likely tenant, but three of them had within the past two days personally conducted likely tenants through the empty apartment. The last of these, a man and a woman, had inspected the flat early on the morning of the outrage.

'And whilst they were going through the rooms,' said Jiggs, 'the front door would be open and anybody could come in.'

The hall porter remembered 'a dark looking man,' carrying a heavy suitcase, which he said had to be personally delivered to a tenant on the floor whence the shots were fired. He had gone up in the elevator, but the lift attendant did not remember his coming down again. It was exactly at the hour when the prospective tenant was making his inspection.

'That's the explanation,' Jiggs nodded. 'It was easy to get up and down the stairs when the elevator was working and miss seeing the attendant. Probably two of them were in the flat; one was certainly there before the people who were looking the flat over had left the premises.'

All London was scoured that night, and particularly that section of London where the alien had his quarters. Firearms experts and ballistic authorities examined the machine-gun. Terry Weston, in the course of an inspection of the murder scene, discovered what had been obvious yet had been missed – that two of the park railings had been neatly painted white for a depth of about four inches from the crossbar.

'I didn't notice it either,' said Jiggs, 'and that's the one thing I should have looked for – the choppers had to have a target to make absolutely sure. Those marks on the rails gave them the distance and the direction without fail. Gosh! I was mad not to have seen that whilst we were waiting for Salaman to come along.'

Scotland Yard waited in some trepidation for its Press, and there was relief in high quarters when Fleet Street, with singular unanimity, agreed that it was not the moment to blame Scotland Yard, but to devise methods for preventing a recurrence of the outrage. Said the *Megaphone*:

> We do not yet know the full particulars as to what preliminary precautions the police took, and what steps were taken to minimise the danger to this unfortunate gentleman. Until we know this it would be unfair to offer any criticism of Scotland Yard and its system. Neither Scotland Yard nor the public could possibly expect an outrage of this character, committed with cold-blooded ferocity and the reckless employment of machine-guns.

It was generally believed at the time that there were two machine-guns employed, and indeed an erroneous statement to this effect had gone out to the Press.

Early the next morning Terry had a phone message from the last person in the world he expected to hear from.

'It's Eddie Tanner speaking. I wonder if you could find time to come round and see me? It's on a purely personal matter, and I would come to Scotland Yard, but I don't think it's particularly advisable at the moment.'

When Terry arrived he found the young man sitting at the very desk where, forty eight hours before, his uncle had sat, and at which he had been murdered in cold blood. He was smoking a cigarette, and before him was a newspaper opened at the news page.

'Bad business, this,' he said, tapping the black headlines with his finger. 'You must be having a pretty lively time at Scotland Yard.'

Terry was not favourably disposed towards him, but even now could not believe that this man had deliberately shot to death a harmless old man, cold-bloodedly and without compunction.

'Do you want to talk about this?' he asked.

'No, it's rather out of my line.' Eddie pushed the paper aside. 'Miss Ranger will be here in half an hour and I intend dismissing her.

He waited, but Terry made no comment.

'I have been thinking the matter over, and I've decided the situation is a little dangerous for her. Within an hour or two of my uncle being killed she was picked up by a gang, who are probably the murderers, and she went through an experience which must have terrified her. Evidently the people who are responsible for this murder' – he tapped the paper again – 'are not very fond of me, and I'm very anxious that her experience shouldn't be repeated. You're a friend of hers – at least, you know her – and I am anxious to get you to help me.'

'In what respect?'

Eddie swung round in his swivel chair so that his profile was to Terry Weston. He dropped the end of his cigarette into a water-filled vase and lit another.

'That young lady lives in an out of the way place: rather cheap lodging, no telephone – a particularly dangerous situation, if these birds still think she can supply them with hot news. I want Miss Ranger to take a flat in the West End, right in the very centre and in a good class neighbourhood. It's rather a delicate matter to suggest to her, because I am willing to pay the rent of that flat, and naturally, being a charming young lady, she'll kick at the idea. I am not only willing to pay the rent, but I will furnish the flat.'

'Why?' asked Terry.

The other shrugged.

'It's a small price for a large peace of mind,' he smiled. 'In other words, I don't want this lady on my mind.'

'That is a very generous offer,' said Terry, 'and I quite see your point of view, although you may have another one at the back of your mind which you haven't given me.'

Still smiling, Edwin Tanner shook his head.

'I have no *arrière pensée*. I am telling you just how I feel. I like this young lady – which doesn't mean that I'm in love with her, or that I should like to be any better acquainted than I am. She's one of the few women I have met in this world whom I would trust, in spite of the fact that she notified you of something which I asked her not to communicate to the police. But I think I understand that. The circumstances were unusual. But I want, as far as possible, to protect her from her accidental association with me. If you think there's anything behind my very simple suggestion, I can't help it.'

'What do you want me to do?' asked Terry.

'Merely to persuade her to accept my suggestion.'

'I have no influence with Miss Ranger,' said Terry, and again came that quick smile of Eddie's.

'I think you have a greater influence than you imagine, and, if this is the case, will you help me?'

'I'll have to think about it,' said Terry.

When Leslie arrived, a quarter of an hour later, she found Eddie Tanner sitting on her desk.

'No work today, Miss Ranger.' He was almost gay. 'You're pleasantly fired.'

She looked at him in consternation.

'Do you mean you don't want me any more?'

'I mean that there's no more work to do. There's plenty of work,' he said, 'but I have decided that it is a little dangerous for you to be in my employ any longer.'

He told her practically what he had told Terry.

'I've asked Terry Weston here this morning,' he explained quite frankly, 'and I have asked him to help me by adding his influence to mine.'

'But I couldn't possibly accept money for – '

Eddie nodded.

'I see your point of view, and in fact I have anticipated it. The offer of a furnished flat is not one which any decent girl could accept from any man, decent or otherwise. I am greatly obliged to you that you are not furious with me. But that is exactly how the matter stands, Miss Ranger, and you would be taking a great load off my mind if you would see my point of view. I owe you fifty thousand pounds – '

'You owe me fifty thousand pounds?' she gasped.

She had forgotten a promise which she had regarded at the time as a piece of extravagance, not to be seriously considered.

He nodded.

'I haven't fifty thousand pounds to give you at the moment, because it will be some considerable time before my uncle's fortune passes into my hands. But I haven't forgotten.'

'Mr Tanner' – she stood squarely before him – 'you know exactly what Mr Weston thinks, and I'm afraid it's what I think – that in some way you secured possession of that will and that you put it in the gazetteer for me to find. As I believe you found it before I did, that absolves you – '

'It does nothing of the kind,' he interrupted, 'even supposing Inspector Weston's fantastic theory were well founded. In any circumstances I am the executor of my uncle's estate, and he left you a thousand pounds, which I shall give to you today. But I want you to let me add to that the service I suggest.'

She shook her head.

'I'd even forgotten about the thousand pounds,' she said with a faint smile. 'That will be ample for me. I promise you this, Mr Tanner, that I will move my lodging to a more central position. In fact, I had already decided to do that. I have some of my mother's furniture stored and I shall be able to make myself a comfortable home. I am very much obliged to you all the same,' she nodded. 'I didn't somehow think it was going to be very easy, and I doubt whether even the influence of Mr Terry Weston would make me change my mind.'

'I respect you for it,' said Eddie curtly.

He paid her her salary and that for another week in lieu of notice, with punctilious exactness, and half an hour later she was in her little room, packing in preparation for the move, which she had long since regarded as inevitable.

# 13

She would not be sorry to leave behind that dreary little home of hers. It was a lonely place, and at nights when she went home she would sometimes walk for a hundred yards without seeing a soul.

'I shall be sorry to lose you, miss,' said the landlady.

Yet apparently mingled in her sorrow was a certain satisfaction which made it possible for her to be sprightly, even in the moment of her misfortune – if misfortune it was to lose a single young lady who very rarely had a meal in the house.

'The truth is, I have let one room on your floor and I could have let yours. They're coming about it tonight. As a matter of fact, miss, I was going to ask you whether you minded moving upstairs. They're two nice young foreign gentlemen who are studying at the University.'

Just about that time quite a number of young foreign gentlemen studying at the University were seeking lodgings in the West End.

It was a relief to Leslie to know that her departure would not at any rate bring any gloom to a woman who had always been kindly, if sometimes a little tiresome.

With all the morning before her, she intended to do a little shopping, lunch in town, and then go out to the repository where her mother's furniture had been stored since that dreadful day three years before when Leslie had had to face the world alone.

She had been guided by a fussy relative who always appeared on such occasions, and who had induced her to store the goods in a pet repository of his own situated in one of the most inaccessible spots.

At the prospect of a visit to Rotherhithe Leslie made a little grimace. She would, she decided, do the unpleasant task first and leave the shopping, and maybe dinner, till that was completed. In the circumstances she decided upon a taxi.

She dived out of the traffic of London Bridge, down the slope into Tooley Street, and the drabness of Rotherhithe came out to meet her. She was not quite sure where the repository was, and stopped the cab to ask a policeman.

'Zaymen's Repository, miss?'

He gave elaborate directions, in which everything seemed to be on the left and nothing on the right.

'You going to claim your property? You're just about in time. They've been advertising for a week. Old Zaymen's been dead two years; young Zaymen...' he lifted his eyes and shrugged his shoulders.

Leslie supposed that young Mr Zaymen was not all he might be, and began to fear for her furniture.

'Some say they've gone broke,' said the policeman, 'some say they're just selling out, but whichever way it is it can't be right.

She excused herself from his philosophy and directed the taxi onward, and after a lot of searching they came to the repository, which was not on the roadside, as she had expected, but through a labyrinth of small lanes, down one more dirty than any, past walls which seemed to exist for the purpose of giving a resting place to rusting iron, and eventually they came to a stark looking warehouse which she dimly remembered having seen before, though in point of fact she had never been in the neighbourhood until that moment.

There was a certain amount of activity. Men were going in and out; there was an unclean looking clerk sitting behind a glass covered partition, and to him she addressed her request for information, producing the receipt for the furniture and a smaller receipt for the money she had paid from time to time in Zaymen's London office.

The clerk looked at them, scowled at them, held them up to the light, brought them close to his eyes and far away from him.

'You're just in time, young lady. That deposit was going to be sold off tomorrow.'

'You'd have been sold off the next day,' said Leslie, with spirit.

She was handed over to the care of a young clerk who was beautifully tailored and whose hair was glossy and perfectly brushed. He was very young, very important, and spoke continuously of 'we,' and she presumed he was the younger Zaymen until he admitted he only had a 'position' with the firm. After a while he came down to earth and was quite agreeable as he showed her over the floor and when she had identified her furniture summoned white aproned men to remove it in a truck which providentially was there at the moment.

'It's a shame' (he almost said 'shime' but corrected himself), 'Zaymen's busting up like this, but I suppose they couldn't refuse the offer. It's one of the soundest warehouses on the river, with a wharf in front, hauling gear, wood panel walls, fireproofed throughout – '

'In fact a very good warehouse,' said Leslie, a little amused.

'It's young Mr Zaymen.' He shook his head and heaved a sigh.

'Is it women or drink?' asked Leslie, and he was a little shocked.

Apparently Mr Zaymen was a gambler.

'He's gambled away the old family warehouse with wharfage and haulage in good condition.'

'I agree with you it's a shame.'

He became more and more gallant. She felt that at any moment he might take off his coat and lay it over a puddle, if there was a puddle, that her feet should not be soiled.

'When I saw you first,' he admitted at parting – he gave her a very moist hand – 'I thought you were a bit stuck up.'

'When I saw you first,' she said very gravely, 'I thought you were a bit stuck down. And now we're both wrong.'

She went round to the wharf, saw her furniture being loaded on to a trolley, and gave the address to which it should be sent. She was taking rather a wild risk, for the little flat she had applied for had not yet been assigned to her. Tipping the workmen, she was going on, when she heard two men talking. They were American, and she was passing on, when she heard the voice of the second man.

'Say, listen, you couldn't compare this with the Hudson. Why, right up by the palisades it's more'n six times as wide.'

Her heart leapt almost into her mouth. She did not forget voices, and the voice she heard was that of the man who had told her to get into the car that night when she was wanted at Scotland Yard.

He spoke again – some triviality about the colour of the river – and she was sure. She looked round out of the corner of her eye. She did not wish them to recognise her. There were two men; they both wore untidy looking pullovers; both were dressed in blue dungaree trousers, over which had been pulled heavy gumboots, knee high.

'Well, boy,' said the voice, 'let's go and shoot the works, and after we're through you can take Jane and I'll take Christabel and we'll go to the movies.'

The second man laughed at this, a short, hard little laugh that finished as abruptly as it had begun. They were both of moderate height, she noticed, both lithe, unusual looking men. They lurched along past the workmen who were loading her furniture, and presently disappeared behind the trolley. She went back to her taxi, a little uncertain as to what she should do. Though she was confident in her mind that this was the man who had led her into danger that night, she could not be sure. She had once heard an American woman say that all English voices sounded alike, but that she could pick out one voice in a thousand when Americans were speaking. It seemed to Leslie that the reverse held now. All American voices did seem alike, and only the English had a subtle difference.

Who was Jane, and who was Christabel, she wondered as she got into the cab and went bumping over the uneven surface of the lane back to the main road. Some private and possibly ribald jest of their own that did not bear investigating she decided.

They had reached the main road, and the cabman was waiting for a trolley with a trailer to pass, when she heard the chug-chug of a motorcycle, and the rider came immediately abreast of the window. He grabbed the top of the open taxi with his hand and looked in. It was the man she had heard speaking. He gave her a long, swift scrutiny, and she returned his stare.

'What do you want?' she asked.

He muttered something, and dropped behind as the cab moved forward.

There was a possible explanation for his conduct. He may have heard the warehousemen mention her name as he furniture was being loaded, and had come after her to make sure. But if that were so, there could be no question about the accuracy of her recognition. It was the man who had come to her house that night Mr Decadon was killed. What was he doing there? Perhaps he was a sailor; he was dressed in the clothes she had seen men wear on tramp steamers, and just at that period the Pool was full of shipping. She wondered if she should call up Terry…she was always thinking of excuses for calling up Terry.

The cab turned down Cannon Street. Near to the junction of Queen Victoria Street she was held up in a block of traffic. Then, to her amazement, she heard her name called. She looked round. A man was standing by the open window, a small faced man with a waxed moustache.

He lifted his hat with elaborate politeness.

'You don't known me, young lady, but I know you – Inspector Tetley from Scotland Yard…a friend of Mr Terry Weston's,' he smirked.

Then, without waiting for her to speak:

'What have you been doing in this part of the world?'

'I've been down to see my furniture loaded. It was in a repository,' she said.

She felt it was not the moment to challenge his right to speak to her without an introduction, or to stand on ceremony of any kind. In a few moments the block would break and her car would move on.

'Where was that, now?' asked Mr Tetley, 'Rotherhithe eh?' when she told him. 'That's a nasty place! Didn't see anybody you knew, did you? There's some bad characters around here.'

She shook her head.

'No, I didn't see anybody I knew. I hardly expected to.'

'I don't know,' he said, still watching her with his ferret eyes. 'There's something queer about Rotherhithe: you're always meeting people you've met before – it's almost a saying.'

'It isn't my saying,' she said, and at that moment the cab went on.

She dimly remembered now having seen the man. He had come to the house once, after Mr Decadon's death. How odd of him to accost her in the street! She wondered if she would tell Terry…

She heaved a long, impatient sigh.

'You're a fool, Leslie Ranger. Keep your mind off policemen.'

The cab set her down in Cavendish Square and she got out. The cabman, after the manner of his kind, came down to the pavement to stretch his legs.

'Hullo!' he said. 'What's the lark?'

She followed the direction of his eyes. Pasted on the leather hood of the car was a white circle. When he pulled it off the gum was still wet. He walked round the cab: there was another white circle behind, and a third on the opposite side of the hood.

'That wasn't there when we left Rotherhithe,' he said. 'I wonder if that chap on the bicycle…'

For some reason or other which she could not explain, a cold shiver ran down Leslie Ranger's spine, and for a second she had a panic sense of fear which was inexplicable, and therefore all the more distressing.

When she had successfully negotiated the hire of her flat she was terribly tempted to go into the nearest call box and ring up Terry. There must be some good excuse for ringing him up, and it seemed to her that she had half a dozen.

# 14

Terry hurried back to Scotland Yard for the secret conference which was to be held that morning. At that time the Chief Commissioner was Sir Jonathan Goussie, a military man who all his life had lived according to regulations and had succeeded in reaching the highest rank by the careful avoidance or delegation of responsibility. He was a fussy, nervous man, in terror of Press criticism, and just now he had completely lost his head. It was a shocking discovery to his executive that this suave, easygoing, and rather amusing gentleman could so lose his balance and nerve that he was almost incapable of leadership at a critical moment.

He sat at the end of the long table and glowered left and right.

'This is a fine state of affairs!' There was agitation in his voice. 'The finest police force in the world, baffled and beaten by a gang of murdering ruffians...'

'Well, sir, what are we going to do about it?'

It was Wembury, Chief Constable, brisk, brusque, who broke in upon the tirade.

'I am not suggesting that every precaution wasn't taken,' said the Chief Commissioner. 'Tetley, I'm sure, did everything that ingenuity could suggest.'

'I did my best,' said Tetley.

He was a favourite of the old man, and, although he had no right to be in the meeting of the inner council, in the circumstances Wembury had called him.

'I don't want to make any complaint,' he went on, 'but there was a lot of interference which there shouldn't have been.' He glanced malevolently at Jiggs. 'American methods are all very well in their way but you can't expect American police officers to understand the routine of work in London.'

'What interference?' demanded Terry wrathfully. 'He gave you every assistance – '

'We don't want any wrangling,' said Sir Jonathan testily. 'The point is, we've got to find some method by which a recurrence of this ghastly affair can be avoided, and I think Inspector Tetley's suggestion is an excellent one.'

Terry looked at the Chief Constable; the Chief Constable looked at him. It was the first news they had had that a system had been devised.

'I don't mind any suggestions,' said Wembury gruffly, 'but I hardly like to have them sprung on me at a meeting. What is Tetley's idea?'

'Mr Tetley's idea,' said Sir Jonathan, 'is that we should issue a notice giving an enormous reward for information that will lead to the arrest of the murderers, and that the reward should not, as is usually the case, be confined to people outside the police force.'

'That seems fairly original, sir,' said Wembury coldly, 'but I doubt very much if it's of much value. We shall have to take every case individually and on its merits. Nothing is more certain than that there will be a regular flooding of London with these notices – "Pay or be killed".'

'One has been received this morning,' said Sir Jonathan soberly. 'I have it in my pocket.'

He searched in his pocket and produced a folded sheet. From where he sat Terry saw that it was printed in blue.

'It came to a very dear friend of mine, or rather the nephew of a dear friend of mine, and he particularly requested that I should make no announcement whatever to my colleagues, and certainly not to the public, as to who he was.'

Terry stared at the old Chief, amazed.

'Do you mean to say that you're not telling us, sir?'

'I mean to say that I'm not telling you or anybody else,' said Sir Jonathan stiffly. 'I have practically pledged my word of honour on the telephone that I would not reveal the name of the recipient.'

Jiggs sniffed.

'Will they keep his name secret at the inquest?' he asked, and Sir Jonathan glowered at him.

'There will be no inquest, sir,' he rasped. 'If the police do their duty, and if our newly found allies really are the clever people they're supposed to be – '

'I'm all that,' interrupted Jiggs.

Wembury, white with anger, broke in:

'I don't think you quite realise what you're saying, sir. This man, whoever he is, will have to have some form of protection, and we can't protect him unless we know who he is. I must insist upon knowing his name and where he lives.'

The old soldier sat bolt upright, and in his eyes was a court martial and a firing squad.

'No person insists when I'm in the saddle, sir,' he said, and Terry groaned inwardly, for he knew that when Sir Jonathan talked about being 'in the saddle' the situation was hopeless.

The conference broke up soon afterwards, with a mysterious hint from the Chief Commissioner that he intended issuing a statement to the Press.

After the party dispersed there was a private conference in the Chief Constable's office.

'We've got to stop that statement to the Press going out until we've seen it,' said Wembury. 'The old man has never been particularly clever, but now he's gone stark, staring mad. I'm going over to the Home Office to see the Home Secretary, and I'm chancing ignominious dismissal from the service for going behind my superior's back.'

His interview with the Home Secretary, however, did not take place. The Minister of State was not in London, though they had had a wire at the Home Office from him that he was hurrying back to town.

'Perhaps,' said the permanent under-secretary, 'if you saw Sir Jonathan and had a private talk with him – '

'I would sooner see Balaam's ass and have a private talk with him,' said the exasperated Chief Constable.

Nevertheless, when he returned to the Yard he sought an interview, which, however, was refused.

At four o'clock that day the afternoon newspapers carried the Chief Commissioner's 'official statement,' which he had carefully penned at his club during the lunch hour. This statement will go down to history as the most extraordinary document that has ever been issued from Scotland Yard. It ran:

Two desperate crimes, which may or may not have a connection, have been committed in the Metropolitan police area during the past week, and have followed the receipt of threatening communications in which the writer has demanded a big sum of money, failing which the recipient will be killed. There is reason to believe that the killing of Mr Salaman at Marble Arch was a direct consequence of one of these threats. The writer of the letter has stated that if any communication is made to the police, directly or indirectly, the person who receives the message will be murdered. Despite this threat, the Chief Commissioner of Police earnestly requests any person who receives such a communication, whether accompanied by threats of murder or otherwise, to forward it immediately to Scotland Yard, and to communicate by telephone with the Chief Constable that the letter has been forwarded. If the threatened person desires to remain anonymous his wishes will be respected. It may be perhaps advisable that the police should know his name, his address, and his movements. In a fight against organised crime it necessarily follows that there must be occasions when the threat will be executed, and the Chief Commissioner is not able to guarantee, either on his own behalf, or on behalf of the Metropolitan police, complete immunity to any person who forwards particulars of these communications, but every effort will be made to afford protection to law-abiding citizens.

It was signed with the Chief Commissioner's name and all his titles.

Jiggs was the first to get a copy of the paper, and he flew into the Chief Constable's office and found Terry and the big man in conference.

'Read that.'

Wembury read it through quickly, and his jaw dropped.

'For the love of Mike!' he said softly.

'You know what that means, don't you?' said Jiggs. 'This old boy had told the world that Scotland Yard is unable to protect people whose lives are threatened.'

Wembury snatched up the paper and raced along the corridor to the Chief Commissioner's room. He was just coming out, and with him was Inspector Tetley.

'Well, well, well?' he asked.

'It isn't well at all,' said Wembury. 'Is this your communication to the Press?'

The old man fixed his glasses deliberately and read the paragraph from end to end, the while Wembury fretted himself hot with impatience.

'Yes, that is my communication.'

'I'm taking it to the Home Secretary at once,' said Wembury. 'You've given murder a licence – told these thugs in so many words that they can go right ahead and that we're not in a position to protect their victims.'

'I wrote that after full consideration – ' began Sir Jonathan.

The telephone bell in his room was ringing.

'Answer that, Mr Tetley,' he said, and, turning to Wembury: 'You understand this is a gross act of insubordination on your part, and it's a matter which must be reported to the highest quarters.'

Tetley appeared in the doorway.

'It's for you, sir.'

The old man went back. His conversation was a short one. Wembury heard him answering, 'Yes, sir,' and, 'No, sir' and knew he was speaking to the Home Secretary. He started some sort of explanation, which was evidently cut short When he came out of his room he was very white.

'I am going to the Home Office,' he said. 'The matter had better remain in abeyance until I return.'

He never did return. Ten minutes after he was ushered into the room of the Secretary of State he came out again, and the late editions of the newspapers that night carried the bald announcement, without any equivocation, that Sir Jonathan Goussie had been dismissed from his office.

'They didn't even let him resign,' said Terry.

'Hell! Why should they?' growled Jiggs. 'It's the same thing, ain't it?'

They were having a late tea in Terry's office, and the inspector remembered his conversation with Eddie Tanner that morning, and related the interview.

'Maybe he's genuine,' said Jiggs. 'There are funny streaks of generosity in Eddie.'

Terry shook his head.

'I couldn't make myself believe that he killed his uncle in cold blood – ' he began.

Jiggs scoffed.

'Kill him, in cold blood? You don't understand these fellows, boy!' he said. 'That's just the way they kill. There's no emotion in it, no hate, no hot blood at all. They treat human beings the same as the stockyard butchers in Chicago treat hogs! You don't have to hate a hog to cut its throat. Very often you say, "Poor guy!" but you cut his throat just the same because it's your job. Do you hate a fly when you swat it? No, sir! The fact that old man Decadon was his uncle and was old, wouldn't make any difference to Eddie or to any of that crowd. Killing to them is just brushing your coat or putting your tie straight.'

He thought for a moment.

'Naturally he wants the girl out of the house. All the other servants will go too. His own crowd's there by now, I'll bet you. Do you know the names of any of the other servants besides…well, she wasn't a servant exactly.'

'There's a boy called Danes, an under footman,' said Terry after a moment's hesitation.

Jiggs reached for the phone and dialled a number. After a while:

'I want to talk to Danes, the under footman – that is Mr Tanner's house, isn't it?'

He listened for a few seconds.

'Is that so?' he said at last, and hung up the receiver.

'Danes left this afternoon. What did I tell you?'

He took a cigar from his waistcoat pocket, bit off the end and lit it.

'You couldn't expect anything else. Eddie couldn't have that house run by a bunch of servants he knew nothing about.'

'He'll have his own crowd in?' suggested Terry.

'Not on your life,' chuckled Jiggs. 'That'd be too easy. No, he'll get a lot of daily folks in – people who sleep home at night. Maybe he'll have a "secretary," but if you go to the house and ask for him you'll find he's just gone out. He'll have a couple of workmen fixing electric bells and things. They'll be there most of the time, but if you ask for them they'll not be there – they'll just have gone out to dinner. You'll find the only person he hasn't fired is the cook.'

'Why?' asked Terry.

'Because she's a daily woman anyway, and lives in the basement and never comes up, and she cooks good stuff. Now about this young lady you're in love with – '

'I'm not in love with her at all,' protested Terry loudly.

'Your ears have gone red,' said the calm Jiggs, 'which means either that you're in love or you're conscious that you're telling a lie! Anyway, what's her name? Leslie Ranger. There may be a lot in what Eddie said. They might pick her up any night and find out things that she knows without knowing she knows.'

'If she told them,' said Terry.

Jiggs smiled grimly.

'She'd tell 'em all right. You don't know these guys, Terry! You've heard the expression about people stopping at nothing – well, that's them! You look up any old book on the way mediaeval executioners got people to talk, and that won't be the half of it. These birds have improved on Nuremburg – especially with a woman. I could tell you stories that'd make your hair pop out of your head, follicles an' everything! There was a gang in Michigan that was after a member of another gang, and they picked up his girl – a reg'lar redhead and full of fight – and like a fool she said she knew, but she wasn't going to tell where her John was.'

He took the cigar out of his mouth and looked at it. 'Well, maybe I'd better not tell you. Anyway, she told them! They got the John in a Brooklyn speakeasy. The girl was dead when we found her, but there were a lot of signs. They had no feelings against her, you understand – they just wanted to know. And they hadn't any feelings against the guy they bumped – they just had to kill him, and that's all there was to it.'

He thought for a moment, and consulted his cigar again.

'Pretty girl, too.'

'The one that was killed?' asked Terry.

Jiggs shook his head.

'I didn't see her till after she was dead, and she wasn't pretty then! No, this Leslie girl. I've seen her twice – she's lovely. Where's the old boy?'

'The Chief Commissioner? He's gone home. Wembury's seen him, and tried to get him to give the name of the man who's been threatened. All he could find out was that the old man had advised this fellow to keep absolutely quiet and slip away to Scotland tonight.'

Jiggs groaned.

'Well, there must have been lots of other letters received by people in London. Have you heard about them?'

Terry shook his head. He was uneasy.

'No, we haven't had one case reported, and I'm a little worried. Orders have been given to all the men on duty – the uniformed policemen, I mean – to report any house that shows a candle tonight.'

Jiggs shook his head.

'There'll be no candle. This is a blue assignment.'

'There may be green as well,' said Terry. 'We can't keep track of the phone calls, but we can watch for the candles.'

Jiggs got up.

'I'll be changing my hotel from tonight,' he said. 'I'm a little bit too conspicuous and easy to get at, and if any of these guys have got an idea that I'm being useful to Scotland Yard I shall hear from them! If nobody tries to kill me in the next fortnight I'm going to feel mighty insulted!'

He left Scotland Yard and went on foot down Whitehall to his hotel. His hands were in his coat pockets and the cigar between his teeth and the rakish set of his hat contributed to the picture of a man who found life a very amusing experience. But the hand in each pocket gripped an automatic and under the brim of the down-turned hat which shaded his eyes was a slither of mirror.

Whitehall was filled with junior civil servants homeward bound; Trafalgar Square a whirling roundabout of traffic. He crossed Whitehall where the Square and that thoroughfare meet, and without any warning of his intention suddenly swung himself on to a westward-bound bus. Five minutes later he passed through the door of his hotel. He had not told Terry that he had already changed his place of residence, though he had notified the telephone exchange at Scotland Yard where he could be found.

He went up to the first floor, where his suite was, unlocked the door and, reaching in his hand, switched on the light. The next second he was lying half stunned on the floor, covered with plaster and the debris of a smashed party wall. The hotel rocked with the crash of the explosion. When he got painfully to his feet he saw the door hanging on its hinges, and clouds of smoke were coming out of the room.

The right hand which had turned on the switch had escaped miraculously. He examined it carefully: there was a scratch or two, but no serious damage. All the lights in the corridor were out. Indeed, for five minutes the whole hotel was in darkness.

He heard shouts below; the loud gong of the fire alarm was ringing, and voices were coming to him up the stairs.

He took a flat electric torch from his hip pocket and sent a ray into the room. It was wrecked. Part of the ceiling had fallen in, the windows had been blown into the street. The wreckage of a table was scattered round the room, and pieces of chairs with torn upholstery lay about the floor.

Jiggs stared and blinked.

'Pineapples and everything!' he said.

# 15

The bomb had been placed on the table, and had been connected with the electric light. If Jiggs had gone into the room before he had turned the switch, he must have been killed.

The clang of fire engines came to him as he walked back along the littered corridor. At the head of the stairs he met the manager, pale, almost speechless.

'It was only a bomb,' said Jiggs. 'Go along and see if anybody's hurt in the other rooms.'

Fortunately at this hour of the day the rooms were empty. His own sitting room was immediately above an hotel cloakroom, the ceiling of which had been blown in, but, except for a slight cut, the attendant had been uninjured.

After the firemen had come and extinguished an unimportant blaze Jiggs inspected his own bedroom. The wall had been breached; a two foot jagged hole showed where the wardrobe had been.

'I shall have very little to pack,' said Jiggs philosophically.

He tried to telephone to Scotland Yard, but the whole telephone system of the house was out of gear.

A huge crowd had collected before the hotel, and crowds at the moment were fairly dangerous. Jiggs went out the back way, found a telephone booth and acquainted Terry.

'Would you like to be host to a homeless American copper who has got one pair of burnt pyjamas and a mangled toothbrush?'

Terry gave his address.

'I'll come round and pick you up,' he said.

'Take the back way,' warned Jiggs. 'There's a crowd of guns in front.'

Here he may have been exaggerating, but, as he told Terry later, one gun in the hands of an expert chopper can be as deadly as fifty.

They drove back to Scotland Yard with such of Jiggs' baggage as could be retrieved.

'Pineapples, eh?' said Jiggs, as they drove along. 'I wondered if they would use 'em.'

'By "pineapple" you mean "bomb"?'

'By "pineapple" I mean "bomb",' said Jiggs gravely. 'It's part of the racketeer's equipment.'

Then suddenly he brightened up.

'That's a compliment, anyway. These birds think I mean something! Who's in charge?' he asked suddenly.

'Tetley,' said Terry. 'The Chief Constable brought him into the Yard for special duty. Tetley's a pretty shrewd kind of fellow,' he explained, 'with a more or less good record. He's too well off to please me, but he may have got it honestly.'

'Sure he may,' said Jiggs sardonically. 'But what he's got now will be nothing to what he'll have this time in three months – he gets right away with it, and that's doubtful.'

Later in the evening fragments of the bomb were brought to Scotland Yard and examined by the experts.

'Good stuff, well made,' was Jiggs' verdict. 'They've got a factory somewhere in London, but the bomb itself was cast in America. I think your chemists will find that when they start analysing it.'

Tetley, who had brought the pieces, made a brief but not particularly illuminating report. Nobody had been seen to enter the room, and three quarters of an hour before Jiggs' return a chambermaid had been in and seen nothing unusual.

'Here is a list of all the guests in the hotel,' said Tetley, and laid a typewritten paper on the table. 'You see, sir. I have divided them into floors – on Mr Jiggs – '

'Captain Allerman,' said Jiggs.

'I beg your pardon. On Captain Allerman's floor there were Lady Kensil and her maid, Mr Braydon of Bradford, Mr Charles Lincoln, the American film actor, and Mr Walter Harman and family from Paris.'

Jiggs bent over and looked at the list.

'And Mr John Smith of Leeds,' he said. 'You seem to have forgotten him, Inspector.'

Tetley looked round at him.

'That's the list that was given to me.'

'And Mr John Smith of Leeds,' repeated Jiggs. 'I've been on the telephone to the manager and got the list of people on my floor, and it included Mr John Smith.'

'He didn't tell me,' said Tetley quickly.

'He not only told you' – Jiggs' tone was deliberate and offensive – 'but he also said that he was rather suspicious of Mr John Smith, who spoke with a curious accent.'

There was a dead silence.

'Yes, I remember now,' said Tetley carelessly. 'In fact, he talked so much about him that I forgot to put him down.'

He scribbled in the name.

'Did he tell you,' Jiggs went on, 'that Mr John Smith was the only person he hadn't seen since the explosion, and that when he opened the door of his room he could find no baggage?'

'Did he?' demanded Wembury when Tetley hesitated.

'No, sir,' said the Inspector boldly. 'He may have told Captain Allerman that, but he didn't tell me. As a matter of fact, I haven't finished my investigations. I thought you wanted the pieces of the bomb over as quickly as you could get them.'

'Go and find John Smith – of Leeds,' said Wembury curtly.

Jiggs waited till the door had closed upon the inspector.

'I don't want to say anything about the investigating methods of Scotland Yard, Chief,' he said, 'but it seems to me that that is a piece of information that should have been reported.'

Wembury nodded.

'I think so,' he said.

'Did the Commissioner tell you the name of the man who's been threatened?' asked Terry.

'No – I don't know why, but he flatly refused. When I say I don't know why, I'm not quite telling the truth. The old man has got the old Army code, which is a pretty good code in the mess-room, but not so good at Scotland Yard. Apparently he promised this fellow, or his uncle or whoever it was communicating with him, that the name should not be given, and not even the Secretary of State can compel this stubborn old dev – the late Chief Commissioner to give us any information on the subject.'

'That's tough.' Jiggs shook his head.

He looked down at the table thoughtfully.

'Suppose we get somebody under suspicion, what are the rules at Scotland Yard? Do you treat him gently and ask him a few questions, or do you slap his wrist or anything?'

A glint was in Wembury's eye.

'No, we treat them like perfect citizens,' he said, 'and if we dare ask them a question or two about their antecedents, somebody gets up in Parliament and that's the end of the man who asked the question.'

Jiggs nodded slowly.

'Is that so? Well, I hope you realise that if you do catch any of this crowd – and you're pretty sure to – you're dealing with the toughest bunch of babies that ever shook hands with the yellow jury that acquitted 'em on a murder charge. If that's the law, Chief, I'm all for breaking it.'

The Chief Constable shook his head.

'I'm afraid you can't break it here, Jiggs.'

'Maybe I'll find some place where I can,' said Jiggs, and nobody protested.

He drove home with Terry and was glad to walk into the cosy flat where Terry had his habitation. It was a block just off the Marylebone Road. Terry kept no servants, except a woman who came in daily to clean for him. Fortunately there was a spare bed made up, for Terry was expecting a visit from an aunt who occasionally stayed with him when she was in London.

'If auntie comes in the middle of the night she's got to be a loud knocker to wake me,' said Jiggs.

'She won't. As a matter of fact, I had a wire from her today telling me she's postponed her visit.'

Terry yawned. Neither he nor Jiggs had had two hours of consecutive sleep during the past two days.

'Personally,' said Jiggs, 'I don't believe in sleep. I shut my eyes occasionally as a sort of concession to human practices.'

Yet ten minutes later he was in bed, and was asleep when Terry knocked at his door to ask if he wanted anything.

They both slept heavily, so heavily that the consistent ringing of the telephone failed to waken them for ten minutes. It was Jiggs who heard it first, and by the time he was in the passage Terry was out.

'What time is it?' said Jiggs.

'Half-past two,' said his host.

'Where's the telephone?'

'In the next room.'

Terry followed him and stood by when Jiggs took up the instrument.

'It's probably for me,' he said. 'I've got a few boys looking around on behalf of the Chicago Police Department.' Then: 'It's Scotland Yard. All right, I'll take the message... Yes, Inspector Weston's here, but it's Captain Allerman speaking.'

He listened in silence for a long time, then he looked up.

'The name of that feller that the Chief Commissioner was so stuffy about is Sir George Gilsant.'

'How do you know?' asked the startled Terry.

'He was picked up by the side of a railway at midnight,' said Jiggs, 'in his pyjamas, and chock full of slugs.'

Terry snatched the phone from him.

'That's all I can tell you, sir,' said the operator. 'We got a message in just a few minutes ago from the Hertfordshire police. They found him lying on the bank by the railside. He'd evidently been in bed.'

'Dead?'

'Oh yes, sir. The Hertfordshire police believe he was on the Scottish express. The body was found half an hour after the train passed, by a platelayer.'

'All right,' said Terry after a moment's pause. 'I'll be down.'

Jiggs squatted down in a chair, his elbows on the table, his head in his hands.

'The old man advised him to go to Scotland, eh?' he said savagely. 'He went! Who is Sir George Gilsant?' he asked.

As it happened, Terry was in a position to inform him. Sir George was a very wealthy landowner, who had a big interest in a North Country steel corporation. He himself was of foreign extraction, and had been naturalised a few years previous to the war, when his father had taken out papers. He had a house in Aberdeen.

Jiggs nodded.

'He might have been safe if he'd got there,' he said surprisingly. 'I think your old man was every kind of a fool, but if you can get any of these threatened men out of London, into the wide open spaces – if you'll excuse the cinema expression – the gangs are not going after them – it's too dangerous. Open country roads are easy to watch. But if you try to get away from London in a train you're liable to end in the mortuary. We've got to know these fellows – know their names and where they live – the minute the threatening letter reaches them, and then we can save them. When I say we can, I mean we may,' said Jiggs.

He looked at the clock ticking on the mantelpiece.

'It's too late for a morning sensation – or is it?'

Terry shook his head.

'No; the last editions go at four o'clock. It'll be in the morning papers all right.'

He had a bath and dressed, and waited an interminable time till Jiggs was ready.

'You had to wait till a squad car arrived, anyway,' said Jiggs.

'We could have taken a taxi,' said Terry fretfully.

'While you're talking about taking things, will you take a word of advice, Terry?' Jiggs was very serious. 'In no circumstances hire a taxi on the street till this little trouble's through. And if you don't follow my advice, maybe you'll know all about it!'

All Scotland Yard was illuminated as though it were early evening when they reached there. The Chief Constable was in his office, and Terry heard the full story of the murder. It had been compiled by investigators on the spot and by the reports which had been telephoned from Hertford.

Sir George had left his house shortly after ten, accompanied by his valet. He carried two suitcases, and the valet had booked two sleeping compartments for the ten-thirty to Scotland. They had driven to Kings Cross, arriving there about ten minutes past ten, and Sir George had gone straight to his compartment, and (apparently on the advice of the Chief Commissioner) had locked himself in.

The valet's compartment was at the farther end of the train. He had waited till the train started, then knocked at the door and had gone in to assist Sir George to retire for the night. During that period the door was locked. He had left his employer at five minutes to eleven and waited until the door was locked after him.

Between Sir George's sleeping berth and the next compartment there was a door, which was locked. The next compartment was occupied by an elderly lady, who had booked her compartment in the name of Dearborn. She was apparently an invalid and walked with difficulty and she was attended by a dark and elderly nurse who wore glasses.

After the discovery of the body a telegram had been sent up the line to York, and the station officials and the local police conducted a search of the train. The compartment occupied by the lady was found to be empty. The attendant said that the lady and her nurse had left the train, which had been specially stopped, at Hitchin.

Sir George's compartment was locked on the inside, and so also was the communicating door. The bed in which the unfortunate baronet had slept bore marks of the tragedy. Pillow, sheets and blankets were soaked with blood. There was blood, too, on the window ledge, but the window itself was closed and the blinds drawn. Also, the report stated, the extra blanket which is carried in the rack had been taken down and covered over the bed, so that at first, when the inspecting officers entered the compartment, they saw no sign of the murder.

The Hitchin railway authorities confirmed the fact that the two women had left the train at that station. A big limousine car was waiting to receive them. The porter on duty was struck by the fact that neither of them carried baggage.

By the time this information reached Scotland Yard it was too late to establish a barrage on the roads. It was not until the next day that any reliable information came through as to the movements of the black limousine.

Sir Jonathan Goussie was aroused from his bed in the early hours of the morning and told of the tragedy. He was shocked beyond measure.

'Yes, that was the gentleman who communicated with me,' he said. 'And perhaps…on consideration…it might have been better if I had broken my word. It was on my advice he went to Scotland…oh, my God! How dreadful!'

They left him, a shattered old man, and came back to Terry's room as the first light of dawn was showing in the sky.

'Things are certainly moving,' said Jiggs. 'I wonder what the rake-off will be today.'

'Do you think they've sent to other people?'

Jiggs nodded.

'And that they've paid?'

'Sure they've paid,' said Jiggs. 'Don't you see the psychology of it? These guys are not asking for a lot of money. They wanted two thousand from Sir George Gilsant, and he could have paid two thousand pounds without remembering that he ever had it. It isn't as though they were asking for twenty or fifty thousand, or some colossal sum. They're making reasonable demands – and in two months' time they'll make more reasonable demands. Any man they catch for money will be caught again. That's the art and essence of blackmail. You can always afford to pay once. It's after you've paid about ten times that it becomes monotonous. After this train murder the letters are going out by the hundred.'

'But you don't suggest,' said Terry hotly,' that Englishmen will submit – '

'Forget all that English stuff, will you?' said Jiggs, scowling at him. 'Lose the notion that the English are just godlike supermen that won't react the same as every other nation reacts. We can sit outside and criticise – say they're yeller, and that we wouldn't pay – but our job is to get killed – it isn't their job. Who was the grandest Englishman that ever lived? Richard Coeur de Lion, wasn't it? And when that Emperor of Austria, or whatever dump it was, said he'd bump him off unless he paid, didn't Mr Lion G. Heart send home and collect all the rates and taxes and babies' money boxes and everything to get himself freed? Sure he did! People ain't yeller because they want to live, or else we're all that colour, boy!'

When Jiggs said he had a few people scouting round for him he spoke no more than the truth. It is true they were not attached, officially or unofficially, to the Chicago Police Department, but they were recruited from a class with which he was very well acquainted. Jiggs' journey to England had originally been arranged in connection with an international conference of police, to deal with a considerable body of cardsharpers and confidence men which spends its life travelling between the United States and Europe. Jiggs had got into touch with half a dozen right fellows, and was getting useful information from them.

He invited himself to breakfast with one Canary Joe Lieber that morning. Joe lived in good style at a railway station hotel in the Euston Road. It was quiet, a little off the beaten track, and it was the kind of place where he was unlikely to meet anybody with whom he had played cards on his late transatlantic journey.

Lieber was stout, red faced, slightly bald. He had a sense of humour; but his principal asset lay in the fact that he was well acquainted with the Middle West and its more undesirable citizenry. He looked up as Jiggs walked unannounced into his sitting room, where he was about to have breakfast.

'Eggs and bacon? That goes for me too, Joe. Anything doing?'

Joe stared at him solemnly.

'See the morning paper, Jiggs? Put a pineapple on you, didn't they? Is that the same crowd that bumped off that Sir Somebody?'

Jiggs nodded.

'It's going to be hot for some of us,' he said.

'I guess you'd better count me out as a well of information.'

'Cold feet, Joe?'

Jiggs pulled up a chair.

'Why, no, but I'd like 'em to stay warm, Jiggs. I didn't know the racket was jigging like it is. You've got a pretty bad bunch here.'

'Have you seen anybody?' asked Jiggs.

Joe pursed his lips.

'Well, I'm not so sure that I want to tell you anything – I never was a stool – but Eddie Tanner's here, and so is Kerky Smith. You know that, of course?'

Jiggs nodded.

'Any little men?'

'Hick Molasco's here. His sister's married to Kerky.'

'She's got his name anyway,' said Jiggs. 'Anybody else?'

Joe leaned back in his chair.

'I'm thinking, Jiggs, whether it's worthwhile telling you – they're yeller rats, all of 'em, and I'd sooner see 'em in hell than eat candy. But I'm a married man with a large and hungry family.' He looked round the room. 'Just have a peek outside that door, Jiggs.'

A waiter was just coming in, in answer to Joe's bell.

'Order what you want,' said Joe.

When Jiggs had closed the door on the waiter:

'I don't like them Sicilian looking waiters,' he said. 'Sit down.'

He leaned across the table and lowered his voice.

'Do you remember Pineapple Pouliski – the guy that took a rap for ten to life in Chi?'

Jiggs nodded.

'I knew him,' Joe went on, 'because he stood in with the crowd that was working the western ocean twelve – it must be fifteen years ago. Then I heard he'd gone into a racket in Chicago, and met him wearing everything except earrings. He was working for the advancement of American labour when the stockyard strike was on – '

'Bombed the State Attorney's house or sump'n – ' Jiggs nodded. 'That's what he got it for.'

Again Joe looked round, then, almost inaudibly:

'He's here.'

'In this hotel, or in London?'

'In London. It's a funny thing. I saw him in a shop on Oxford Street, buying clothes for his old mother. He didn't see me, but I heard him tell the girl who was serving.'

'He didn't see you?' asked Jiggs. His eyes were all alight with excitement.

'No, sir,' Joe shook his head.

'Can you remember the store on Oxford Street?'

The other pursed his large lips.

'No, sir. Rightly it wasn't on Oxford Street, it was just off – one of those side turnings where you can buy cheap wardrobes. As a matter of fact, I was in there getting something for my wife, one of – um – ' He made ineffectual gestures.

'Does it matter?' said Jiggs politely. 'You don't remember what he bought?'

'No. They were still handing out stuff to him when I went away.'

He could, however, give a fairly accurate description of where the shop was situated.

'You don't know where he's living now?'

'You know all I know, Jiggs,' snapped the other, for once coming out of his genial character. 'I tell you, I'll be glad not to be in on this racket, because it looks mighty dangerous to me – somebody blew out an hotel yesterday.'

'They're yeller rats – they got my brother-in-law's home with a pineapple because he wouldn't join their plumbing association, and I don't feel very good towards 'em.'

Then, inconsequently:

'Pineapple was wearing glasses, and there was a yellow taxicab with the wheels painted green waiting for him outside.'

Suddenly he struck himself in the mouth with the flat of his hand.

'Shut up, will you?' he growled. 'Won't you never learn? At the same time, Jiggs, it mightn't have been his taxi, but there it was with the flag down.'

Jiggs went back to Terry's flat and called him on the phone. Briefly he gave the gist of what he had heard, without, however, disclosing the name of his informant.

'You've got a taxi department at Scotland Yard... Public Vehicles, is it? Well, can you get on to the fellow in charge and find if he's heard of such an atrocity as a yellow taxi with green wheels? And listen, Terry, get the Chicago Police Department on the long distance. Put a transatlantic call in for me, and I'll be there in your bureau – well, office.'

He had hung up the telephone, when it started ringing again. He thought that the Scotland Yard operator had forgotten to ring off. He picked up the receiver.

'Hullo! Is that you, Jiggs?'

Allerman had not spoken.

'Hullo, Kerky! Thought-readin'?'

'No, sir!' He heard a little chuckle from the other end of the wire. 'Nothin' mysterious about it. I was trying to get through to you, and maybe I didn't get tangled up with the last part of your talk with little old Scotland Yard. Everything all right in Chicago? Nobody sick, Jiggs?'

'That's just what I'm going to find out,' said Jiggs. 'How did you know I was here?'

'The operator at Scotland Yard told me,' said Kerky. 'Wondered if you might like to come and have a bit of lunch with me at the Carlton or any place you like. Nothing's too swell for you, Jiggs. I'd like to have you meet my wife too.'

'Which one is this?' asked Jiggs rudely.

'Say, listen! If I told her that she'd be so sore! Is it a date?'

'Mark it,' said Jiggs.

If there was one thing more certain than another, it was that Scotland Yard's very secretive operator had not given Albuquerque

Smith the private telephone number of Inspector Weston. He took the trouble to inquire when he reached headquarters, and had his views confirmed.

'They're tailing all the time – they knew I was there,' said Jiggs thoughtfully.

When he had come out from seeing his friend of the morning, he had noticed the waiter emerging from the room next to the suite occupied by Joe. Jiggs took a bold step. Accompanied by two officers from Scotland Yard, he went back to the hotel. His friend was out, but he saws the dark faced waiter who had served them that morning. The manager of the hotel was present at the interview, which took place in Joe's sitting room.

'I'm putting this man under arrest on suspicion, and I want you to take one of these officers to his room,' Jiggs said to the manager.

He was drawing a bow at a very large venture. Luck was with him. The waiter, having been at first amused and indifferent, suddenly made a dart for liberty. When he was captured he committed the unpardonable sin from a policeman's point of view; he pulled a gun on the detective who held him. Jiggs knocked it out of his hand, and they put the irons on him.

In his room was a half finished letter, written in English. It began without any preliminary compliment.

*Jiggs came up to see Canary Joe Lieber, and they had a long talk. Joe said something about Pouliski – Pineapple Pouliski. I could not hear; they were talking in a very low voice.*

Jiggs read the letter and put it in his pocket.

'Don't take that man to the Yard, take him to Mr Weston's house,' he said. 'Frisk him first, and then take the irons off him. We don't want to attract any attention.'

He walked out arm in arm with his prisoner, and came to Terry's flat without any unusual incident.

'You two boys can wait outside while I talk to this feller,' said Jiggs, and a look of alarm came to the dark man's face.

The two officers demurred, but they retired.

'Now, sonny boy,' said Jiggs, 'I've got a very short time to get the truth from you, but I want to know just where you were sending that letter.'

'That I shall not tell,' said the man, who called himself Rossi.

'Ever heard of the third degree, kid?' asked Jiggs. 'Because you're going to get it. Where was that letter going?'

'I'll see you in hell – ' began the man passionately.

Jiggs yanked him on his feet again by his collar.

'Let's talk as brothers,' he said kindly. 'I don't want to beat you up. It breaks my heart to do it. But I've got to know just where that letter was going.'

The trembling youth thought awhile.

'All right,' he said sulkily. 'It is for a young lady I make these notes. Her name is Miss Leslie Ranger.'

Jiggs gaped at him.

'For whom?' he asked incredulously.

'Miss Leslie Ranger.'

Then, to Jiggs' astonishment, he gave Leslie's address.

'Do you send it to her?'

'No, mister.' The young man shook his head. 'A boy comes for it and he takes it to her.'

Jiggs heaved a sigh.

'Oh, just that! Now, what boy comes for it, and when?'

Here Rossi could tell him nothing except that those were the orders he had received on the night before. He was told by a compatriot on the telephone (Rossi was a Sicilian) to keep an eye on the guest, to note the names of his visitors, and to hear, if he possibly could, any conversation between them. The compatriot had invoked the sacred name of a common society, and Rossi had obeyed.

'A very simple little story,' said Jiggs. 'Now perhaps you'll explain why you carried a gun loaded in every chamber, and why you pulled it on the officer who arrested you? What were you expecting?'

The man was silent here.

'Are you going to talk?' asked Jiggs wearily.

Ten minutes later Rossi broke, and, after allowing him time to compose himself, Jiggs took him off to Scotland Yard and handed him over to the station sergeant at Cannon Row.

He reported to the Chief Constable.

'There's a member of the gang in every big hotel. As a matter of fact, there's one on every floor. This boy Rossi is from New Orleans, of all places in the world. He was doing badly and was tipped off there was good money in England. He reported to the chief of his society in New York and got his assignment right away – there's some arrangement by which countries exchange waiters, and Rossi was put into this particular job. The gunplay was easy to explain. He's served one term, having been sentenced to from one year to twenty for unlawful wounding – he's not a fully fledged gunman, but he's got the makings.'

'What about his passport?'

'It's in order,' nodded Jiggs. 'No, we've got nothing on him and we can't connect him with anybody in town – doesn't know Eddie Tanner or Kerky or any of them. If he had he'd have spilt it, because he's soft.'

The Chief looked at Jiggs suspiciously.

'Did you get all this as a result of questions?' he asked.

'More or less,' said Jiggs.

Then, suddenly, leaning over the table:

'Listen, Chief: you've had five people killed in less than five days, and there's a whole lot of people who are due for the death rap. Are you putting the tender feelings of this wop before the lives of your friends and fellow citizens? Is that the way it goes in England, that you mustn't hurt this kind of dirt?'

'It's a rule, Jiggs,' said the Chief Constable.

Jiggs nodded.

'Sure it's a rule. Get yourself assassinated like gentlemen, eh? You can't fight machine-guns with pea-shooters, Chief, nor with pillows. I just slapped his wrist and he fell. If he'd got his finger inside the trigger-guard of his Smith-Wesson one of your detectives would either be dead or feeling more hurt than Rossi is.'

The argument was unanswerable.

'You'd better have a talk with Terry,' said Wembury. 'I couldn't say any more to you without approving, and that I mustn't do.'

Jiggs had hardly been in Terry's office five minutes when the transatlantic call came through. In another second he heard a familiar voice.

'Oh, Hoppy!' he hailed him joyfully. 'It's Jiggs speaking, from London, England. Listen – don't waste your time on all that "sounds like in the next room" stuff. Remember Pineapple Peter Pouliski?... Sure. Isn't he in Joliet?...'

Terry saw him pull a long face.

'Is that so? Have you got a good picture of him?... Yeah, that'll do. Send it down to the Western Union and have 'em telegraph it across. If they haven't got an instrument they'll tell you where you can get it. When did he come out of Joliet?... Only served two years? Poor soul!'

# 16

Terry Weston had Inspector Tetley with him when he went up for the preliminary hearing of the inquest on Sir George Gilsant. By a special Home Office order the inquiry had been moved from Hertford to London.

'Life,' said Tetley, 'is just one darned inquest after another.'

He twirled his little waxed moustache and grinned expectantly.

'When you say anything funny I'll laugh, Tetley,' said Terry. 'At the moment it's taking a hell of a lot to amuse me.'

'You take things too seriously,' said the inspector. 'After all, you can't help crimes like this being committed, and the great thing is not to lose your head. If Sir George had taken our advice – '

'By "our" I presume you mean the Chief Commissioner and yourself?'

Tetley nodded.

'We wanted him to go out of town by car.'

'Did he tell you – the old man?'

Tetley nodded. He was rather proud of himself.

'Yes, sir, he told me. In fact, I'm the only person he did tell that it was Sir George who was threatened.'

Terry Weston said nothing; he could hardly think about the blunder without wanting something particularly exciting to happen to the late Chief Commissioner.

Tetley was right. He saw before him a ghastly procession of inquests. That on the detectives and Salaman had been adjourned. The coroner who was inquiring into the latest fatality only heard formal

EDGAR WALLACE

evidence of identification, and agreed to an adjournment of a fortnight.

Terry stayed behind to talk to him and to make arrangements for future sittings.

'I suppose you'll want more than a fortnight, Inspector?'

'It looks as if we'll want years,' said Terry ruefully, 'for unless we get a lucky break – I mean a bit of luck; I've been associating with an American detective lately, so my language is not all that Mayfair could desire – I can't tell you when we shall want the next sitting.'

The coroner scratched his chin.

'It's a curious business,' he said. 'I met a man this morning, a very rich man called Jenner, who's in a terrible state. He shook like a leaf when you talked to him, and it occurred to me that he might have had one of these letters.'

'Really?' Terry was interested. 'I think I know the man you mean – Turnbull Jenner, the coal man?'

'That's the chap,' said the coroner. 'He was saying what a disgraceful thing it was that Scotland Yard couldn't give protection to people. He was quoting the Commissioner's letter.'

'That will be quoted for a long time,' said Terry grimly.

When he came out of the court he saw Tetley speaking very earnestly to a man who was a stranger to him. He was fair enough to be described as an ash blond. His log face and his heavy chin made him rememberable to Terry. As they were speaking a third man passed them, turned back and said a few words to the two. He was a round, plump faced man below middle height; he wore horn-rimmed spectacles and was carefully tailored. The two men went off together, and Tetley strolled back towards the courthouse. He was visibly disconcerted to see Terry watching him.

'Hullo, Chief! I've just been talking to those fellows. They wanted to know which was the nearest way to Highgate, and as they seemed foreign I improved the shining moment, so to speak, by asking them who they were.'

102

'I didn't even notice them,' said Terry, and he saw a look of relief on the other's face. 'You can take the police car back to headquarters, Tetley,' he said. 'I shall want to see you this evening.'

'I thought if you drove me back in your car we might talk things over,' began Tetley.

'Go the way I suggest,' said Terry, and the Inspector's face went livid with fury.

'You're not talking to a flat-footed copper, you know, Weston,' he said. 'All this high-hat business – '

'When you speak to me, say "sir",' said Terry, 'and touch your hat – will you remember that, Inspector?'

He left the man so shaken with rage that he could not have spoken even if he had thought of an appropriate answer.

Terry got back to headquarters just before five. He was a very tired man, in no physical condition to undertake any further investigation. He had promised himself that he would seek out Leslie Ranger. He knew she was changing her lodging that day, and up to the moment had received no information as to her new address.

Jiggs came in, looking as if he had just woken up and had all the day before him. He could do no more than point to a chair.

'Sit down, and don't be energetic. I'm all in.'

Jiggs relit the stump of his cigar.

'That picture has come through on the television apparatus or whatever you call it – the picture of Pineapple Pouliski. The funny thing that, though I pinched him, I don't remember what he looks like – I'm confusing him with somebody else all the time. How much did they ask from Sir George Gilsant?'

'Two thousand pounds,' said Terry, and took up the phone. 'That reminds me,' he said. 'Is the Chief Constable there?… Can I speak to him?'

'He's on his way down to you, sir,' said the secretary's voice, and at that moment the Chief came in.

'What are we going to do?' said Terry. 'A man named Jenner has been threatened – at least, the coroner thinks so.'

Wembury nodded and dropped into a chair.

'That's what's worrying me. I've had a tip about another man who has had a letter of demand and has not communicated with Scotland Yard. What are we to do? If we start making inquiries we're responsible for the man's death, supposing he is killed. I think we've got to make it a rule, Terry, that we do not move in any of these cases until we are requested to do so by the threatened party. It's an act of cowardice, I admit, but what are we to do? We cannot be responsible for the lives of these people, and for the moment I certainly can think of no method of offering them protection. That man you put into Cannon Row, Jiggs, has asked to see a lawyer. He has also complained to the station sergeant and the divisional surgeon that you beat him up.'

'I'll talk to him,' said Jiggs.

It was at that moment that a messenger came in with a photograph in his hand.

'This has come over the wire, sir. The man who brought it is outside.'

'Show him in.'

The operator was admitted, and carefully stripped the cover from the photograph, which was still a little wet.

'That's the boy,' said Jiggs. 'Why, how could I forget him! Pineapple Pouliski!'

He handed the photograph across the table to Terry, and the Chief Inspector gasped, for the photograph was the picture of the little man who had spoken to Tetley that afternoon outside the coroner's court!

# 17

There is a special department at Scotland Yard which is never written about. Its duties are very often painful. Its very existence might be taken as a slight upon the finest police force in he world.

The head of that department was summoned to the Chief Constable's office.

'Put Inspector Tetley under close observation,' was the Chief's order. 'He is not to be left day or night. His room is to be searched without his knowledge, and he may be arrested without warrant on the instructions of Chief Inspector Weston or myself – or Captain Allerman,' he added.

The head of the department had heard too many surprising things to be surprised now.

'I'll see to that personally,' he said.

Twenty specially chosen detectives came into Terry Weston's office and examined the photograph of Pineapple Pouliski. They examined it intently, rephotographing it on to their minds, and then went away.

Just before midnight, in one of the most fashionable of night clubs, a pleasant-spoken man, who was accompanied by a beautiful girl, came on to the floor and asked for a table. He was round faced, wore glasses, and spoke with a soft, southern accent. Five minutes later, a man who was not in evening dress, and against all the laws of the club, strolled on to the floor and pulled out a chair immediately opposite the round faced man.

'I want to see you outside,' he said in an even tone. 'If you put your hand in your pocket I'll shoot you – those are my instructions.'

'Who are you?'

The inquiry came after a pause.

'I am an officer from Scotland Yard.'

'Sure I'll come with you.'

The man got up, spoke a reassuring word to his companion and strolled out. In the vestibule he asked for his coat.

'It's a nice warm evening and you won't want that,' said the detective.

Then Pineapple Peter Pouliski became aware of the fact that there were half a dozen tough looking men in the vestibule, and none of them appeared friendly.

A phone message came through from the Yard. Jiggs heard it without enthusiasm.

'Sure I'll be present when you question him,' he sneered. 'I'll hold the scent-spray!'

As they walked Pouliski into Terry's room he saw Jiggs and momentarily stopped, looked at him from under bent brows, and then, with an effort that was palpable, took two steps into the room.

'Let me offer you a chair,' said Jiggs politely. 'How are you, Pineapple? Haven't seen you for a very long time.'

Pouliski did not answer. He looked at the chair, tested it and sat down on it.

'My name is George Adlon Green,' he said. 'You will find it on my passport. There has been some mistake made.'

'Sure,' said Jiggs. 'George Adlon Green, Earl of Tarrytown and Cicero, Marquis of Michigan, and King of all the hoodlums.'

Pouliski had gained a little courage. He stared insolently at the American officer, then looked round at the Chief Constable.

'Who is this man?' he asked.

'Three old knife wounds under the right shoulder,' said Jiggs. 'I guess you haven't got rid of them, Pineapple.'

He saw the Chief's frown and remained silent through the questions which followed. There was Mr Green's passport, all in order. It was significant that he carried it in the breast pocket of his dinner jacket. He had no firearms. Though a shrewd detective had watched him from the other side of the table he had not seen Pouliski pass his gun to his fair companion. Moreover, he had a satisfactory account of his movements to make.

Yes, he remembered speaking to Tetley. He had asked him the way to Highgate. He had gone to the coroner's court that morning to hear the inquest; he was naturally interested in this extraordinary crime. He knew nobody in town; he was in London on a holiday with his sister-in-law, and he had a lodging in Bloomsbury.

The railway porter who had helped the 'aged lady' into her compartment, and the conductor attendant of the coach, who had been brought back from York, were waiting in an anteroom. Neither could identify him. The conductor was almost sure, but could not swear. They had him removed from the room and there was a hasty conference.

'There's hardly enough evidence to hold him,' said the Chief Constable. 'Suppose he is this man Pouliski, we can't even charge him with falsification of passport. That is a matter for the Federal authorities and not for us.'

Jiggs was standing by the table, his face set and gloomy.

'Chief,' he said, and he spoke slowly, as though he was weighing every word, 'you've got in that next room the man who murdered Sir George Gilsant. Whether his confederate did any shooting is another matter. Pouliski's a killer, an expert bomb maker. What are you going too – expatriate him?'

The Chief shook his head.

'There's no way of learning the truth. Our powers are very limited.'

Jiggs thought a moment.

'Well, let him go,' he said. 'I'll take him home. If I do anything I shouldn't do he can have me arrested. Whatever happens will bring no discredit on Scotland Yard, because I don't belong there. But I'm not going to see a cold-blooded murderer walk straight out of Scotland Yard laffin'!'

The Chief Constable thought for a long time, and then: 'All right, take him home,' he said.

Jiggs drew a long breath.

'Let me do a little investigating,' he said.

They brought in the prisoner.

'We are not detaining you, Mr Green. Captain Allerman will see you to your house.'

Green's face turned white.

'I don't want any escort,' he said violently. 'I guess I'll stay here for the night. I don't like that guy, anyway.'

'You come with me, sweetheart,' said Jiggs, and took the other's arm in his.

Terry Weston's car was waiting near the entrance.

'Can you drive, Kid?'

'No,' said Green loudly.

'Just try. You used to drive a machine pretty well in the old days. I'll just sit behind and tell you where I want you to go.'

Terry, who had followed them down, saw the car turn on to the Embankment, not towards the West End, but to the city and what lay beyond.

Three men saw the departure from Scotland Yard, watched the car disappear, saw the frightened looking Pouliski driving, and caught a glimpse of Jiggs Allerman's grim visage behind. A second car trailed behind, keeping at a distance, followed it through the City of London, through Whitechapel, the Commercial Road, on to Epping, saw the car stop there for an hour, and maintained a watch at the same respectful distance.

At a quarter to three in the early morning the car turned and came back towards London. This time Jiggs was driving and Pouliski sitting on the rear seat.

They drove to Scotland Yard, and Jiggs handed him out and accompanied him upstairs to the Chief's room. Wembury was still there, and he looked up in amazement, for there was no sign that Pouliski had suffered any ill treatment.

'I guess we'll let this gentleman go, Chief,' said Jiggs. 'I'm convinced I've made a mistake about him.'

Terry, who came in at that moment, stood still and stared in amazement.

'All right,' said Wembury. 'Let him go.'

Jiggs accompanied the prisoner, who was a prisoner no longer, on to the Embankment and called a cab for him. Three watchful men saw this, and one went to the telephone and called a number.

'Pouliski fell apart.'

A silence, and then a voice said:

'All right. Put him where he belongs.'

'What the devil does all this mean?' asked the Chief when Jiggs came up.

'That fellow's a murderer all right. I don't know who his pal was, and probably he doesn't know himself. But he not only murdered Sir George Gilsant, but he put the bomb in my room, and that was unpardonable.'

'Then why have you let him go?'

'I haven't let him go, I've killed him,' smiled Jiggs. 'I was trailed all the way out to Epping by a car, and trailed all the way back to Scotland Yard by that car. I'm banking on psychology.'

Jiggs was right. A policeman patrolling St James's Park in the early hours of the morning saw two well shod feet protruding from some bushes. Investigating, he found a man who had been shot at close quarters, and there was enough of his head left to identify him as a gentleman who carried a passport in the name of Green. Psychology had won.

'It stands to reason,' said Jiggs explaining his peculiar theory the following morning, 'that if the gang saw a fellow like Pouliski, who everybody knows is yellow, talking with me, driving out into the country with me, and driving back to Scotland Yard with me, and then being released and having a taxi found for him – as I say, it stands to reason that the psychological head of the gang said, "Pouliski's fallen apart – put him where he belongs," and I'll bet those were the words, almost to a comma. They thought he was betraying them, so they just did the right thing by him – they put him on the spot, and they've lost the best pineapple man that Chicago has ever produced.'

# 18

It has come to this (said the *Megaphone* in its leading article), that we have almost accepted the fact that every day should produce its new outrage. The killing of this man Green in peculiar circumstances, the slaying of Sir George Gilsant, the wicked outrage which killed four people at Marble Arch and which shocked the civilised world – are they to become everyday happenings? Are we to be so callous to these monstrous outrages?…

There was much more in the same strain. Leslie Ranger read the leading article and put it down with a sigh.

She was living in some disorder; her furniture had been moved the previous night, and every room was a scene of confusion. By great good fortune she had secured, at a bargain price, a small flat on the fourth floor of a newly erected block, overlooking Cavendish Square.

A thousand pounds had been paid to her the day she left Mr Tanner's employment and most of this was still intact.

Though the flat had the appearance of a bargain, the rent was high enough to compel her to keep in mind the immediate need of securing new work. Curiously enough – or it seemed curious to her – the thing she most missed about her work in Berkeley Square was the opportunity it gave her of meeting Terry Weston. She told herself this was because he was an extremely pleasant man, the kind of friend any girl could have without there being any nonsensical suggestion of love making. She liked the brightness of him, but supposed, with a rueful little smile, that he wasn't feeling particularly bright now.

It was another odd circumstance that she very rarely thought of that amazing experience of hers on the night Elijah Decadon was murdered. If it came into her mind she dismissed it instantly, as one dismisses the memory of a bad dream. She had been half asleep when the dream began, quite asleep when it ended. She could never wholly grasp the reality of it or feel the fear which such a happening should inspire. Certainly she did not even remotely associate herself in her mind with any of the tragedies which had been enacted so swiftly in the past days, and could not dream that she was still a factor, and an all-too-important factor, in the war which was developing under her eyes. That she had been Decadon's secretary was merely an accident. It gave her a certain personal interest in that one, but to her the most hideous, crime.

She spent the afternoon fixing the carpet with the aid of two men who had been sent from the store, for her carpets had been new. By night she had the flat in something like shipshape. It was very small, an afterthought of the architect's, and, because of its smallness, rather difficult to let. But it was big enough for her. She made a study out of what was little bigger than a cupboard; a sitting room out of the hall vestibule; and reserved for her bedroom the largest room in the flat. The study might be profitable: she had her own typewriter, and at a pinch could do copying work. But the pride of the place was a new pattern telephone, which had been left by the last tenant and which she was able to get connected up with her new number in an incredibly short space of time.

The occupants of the flats were members of the well-to-do professional classes. Most of them paid ten times the rent which was levied from her. The address was therefore a very good one, and it had distinct advantages. There were porters on duty day and night, and central heating which really heated.

She had registered her name with a stenographer's agency, without hoping, however, to get the kind of work she required. Leslie was an ideal secretary, one who forgot nothing, and could be relied upon to think back with the accuracy of a filing index.

She was cooking herself a very frugal supper, when the doorbell rang. It must either be somebody who thought the previous tenant was still in occupation, or –

Terry would be too busy to call. Besides, he did not even know her address. She opened the door, and the moment she saw the beautiful girl standing outside she knew that some mistake had been made. Then, to her amazement:

'Are you Miss Ranger?'

'That is my name,' said Leslie, in surprise. 'Leslie Ranger.'

'May I come in?'

Leslie was feminine enough to apologise for the untidiness of the flat and to explain the reason all in one breath.

'I think you'd better come into the kitchen: it's the only place where there's any kind of order,' she said.

Her visitor was most expensively dressed. She wore a sable wrap, though the evening was quite warm, and the diamonds on her fingers were blinding. It was the first time Leslie had ever seen a platinum blonde close enough to receive an impression of its pale splendour.

'Do you mind if I sit down? Any old place will do.'

She pulled up a hard wooden chair and sat. Her stockings were so thin that she hardly wore stockings at all, Leslie saw, and decided that her shoes were American made. They had buckles which might have been diamonds, and probably were; they were splendid enough for diamonds. There were big diamonds in her ears, and a great stone, suspended by a thin pearl chain, lay on her breast.

'You don't know me, I'm sure.'

She spoke with the burr of the Californian, but Leslie could not know this.

'I'm Mrs Smith. My husband's the gen'leman who's called Albuquerque Smith because he comes from Albuquerque. I come from farther west – Los Angeles Maybe you've heard of it; it's where the motion picture people work – movies, you know.'

112

Leslie nodded breathlessly. To be brought into touch with Hollywood was rather a thrill.

'My husband, Mr Smith, is here for a vacation and he's just lost his secretary. She's gone abroad to marry a feller in Bombay, India. I heard about you, and I thought maybe you'd like to come along and see Mr Smith.'

She said this all in one breath, without a pause to denote where one sentence ended and another began. Her tone was monotonous and a little unpleasant, and all the time she was talking she was looking alternately from Leslie to her kitchen furniture, and obviously looking but to disparage.

'That's very nice of you, Mrs Smith,' said Leslie at last – even platinum blondes have to breathe. 'I am looking for a secretarial position.'

'You used to work for Mr Tanner. Why, I guess we just know Mr Tanner. He's a really nice man and quite a gen'leman. When I heard you'd left him I told Kerky, and he said, "Why, Cora, why don't you go right along and see Miss" ' – she had to pause for a second before she could recall the name – ' "Ranger?" and I said, "Sure." I don't believe in a girl taking a job with a man unless there's a wife or a lady about. Girls get themselves in all sorts of trouble just because they don't have a little discretion. The things I could tell you about girls who've taken jobs with men right here in London – why, you'd never believe it.'

She paused, and uttered a footnote.

'Cora's my name, but not my given name.'

'I shall be delighted to come along and see Mr Smith tomorrow.'

The woman opened a bag of unusual design.

'Cute, ain't it?' she said. 'I bought it in Paris, France. It cost six hundred bucks – would you believe it? – but all these diamonds are real. I lost one the other day, and you wouldn't believe the trouble I had to get the money from the insurance man. Gee, these insurance crooks, they're the worst of all.'

She produced a platinum card case and a card, and sailed out, leaving behind her the exotic aroma of almost everybody's favourite scent. Leslie opened the window. She liked perfumes, but preferred them one at a time.

She looked at the card. It was simply inscribed 'Mrs A Smith,' and under that, in brackets, were the italicised words 'Born Schumacher.' The address had been scribbled across the top of the card. It took Leslie a long time to decipher the name of an hotel which, once decided upon, seemed very familiar.

As she was undressing for bed that night she realised that Mrs Smith could not have come from the agency – how, then, did she know she was in need of a job? Then she found a solution: Eddie Tanner must have told her.

Albuquerque Smith! She repeated the name to memorise it. His wife had called him 'Kerky,' which was rather amusing. He was obviously a rich man, since he could afford so glittering a wife. She went to bed, dreaming about diamonds which scintillated blindingly and emitted a confusion of exotic scents.

She had put out the light and slipped into bed, when she heard the doorbell ring again. It was nearly midnight. Drawing on her dressing gown, she went to the door.

'Who is there?' she asked cautiously.

'Can I see you for one moment? It's rather important.'

Her mouth opened in amazement. It was the voice of Eddie Tanner.

'I'm quite alone in the flat, Mr Tanner. I'm afraid I can't ask you in.'

'Please! It's very, very urgent.'

She hesitated, then drew back the bolt and turned the knob of the spring lock. He was in evening dress, looking rather flushed and more perturbed than she had ever seen him before.

'I'll stay right here,' he said, his back to the door. 'I don't want to come into your flat. Did a woman come here tonight calling herself Mrs Smith?'

'Yes, Mrs Albuquerque Smith.'

114

He nodded, and for the first time she became aware of the squareness of his chin. It seemed to grow visibly squarer as she looked at him.

'Did she ask you to go to work for him – for Smith?' And, when she nodded: 'What did you say?'

'I said I'd see Mr Smith tomorrow.'

'Is that all they wanted to know?'

He had never before sounded so much like an American. Ordinarily he had the rather dull, lazy speech of the London young man.

'That's all I wanted to know, Miss Ranger. I hate to intrude so late at night. I guess you'd better not go to Mr Smith. You won't like it. Did Sally say anything about her previous matrimonial adventures by any chance?'

He saw her look puzzled.

'She called herself Cora, I guess, but Sally's her name.'

'Do you know her very well?' curiosity prompted her to ask.

He nodded, and there came that quick smile of his.

'I guess I should! She and I were married till eight years ago.'

Leslie looked at him incredulously.

'Married? Why, she's only a child!'

'Thirty eight's a pretty old age for a child. If ever you get a chance tell her I said she was thirty eight – she'll be so pleased!'

He seemed to be inspecting her with a sort of long, calculating glance that seemed to sweep over her like the steady roll of a searchlight.

'I don't think I should take that job if I were you, Miss Ranger. Anyway, it's just a try on. Kerky doesn't want any secretarial assistance. Sally was one of the fastest stenographers in Chicago before she hit the big shots.' And then hastily: 'I'm using bad slang. What I meant was, before she became friendly with the more flashy side of the underworld.'

'Before she married you?' he challenged.

'Exactly. You'd never guess it, Miss Ranger, but I once spent half a million dollars on Sally. She was a brunette in those days, and not so

115

refined. That was all I wanted to know, and I guess you've told me everything.'

He reached out, dropped his hand on the knob of the door and stood stock still. She felt the tenseness in his attitude, although she could not see his face.

'Is anything wrong?' she began.

He raised his hand and she was silent. Suddenly he turned round and pointed straight past her, and then to the left, and she knew that he was telling her to go into her little sitting room. The strangest thing of all was that she obeyed without questioning.

When she was out of sight she heard the 'tchk!' as the door had been opened and then Eddie Tanner's voice.

''Lo boy! What are you sniffin' round here for?'

'Why, Ed, I was just going to call on a friend of mine who lives in this block…say, put your gun away. Ed.'

'Stand right up against that wall and touch as near the ceiling as you can,' he said.

A long silence, and then:

'What did you bring this for? To call on your friend?'

'Why, Ed,' whined the voice, 'you just can't be too careful in this town. Say, I never carry a rod as a rule.'

'You won't carry it any more,' said Eddie.

'Sure I won't.'

'That's OK' said Eddie's voice. 'Walk straight to the elevator – I'll be behind you. I've got my car behind the block. We'll go right along and have a little talk.'

'That's OK with me, Ed.'

She heard the door close softly, and presently the moan of the lift coming to fetch them. She never saw the face of the man who was standing outside the door, who had followed Ed Tanner into the building, and who was now going to pay for his temerity – pay the only price that gangland knows.

# 19

Of late Leslie had not been sleeping well, but on this, the first night in her new flat, she fell into a long, deep and dreamless slumber. The sunlight was showing round the edge of her drawn curtains when she woke. The clock at her bedside pointed to a quarter to twelve. She could not believe it until she had consulted her watch, and then she remembered the engagement with Mr Albuquerque Smith, and, even as this was recalled to her mind, she remembered the warning of Edwin Tanner.

She was still debating with herself whether she should go or forget the engagement when she was dressed and sipping her first cup of tea. At one o'clock Mr Albuquerque Smith looked at his thin, jewelled watch.

'That dame isn't coming,' he said to his wife, and she shook her head wearily.

'Say, you'd think a girl like that...say, I'll bet she hasn't three of anything that matches – '

'I wonder if Ed saw her last night?'

She looked at him in astonishment.

'Don't you know?' she asked, and for some reason the question irritated him.

'I don't know everything,' he snarled.

But she was too dumb to be quieted.

'Anyway, I thought you'd know all Ed did.'

He smiled at her, a long, slow, malignant smile.

'I put a boy on to trail him, and I ain't heard from the boy. Does that satisfy that majestic mind of yours?'

Whenever he spoke about her majestic mind she knew he was annoyed with her, and that it was the time to stop asking questions.

If Leslie did not come, Kerky Smith was not to be without a guest for lunch. He looked up as the shadow of the visitor fell over him, and paused, his fork halfway up to his mouth.

'Why, Jiggs!' he said.

'You asked me to lunch yesterday, Kerk, but I kinda forgot it. Howdy, Mrs Kerky! Been buying up London this morning?'

Kerky Smith cut short her plaint about the inadequacy of London stores.

'Say, Cora, I want to have a little talk with Captain Allerman. Perhaps you wouldn't like to have your dinner upstairs?'

He was surprised when she rose without one snap of a remark, without so much as a scowl. She was, in truth, not sorry to leave her husband, who was in his less tolerant mood.

'Everybody's getting going,' said Jiggs. 'There won't be enough coroners' courts in London to deal with this fresh outbreak of hundred per cent Americanism.'

Kerky grinned.

'Stop knocking our native land, Jiggs. I guess they're not Americans at all, just a low-down lot of foreigners. Why don't they go home where they come from – that's what I always say.'

'That's what everybody always says,' said Jiggs, 'especially when they ain't sufficiently intelligent to ask a question that can be answered by somebody more intelligent. When you going home, Kerky?'

'What, me?' Kerky Smith was both surprised and hurt. 'Why should I go home? I thought of going over to Paris.'

'Do you know what happens to people who are caught here on a first degree charge, Kerky? All the best lawyers in the world don't save 'em. There's no pull here. These judges don't care two hoots in hell whether a man's worth a million or just owes it. I'd just hate to step out of the death cell on to a trap.'

Kerky's smile never varied.

'You ain't expecting to get croaked, are you, Jiggs?' he asked innocently. 'Why, I'd be sorry to hear that.'

'That's one aspect of the situation,' said Jiggs, in no sense annoyed. 'I'll give you another. There's a quick-drawin', quick-shootin' son of a gun living around here who's more fatal than a hot winter.'

Again Kerky grinned.

'I'm that thin, Jiggs, that no bullet could hit me!'

'This fellow would hit you,' said the unperturbed Jiggs. 'This fellow's such a grand shot that he could find your brain – and that's the smallest bull that was ever on a target.'

'What'll you eat, Jiggs? Something hot and poisoned? No, I'm not goin' back – not yet awhile. You tell 'em when you reach New York that I'm just stayin' on to see the sights.'

Jiggs got up from the table.

'You're an old traveller, Kerky, and you know what four hoots on a foghorn mean – abandon ship! And if you haven't heard those hoots, you go right along to some good ear man!'

He walked up the Haymarket, reached the corner of Panton Street, and was debating which way he would go, when a dark taxicab came flying down the Haymarket, pulled up with a jerk of brakes, and swung round into Panton Street, so close to the kerb that Jiggs stepped back. He not only stepped back, but ducked. Three shots ripped out from the interior of the cab. The bullets starred a plate-glass window. The cab sped on, going at a remarkable speed for a cab. It did not go as fast as the bullets from Jiggs' .45. Twice he fired, and each time he hit the cab. It darted down Orange Street, and, when he reached the corner, was gone.

A policeman strolled up to him. He was stern of face.

'What's that in your hand?' he asked.

Jiggs looked down, and slipped the .45 back into his pocket.

'That's a gun,' he said, and made an explanation under his breath.

A little crowd was gathering, and people were running from the Haymarket who had seen the shots fired, and he was anxious not to make the policeman look foolish.

'Did you see a taxi pass?'

119

'Yes, sir, a black taxi went down Orange Street. Looked like a drunken man inside.'

'Not drunk – dying, I trust,' said Jiggs cheerfully.

Then the policeman recognised him.

'Captain Ammerman,' he said.

'Allerman is better, but Ammerman will do. Yes, that is about my name.'

'That taxi was moving pretty fast. In fact, for a minute I was going to stop it.'

'You wouldn't have stopped it, officer,' said Jiggs good humouredly, 'and you most certainly would have got a slug in your midriff.'

But this time half a dozen policemen were on the spot. They had come from all directions at the sound of the shots and the police whistle which followed. There was nobody to arrest, and the big crowd, which was swelling every minute, found, after the way of all crowds, that they were the only offenders and were sternly dispersed.

Jiggs reported to Scotland Yard, but matters had reached the stage where nobody was very much surprised, and the Chief Constable was hardly interested. He had just come back from the Home Office, and that afternoon Jiggs, glancing through a newspaper, saw a paragraph which held his eye.

In reply to the Member for West Croydon, the Prime Minister stated that his attention had been directed by the Secretary of State to recent outrages in London, and emergency legislation would be introduced into the House on the following day. (Cheers.) Penalties of a drastic character would be imposed. At all costs the law would be vindicated.

Jiggs Allerman wondered what form the new legislation would take. The British were a peculiarly savage people in moments of crisis, and, if not savage, they were certainly ruthless.

Scotland Yard was worried, not at the murders, but by the fact that no further complaints had been received. On one night eight candles had been seen in as many windows, and the names of the householders had been carefully noted.

'What I want now,' said Terry, 'is some bold fellow to come forward and say, "Here's the letter I've received, here's the threat it contains: now it's up to you fellows to protect me." If I can get a letter like that tomorrow morning I'll be a happy man.'

He had a letter like that by ten o'clock the next day, but he was not happy, for the person who had received a demand for five hundred pounds – a demand supported by the usual printed threat – was Leslie Ranger.

# 20

She brought the letter up herself, rather amused and by no means alarmed. Terry had the phone message that she was waiting to see him, and beamed.

'Ask her to come up,' he said. 'Miss Ranger,' he explained to Jiggs, and Jiggs grunted.

He got up as the girl came in with a smile for both of them.

'Look at this,' she said, 'Isn't it amusing?'

Terry took up the letter, saw the green print, and before he had read a line guessed its contents and went white. He handed the letter without a word to Jiggs.

'Have you got five hundred pounds, Miss Ranger?' frowned Allerman; and then his beetling eyebrows rose. 'Why, of course! You inherited a thousand. 'They're only taking a cut of fifty – that's the idea.'

'But it's absurd,' said Leslie. 'They've sent it as a joke.'

The two men looked at one another.

'Do you think it's a joke, Jiggs?'

Jiggs Allerman scratched his chin and pulled an awful face.

'Why, no, I don't think it's much of a joke. What are you going to do, Terry?'

'I don't know. I'll see the Chief Constable. I think she should stay here. There's a spare room; we could make up a bed for her. I'll speak to the matron about it.'

When Terry had gone flying out of the room:

'Is it really as serious as that?'

In spite of her self possession she had suddenly gone cold.

'Why, no, Miss Ranger,' drawled Jiggs. 'It's not serious, and yet it might be serious. There's one guy in London that won't think it's a joke at all.'

He waited until Terry returned, then excused himself and, taking his hat, boarded a squad car and was driven to Berkeley Square.

Eddie Tanner was in and would see him presently, said the dapper little footman who admitted him, and who gave him a scrutinising gaze which took him in from the top of his sparsely covered head to his square toed shoes.

'Sorry to keep you, Jiggs.' Eddie Tanner closed the door behind his visitor. 'Sit down. Have a good cigar?'

Jiggs accepted the invitation.

'Anything doing?'

'Nothing at all,' said Eddie. 'I thought of running over to Berlin for a week. You can't make these lawyers move any faster than they want.'

'Quite a lot of excitement going on in this town,' said Jiggs.

Eddie Tanner nodded.

'Somebody took a crack at you yesterday, I'm told. A friend of mine was in the Haymarket.'

'A friend of yours was trailing me from Scotland Yard and therefore was in the Haymarket,' said Jiggs pleasantly.

'Anyway, they didn't get you,' smiled Eddie, 'for which we're all very thankful.'

'They're gettin' a few,' said Jiggs. 'Say, Eddie, I didn't know these guys operated with women.'

Eddie looked round.

'What do you mean?' he asked.

'Why, that girl who used to be here – what's her name – Miss Ranger. They put a green 'un on her this morning. Five hundred pounds – twenty five hundred bucks under the old conversion when pounds were pounds.'

'Miss Ranger?' Eddie Tanner for once had lost a little of his imperturbability. 'Greens? Those are the people who send the green printed notices, eh? It's a joke.'

# EDGAR WALLACE

Jiggs shook his head.

'I don't think it's a joke, Eddie.'

Eddie lit a cigarette, which he took very slowly from a gold case.

'What a nerve!' he said. 'But I don't suppose anything will come of it, Jiggs. What are you doing with the young lady?'

Jiggs grinned.

'We're publishing that in the five o'clock editions. You'd better look out.'

Eddie chuckled.

'It was a silly question ask. Are you going, Jiggs?'

Jiggs nodded.

'I just looked in,' he said.

At a quarter-past seven that night Kerky Smith was pacing up and down the broad vestibule of his hotel, stopping every few minutes to look at his watch. He was resplendent in white waistcoat and tie, and in the buttonhole of his tailcoat was a large gardenia.

'My, Kerky, you look grand!'

Kerky Smith dropped his hand carelessly into the inside of his dress jacket and turned without haste.

''Lo, Eddie!' he said.

'Come down to the court and have a drink.'

They went down the steps to the palm court, and Eddie snapped a waiter.

'Going to the Opera, eh?'

'No, I'm going to a theatre. Damn all women! They keep you waiting…Cora went out shopping this afternoon.' He looked at his watch again. 'She takes an hour to doll up.'

'Funny how women keep you waiting,' said Ed.

He blew a ring of cigarette smoke and watched it dissolve.

'Remember that secretary of mine, Miss Ranger? A terribly nice girl. I've been waiting to see her all afternoon, but she's at Scotland Yard. Some joker sent her one of those pay-or-pass letters, and I guess Jiggs and Terry Weston are kinda worried about it. I told them they needn't worry their nuts.'

'Sure,' murmured Kerky, his eye on the door.

'Because I figure it this way.' Eddie was looking at his cigarette, as though reading some esoteric message it conveyed. 'Nothing worse is liable to happen to Miss Ranger than might happen to, say, Cora. Suppose you picked up this Ranger girl dead tomorrow – why, you're just as liable to have Cora's head delivered to you in a fruit basket in time to cheer you up for breakfast.'

Kerky was listening now, his face set, but with a little quiver of his lips which he could not control. He was very fond of this platinum wife of his, very proud of her, and he knew that the man who sat by him, smoking his cigarette so negligently, was entirely without sentiment, and that Cora's head would mean no more than a sheep's head. Kerky was tough, but here was one reared in a school that was steel hard.

There was a very long silence.

'Call it a deal, Eddie,' said Kerky Smith, and coughed. He found his voice surprisingly husky.

Eddie looked at his watch and rose.

'Sorry you've missed your theatre,' he said. 'I've got an idea Cora may be held up in the traffic, and be back around eight.'

It was five minutes past eight when Cora arrived, furious, voluble, a little frightened.

'Listen, Kerky.' (This was in the privacy of their own sitting room.) 'You've got to go after this guy and get him! Keeping me shut up in a room, pretendin' you were sick and wanted me – '

'Shut your mouth, sweetness,' said Kerky good humouredly.

'And I got a headache!' she went on.

He grinned.

'You're lucky to have a head to ache with – believe me! Say, Cora, that guy's clever. I wish him and me were in the same racket.'

Cora Smith knew he was speaking about her former husband. He never spoke about Eddie Tanner except as 'that guy.'

At exactly eight o'clock Jiggs was called on the phone and recognised Eddie's voice.

'Don't you worry anything about Miss Ranger,' he said. 'I got an idea it was a joke.'

125

'That's swell,' said Jiggs, and conveyed the news to Terry.

'But you can't take the word of a man like that.'

'You can take his word, believe me,' said Jiggs emphatically. 'If he says it's a joke it is a joke.'

'Do you believe it's a joke?'

'Not originally,' said Jiggs, shaking his head, 'but now, yes.'

'And that Leslie is in no kind of danger?'

'I mean,' said Jiggs good humouredly, 'if you'll excuse the poetry, that Miss Ranger's in no kind of danger.'

Reluctantly, but to Leslie's great relief, she was allowed to go back to her flat. She was unaware of the plain clothes policeman who stood on duty in the corridor all night, less aware that a car that was parked right opposite the door for the greater part of the night was equipped with a machine-gun, and that the chauffeur was English Jack Summers, the most notorious chopper of foreign origin that Chicago had known.

The next afternoon Leslie had visitors. Jiggs and Terry Weston honoured her with their presence at tea. Both men were anxious to see the place, and more especially its approaches, and both Jiggs and Terry were rather curious to discover what she had been doing in the City three days before. It was Jiggs who approached the matter.

'Met an old friend of mine the other day in the City, didn't you, Miss Ranger – the well known Inspector Tetley?'

She had forgotten Tetley's existence.

'Why, of course. Yes, he came up to me in the street. I was driving back from Rotherhithe, and there was a traffic block. He came into the road and talked to me. I didn't know him.'

'But you were expecting him, weren't you, Leslie?' asked Terry.

She shook her head.

'Well, he was expecting you. He was waiting on that sidewalk for about ten minutes, and then suddenly picked you up. How he did that in a taxicab I don't know.'

'Oh!' she gasped.

Now for the first time she understood the meaning of those three white discs that had been pasted on the cab. She told them what had happened.

'When we got off we found three paper labels had been gummed. I rather suspect the sailor on the bicycle.'

Jiggs sat bolt upright.

'Let's hear all about the sailor on the bicycle.'

She told him of her visit to the depository and her recognition of the voice.

'I don't suppose for one moment it was the same man, because all Americans – if you'll forgive me – talk alike.'

'If you'll forgive me, they don't,' said Jiggs, 'but we'll let that slur upon my national speech pass without any further comment. You're pretty sure it was the same man who drove with you from your house the night of the Decadon murder?'

She hesitated.

'Well, I'm almost sure.'

'You had a good look at him?'

She described the man and his companion. Jiggs rubbed his chin.

'Dressed in top boots and guernseys and hanging round a wharf. Who bought that depository? Well, you wouldn't know that. It was a fool question, and you'll consider it wasn't asked. And that's all they said?'

'That's all – except the little joke about…some girls, that isn't worth repeating.'

'Everything's worth repeating,' said Jiggs. 'What did they say?'

She told them.

' "You take Jane and I'll take Christabel"?' Jiggs frowned. 'It sounds very much like one of those low adventures that sailormen have.'

He caught Terry's eye and abruptly changed the subject. When they were outside:

'What was that halt sign?' demanded Jiggs.

'It's just a wild guess on my part,' said Terry quickly. 'I don't know whether it's the case in your country, but here most of our barges and tugs have double names, generally girls' names. You'll find plenty of

Marys and Anns and Emmas and Margarets, and I daresay that somewhere on the Thames you'll find a Jane and Christabel.'

Jiggs whistled.

'The name of a boat? That was a little joke!'

'They're on a boat called the *Jane and Christabel*, and unless I'm mistaken she is no barge, but a steam tug.'

Back at Scotland Yard, Terry got in touch with the superintendent of the river police, who was a living encyclopaedia upon river craft.

'*Jane and Christabel*? Yes, I know her. She's a big tug – twin engines. She used to belong to the Calcraft Concrete Company, and when they went bust she was sold somewhere. I'll look her up.'

Ten minutes later he came through with the information that she had been sold to a Mr Grayshott of Queensborough, and that she usually lay in the Pool. She had taken a timber load up to Teddington a fortnight before, but she had been laid up with some kind of engine trouble, and they had been tinkering with her ever since. All offers of hire had in consequence been refused.

'Where is she now?' asked Terry.

'She may be in the Pool or she may be down at Greenwich.'

It was three quarters of an hour before she was located. She had gone down under her own steam and was moored off the Isle of Dogs, was the report.

'She has been sold to go to America,' said the superintendent, 'and some of the American crew working across the Atlantic are on board, but there's been a hitch about registration.'

That night Terry Watson went to Greenwich in a fast car, and at Greenwich Pier a police launch was waiting for him. The boat slipped out into mid stream and swung round, heading up river.

'There she is,' said the sergeant in charge.

Terry fixed his night glasses on the big two-funnelled tug that lay close inshore. Except for the lights which indicated that she was moored, the boat was in darkness. A powerful looking vessel, and Terry could well believe she was the fastest on the river.

'Do you want to board her?'

'No,' said Terry, 'I don't want those people to be in any way suspicious that they're under observation; but she's got to be watched day and night, and I've arranged with the superintendent to send down a special relief crew and a launch for that duty. I don't want anything that looks like a police launch watching her, but every move has got to be reported to Scotland Yard, and the launch which comes will have a wireless set and an operator.'

The tide was running up, and the launch continued its progress till it came opposite the high depository building. At the adjacent wharf two bargeloads of bricks were being unloaded by flare lights, and Terry was able to see the façade of the deserted depository. There was nobody on the wharf.

'Would you like to land?'

'No, I don't think it's worthwhile. Take me to Old Swan Pier. I told the car to meet me there.'

'Would you like to land?'

'No, I don't think it's worthwhile. Take me to Old Swan Pier. I told the car to meet me there.'

Again the launch went out into midstream, then suddenly:

'Look out!' yelled one of the officers.

The steersman glanced round and set his helm to port, and the little boat swung over. Quick as they were, they only missed destruction by a hair's breath. The big, black bulk of a great tug loomed over them and swept past. As it came abreast of them its starboard and port lights suddenly flared up. Until then it had been running in darkness. The sergeant yelled something, but the tug sped on.

'He was running without lights.'

He stared furiously after the disappearing stern of the *Jane and Christabel*.

'I'll pull him in for that.'

'I don't think you'd better,' said Terry. 'Let that keep.'

When he returned to his house he found Jiggs poring over a special late edition of the evening newspapers which contained the new emergency measures for dealing with the situation. It was called the Criminal Law Emergency Powers Amendment Act.

'This is going to make some of these birds take notice,' said Jiggs. 'Death for bombing, life imprisonment for being in possession of bombs, twenty five lashes with the cat for being in possession of loaded firearms, seven years and twenty five lashes for conspiracy to extort money...'

He skipped from item to item and shook his head admiringly.

'They won't like the cat, but, on the other hand, who cares what they like? Fourteen years and twenty five lashes for shooting with intent to murder – phew!' He whistled. 'And that's not all. Fifty thousand pounds reward – that's some reward – for information,' he read, 'securing the conviction of the person or persons guilty of the wilful murder of –'

He folded up the paper.

'First you catch your hare,' he said, 'then you lam his head off, and he tells you all about the fox; you catch him and you lam his head off. And presently you get the big bear – and him you hang. What did you find tonight, the *Jane and Christabel*?'

Terry told him of their little adventure on the river. His companion listened without comment.

'They know every move you make. Tomorrow when you go down to search this tug and hand the skipper a ticket for running without lights you'll find there's a new crew on board. Maybe the tug's changed hands and belongs to some little owner who's never owned so much as a rowboat before. Then you stopped to inspect the warehouse? That's a bear point against your Leslie, so mark it down on her.'

'What is going to happen to the warehouse?'

Jiggs shook his head.

'Nothing. These guys could afford to buy a row of buildings and scrap 'em. Anyway, it's not a dead loss: they can put the property in the market and lose a little. But they could lose a lot. Money's flowing in.' He sat back in his chair. 'Forty thousand pounds a day – two hundred thousand bucks. Think it over, boy. And there'll be just enough people getting sassy to justify a little high-powered shooting.'

# 21

Mrs Kerky Smith was fairly accurately described by Jiggs as lovely but dumb. In his more profane moments he called her Gardum. What that meant nobody exactly knew, but it sounded very much like bad language. If she had not been dumb she would have realised that her husband's patience was near to fraying. After her hundredth 'Can't you do sump'n? He put down the newspaper he was studying, folded it carefully and dropped it into the wastebasket as though he were depositing a million dollar bond in a safe deposit.

'Listen, Cora! I don't often talk my business to anybody, and you know that. I know you were put to a whole lot of inconvenience when they pushed you into that little dark room and told you to wait. Shall I tell you why you were there? It seems somebody sent one of these threatening letters to that girl Leslie Ranger. You know who she is, because you've spoken to her; you know who she is because she was coming to be my secretary; and you know who she is without asking any further questions because – why, you know who she is!'

'What has that to do with me?' she demanded.

'Well, I'm telling you. They sort of felt that I might have some influence with this low-down racketeer who's jigging around London. So they put you there until somebody pulled back that letter from Ranger and told her it was a joke. And if somebody hadn't pulled back that letter, shall I tell you what was going to happen, Cora? They were going to slice off your nut.'

She gaped at him.

'Me?' she squeaked.

He nodded rather gravely.

'Yes, they were going to kill you, take off your head, kid, and send it to me as a sort of present.'

She smiled scornfully.

'And take that laff off your voice, kid. They'd have done it. And that's only half of it. Now will you be good and quit whinin'?'

But she was boiling with rage.

'For that dam' little stenographer – say, what do you know about that, Kerky! And you sittin' around and talkin' about it as though – '

'I've finished talking about it, angel-face,' said Kerky, 'and you've finished talking about it. I know just how you're feelin', but you don't now how I'm feelin', because I don't open my trap as wide as you. Something's going to happen sooner than you think – they're not going to get away with that, no, ma'am! I'm short on ideas for the minute, but one'll strike me, and then I'll talk to this guy in a way he'll understand.'

'I'd like to have you get that girl,' she said savagely.

Kerky smiled.

'Wait,' he said significantly.

But something happened next morning, and was reported in the afternoon newspapers, which put the matter of Leslie Ranger entirely out of his mind.

Almost everybody knows Cuthbert Drood. He has an international reputation as a big-game shot, a world traveller, an excellent raconteur, and a man whose courage is guaranteed by the highest decoration that chivalry can offer – the Victoria Cross.

Cuthbert Drood was one of the few colonels in the world who called himself 'Mr' He was a tall, fair, sandy-haired man, who hunted all the winter, and yachted most of the summer. His father had been a brewer. He had had six relatives on both sides of the family who had left him a million sterling each. He boxed well, had been a champion runner at the university, was a squash player, a pistol shot – and a bachelor.

He did not communicate with the police when by one post he received two communications, one printed in blue and one printed in green. He chortled with joy and rang up a news agency.

'There seems to be a certain amount of reticence shown on the part of the people who are getting these tickets,' he said, 'and for fear the police keep this matter quiet I am letting you know before I go to Scotland Yard that I've had, not one, but two!'

A few minutes later his call came through to Terry. He explained what had happened, and added that he had communicated with the Press.

'I feel this thing can't be given too much publicity. I've never asked for it before, but the circumstances call for a brass band, what?'

When Terry called on him he found him in his library with half a dozen tanned looking men of various ages, and within reach of every guest was a large tumbler full or half full of amber liquid. Terry was introduced boisterously. Every man there was a hunter, cronies of the great Cuthbert.

'And we're going to give these fellows a run for their money,' boomed Mr Drood. 'I've been sick to death, the way these warnings have been received by some of the best people in the country. Young Ferthern ought to be horsewhipped – paid and bolted. You wouldn't believe it, but he was in the 184th and had a good war record.'

A deep bass voice growled that it was demoralising.

'It hasn't demoralised me,' roared Cuthbert with a broad grin. 'My friends have done me the honour of running round on a very interesting occasion. They're sleeping in the house tonight; I've told all the servants to go to the devil, and if there's any gun-play we shall be in it.'

Terry left him with a certain sense of hope. Here might be a nut that neither Blue nor Green could crack.

One thing he learned which was interesting: the blue communication had been posted a day before the green, but had been addressed to Ebury Street, where Mr Cuthbert Drood had a second establishment, a small house which he had let for the season. The letter had been readdressed and had arrived a day late, but simultaneous with the green demand.

Terry collected Jiggs and told him exactly the position.

'I read it in the evening newspaper,' said Jiggs. 'It's rather curious, and in a way it's going to bring about complications. If there's any one thing clearer than another,' he said, 'it is that the Blue and the Green crowds have fixed an agreement. I don't know when they fixed it, but it must have been soon after the killing of old Decadon. The fashionable part of London has been divided between the two gangs, and there's been some sort of gentlemen's agreement that one shan't encroach on the territory of the other. That, of course, explains why Drood had two demands. The Blue gang sent it to Ebury Street, thinking he lived there; the Green gang to Park Street. Now the question is, not whether Mr Cuthbert Drood and his boyfriends can shoot off the killers, but what line and what attitude Green is going to take with Blue, and vice versa. I'd give a lot of money to be listening in on the right kind of wire!'

Jiggs Allerman was right. A wire was very busy at that moment. Mr Kerky Smith in his palatial suite was talking with Eddie Tanner. Eddie was in the girl's little study, and he had with him three very respectable looking young men, who sat on the edge of chairs, balancing their bowler hats on their knees.

'Sure,' Eddie said, 'I saw it in the newspaper… One man has had a letter from both parties.'

'Yeah,' said Kerky in his silkiest tone. 'Green wanted five thousand pounds. The poor little racketeer who's mishandling the Blue outfit would be glad to take two thousand. I guess the bigger man wins here.'

Eddie smiled.

'You've got it all wrong. The biggest man isn't the man that opens his mouth widest.'

Kerky Smith thought for a long time before he spoke.

'Anyway,' he said, 'nobody's going to get anythin'. This guy's one of the original veterans of the Great War, and guns are just toothpicks to him.'

'That's so,' agreed Eddie. 'Maybe these Blue and Green fellows will talk it over and fix sump'n.'

'Maybe they will,' said Kerky, 'but I guess they won't. You can't expect big businessmen to come right down and sit in convention with the pedlars.'

'Is that how it strikes you, Kerky?'

'Sure that's how it strikes me,' said Kerky, and hung up the phone.

He was in rather an uncompromising mood that day. Cora had been difficult. She was still sore with the people who had kidnapped her. He had been affronted and was in his best go get'em mood. That question of territory had not been completely and satisfactorily adjusted. Lieutenants had discussed spheres of influence and had made loose agreements, but the Big Boy had sanctioned nothing.

There was a problem to be settled, a very vital one. Who would frame the answer to Cuthbert Drood's defiance? All the world knew that he was standing up against Blue and Green, and it was not good that he should go unpunished. And just the spectacular form of punishment necessary, and administrable, was to hand. Such a case had been prepared for on both sides, though neither knew the method of the other.

Eddie was getting high hat. He had already committed unpardonable offences, and now this new and irritating situation had arisen, as Kerky had known it would. There was no place for two crowds working in a limited and foreign area like London. There had to be either a hook-up or one side had to go out of business, and Kerky knew which side that would be.

His exasperation when he went to his rooms to find Cora, deepened dismally. He hated women who cried, and he had forgotten the cause until she reminded him.

'Can't you get it out of your head, kid? Forget it!'

'They'd have put me on the spot and you wouldn't have cared two damns!' she sobbed. 'I've told you about Eddie. You think he's soft, but he's tough, Kerk — tougher than any guy you know... Why, once when I was sore with him, he took me by the neck and held me out of a window eighteen floors up…in New York City. I was scared to death.'

He left her lamenting and reminiscent. He had rather an important appointment.

In Soho was a little barber's shop that had a very private room for very special customers. Kerky was such a customer. He went in, took off his coat, and the dark skinned barber shut the door and manipulated a comb and scissors; and what the barber told Albuquerque Smith, and what Albuquerque Smith told the barber, was entirely their own affair.

It was a favourite method of Kerky's. Whenever he made his appearance in a new town somebody came along and bought up a barber's shop, fitted an inner room with a big, safe door, employed two assistants who spoke the same language as himself, and there was an office ready made for his intelligence department. As invariably on the first floor was a little bookmaker's office with a dozen telephones, and only two or three clerks.

Kerky finished his conversation, brushed his own hair, strolled out through the shop, and his car, which had been waiting in a little side street opposite came noiselessly to the kerb. He stepped in and the car moved on. Almost instantly another came abreast and a little ahead.

Kerky smelt danger, and in a split second of time, before the machine-guns rattled, he had dropped to the floor of his car. He heard the crash of glass; some pieces fell upon him. His driver sagged over and slumped forward on to the wheel.

There were screams, police whistles; excited people were shouting like the demented. A policeman ran up and assisted Kerky from the car. He was shaken but not hurt.

'My driver's shot, I think.'

They eased the driver from his seat on to the pavement, and somebody rang for an ambulance.

Kerky Smith was not frightened; he was not hurt. He was just a little more than perturbed. But the dominating emotion in him was one of respect for an enemy he had underrated.

One evening newspaper bill stated baldly 'Mystery Shooting in Soho.' Another, guessing rather than knowing: 'Gang Fight with Machine-Gun.'

'Which is the truth,' said Jiggs, stopping at the corner of the Embankment to buy a newspaper. 'Just that. A little pyrotechnic display with green and blue lights, and Kerky Smith not so sure as he was. Terry, he's going to stage something. That guy's got to do something big to retain his self respect.'

'That's what I'm thinking,' said Terry quietly. 'I'm not so confident myself as I was this afternoon.'

'About Drood?'

Terry nodded.

'Whoever gets in there will have a pretty warm reception.'

# 22

Although officially Leslie Ranger's flat was on the fourth floor, it was in reality at fifth floor level. The ground floor was taken up by rather lofty shops, and there was a mezzanine floor which counted for nothing.

She had read the gesture of defiance issued by Mr Cuthbert Drood, and felt a personal interest; for Drood was one of those national characters that appeal to the young and the romantic. Moreover, from her high floor Leslie overlooked, as she discovered, the flat roof of the house in which Mr Drood was creating a fortress. It was across the street, and when Mr Drood came out in the morning and performed his athletic and gymnastic exercises in a costume of the scantiest proportions, Leslie could, and actually did, find herself an interested audience.

It was on the first morning she woke in her new home that she had this gratuitous display, and was curious enough to discover who was the gymnast, dressed in a pair of blue trunks and nothing else.

It was growing dark, but the rain clouds which had covered London had drifted off, and there was a deep orange streak in the western sky. The air was remarkably clear, and objects were visible for a long distance. She could even see the lights of Hampstead by craning her neck.

She was sitting at the window, watching idly and thinking rather intensively, when on the high roof of the next house, a roof which commanded the flat top of the Drood dwelling, she saw a figure appear cautiously from behind a chimney stack, and vanish again. She wondered if it were a policeman. She supposed the police had taken every precaution, and had men posted at all vantage points. She looked, but did not see the man again. Then, obeying an impulse, she went to the telephone and rang up Terry. It was, she told herself, the flimsiest of excuses, but it *was* an excuse.

Terry took a lot of finding. He was somewhere in the building, and the operator, who had apparently acquired a new vocabulary from Jiggs Allerman, said she would "call her back." Ten minutes later Terry's voice gave her a pleasant little thrill.

'It's a silly question I'm going to ask you, but have you put any men on duty at Mr Drood's house?'

'There are one or two officers about, I believe,' said Terry, surprised. 'Why?'

'Well, I can see it from my flat. In fact, I can see the roof, and I thought I saw a man on the roof of the next house. It's dark now, but I distinctly saw somebody, and I wondered whether it was a policeman.'

She heard him consult somebody, and there came a faint reference to hell. She guessed it was Jiggs who was consulted.

'Do you mind if we come along to you – Captain Allerman and I?'

She felt guilty at taking them away from their duties, and said so.

'Rubbish! This is duty. Before I come I'll get on to the officer in charge of this particular job and find out if he has been exploring the roof – probably he has.'

They arrived half an hour later.

'I think it must have been Tetley,' said Terry. 'He's been there all evening and very likely he was the man you saw.'

'Is he the man who put the lights on the roof?'

'The what?' asked Jiggs quickly. 'Which lights?'

She led him to the window, and he almost pushed her aside. On the flat roof of Cuthbert Drood's house were three red lights, placed in the form of a triangle.

'That's funny,' said Jiggs, and pinched his lip. 'Now what the devil are they for?'

'Possibly Tetley has some men on the roof and he wanted to give them a guide,' said Terry. 'He told me he was going to have a marksman in half a dozen windows overlooking Drood's house.'

'Sure,' said Jiggs slowly. 'That's a grand idea.'

Suddenly he snapped his fingers with extraordinary rapidity.

'Who's going to break into that house and start shooting?' he asked quickly. 'Not even a Chicago copper. It's full of dead shots, and if they got Drood they'd be certain to lose half a dozen men. Let's go, Terry.'

Without a word of farewell he flew out of the flat, Terry after him. They crossed the road at a run, dodging a taxi and swift moving car. A policeman stepped forward to intercept him, recognised him and passed him on. In another second Jiggs was knocking at the door of Mr Cuthbert Drood's residence. To his surprise a panel in the door opened and a suspicious face appeared.

'What do you want?'

The panel had been cut that afternoon by the enterprising Cuthbert, with the assistance of a carpenter.

'You can't come in, gentlemen,' said the custodian. 'Mr Drood is admitting no police officers into the house. He's got his own friends here and he'll look after himself.'

'But this is important – absolutely vital. I want to go up on to the roof – '

'You can't go on to the roof or into the basement either.'

The panel was closed with a bang. Jiggs looked in amazement at Terry.

'This is preposterous,' said Terry, and knocked again.

Again the panel opened, and this time the barrel of a log automatic appeared resting on the rough edge of the wood.

'I know who you are, Mr Weston, but those are my orders. You can't come in between now and tomorrow morning. Mr Cuthbert Drood has made his own plans and he doesn't want any police assistance.'

'That's that,' said Terry as they came down the steps.

He was half annoyed, half amused. He asked a detective officer whom he saw on the corner of the square where Tetley was to be found and got into communication with him by public phone.

'It's all right, Mr Weston. I've allowed Mr Drood to have his own way.'

'Have you been on the roof there this afternoon or this evening?'

There was a pause.

'No, I haven't,' said Tetley. 'Why?'

'Did you give any orders for lights to be placed there?' (Jiggs prompted this inquiry.)

Another unusually long pause.

'No, sir. Maybe Mr Drood has got some idea of his own. He's a very masterful gentleman.'

As Terry hung up and was moving out of the booth:

'Do you mind if I phone to the Yard and ask him to send me a rifle? What department do I ask for?'

The astonished Terry told him, and stood by whilst Jiggs got through.

'Send a good sharp-shooting rifle – one of those I saw when Mr Brown took me round...yes, with a telescopic sight if you've got one. Got to come right away to 174 Cavendish Square...it's a block of flats, and it's to be brought up to Miss Leslie Ranger's apartment. Inspector Terry will be there...all right, Chief Inspector Terry, if you're so darned particular.'

'What's the idea, Jiggs?' asked Terry as they walked across the square to Leslie's apartment.

'It's just an idea – gosh!'

He stopped in the middle of the road and would have been run down by a taxi if Terry had not gripped his arm and pulled him back.

'I wish you wouldn't have these startling thoughts in the middle of the road,' said Terry peevishly.

When they reached the sidewalk, Jiggs asked:

'Are there any silencers at the Yard? That'd save me a bit of embarrassment.'

'Rifle silencers? Yes, dozens of them.'

Leslie was surprised to see them back, and a little relieved too. Jiggs got on to Scotland Yard again and supplemented his order.

He was hoping that there was a flat roof on this block of flats, but as he walked across the square he had seen that the roof was tiled and sloping. It was Leslie's window or nothing.

'Now just exactly what are you going to do?'

'I ought to have asked them for a pair of field-glasses,' said Jiggs gloomily. 'My memory's just going dead on me – '

'I have a pair of glasses,' said Leslie.

She went to her bedroom and returned with an old pair of binoculars which had been her father's. Jiggs focused them on the flat roof and grunted his satisfaction.

'Fine! There's a parapet all round. That was worrying me. Look Terry, you see how bright those lights are – well, they're twice as bright from above. You see how one of them throws a light right up the wall of the next house?'

He looked at his watch and groaned.

'How long will it take those people to get from Scotland Yard?' he asked presently.

Terry hazarded a guess.

'I could do it in half the time.'

'Whatever I'd said you could have done it in half the time,' said Terry easily. 'It's a nice, starry night,' he added.

'I've noticed that.'

'Now what is the mystery, Jiggs, and what are you going to do with the rifle when you get it?'

'I'll tell you what I'm going to do with the rifle when I get it,' said Jiggs quietly. 'I'm a pretty good shot – in fact I'm a hell of a good shot, if you'll excuse the transatlantic expression, Miss Ranger – and I'm going to put those lights out.'

'What?' asked Terry incredulously.

'That's just what I'm going to do, sir. I'm going to plonk those three lights right out, and if I don't I'm going to the recruits' class!'

'But, Jiggs, you can't do that in the heart of London!'

142

'If your silencer is any silencer, the heart of London is going to beat no faster.'

The rifle arrived ten minutes before Terry had thought it possible for the messenger to travel between Thames Embankment and Cavendish Square. Jiggs fitted the silencer with a scientific hand.

'I'm taking my hat off to the police,' he said. 'I didn't ask for ammunition and they've sent me a packet – there's brains in London, Terry. I'm saying it.'

He filled the magazine and, leaning down by the window, took aim. There was a 'plop!' and one of the red lights went out. Looking down, Terry saw people passing up and down the street, but nobody seemed to have noticed the explosion. Again Jiggs aimed. This time the 'plop!' was louder, and the whine of the speeding bullet came like the shrill whistle of a gale. The second light went out. They heard the smack of the bullet as it struck brickwork.

'Thank the Lord for the parapet! This one's easier.'

He levelled his rifle; there was a quick spurt of flame, a louder and more booming 'plop!' and the third light went out. This time somebody in the street heard. They saw upturned faces looking vaguely in all directions. Jiggs removed the silencer. On his face was a grin of smug satisfaction.

'All right, miss, you can put the lights on.' And then, quickly: 'No, don't. Do you hear anything, Terry?'

He put his head out of the window, listening. Terry was straining his ears.

'Yes, an aeroplane.'

He heard the quick intake of Jiggs' breath.

'Just in time, eh?'

And then the grind and thud of the bolt as Captain Allerman drove another cartridge into the chamber.

The roar of the engine was plainer now. The machine was coming straight for Cavendish Square. They looked up, but could see nothing. Then suddenly it swept into view: a small, black plane, flying so low that its wheels almost skimmed the roof of a high store building. It dipped a little, came straight towards the northern side of the square. It swept up, turned, and came back.

'Looking for the lights,' said Jiggs.

Then came his favourite Shakespearean quotation.

' "Speak, hands, for me!" ' he snarled.

There was no silencer on the muzzle of the rifle. The crash of the explosion struck Leslie like a blow, and she stepped back. A quick snap as the bolt opened and closed, and again the explosion.

The plane was nearing the centre of Cavendish Square, when it suddenly heeled over. Its tail went down and it fell with a crash in the centre of the garden which occupied the middle of the square.

'Gotcher!' It was Jiggs' triumphant voice.

A big tree eased the fall of the plane; they hardly heard the sound as it struck the ground.

Now the police whistles were blowing. People were flying from all directions.

'For God's sake, what have you done?' asked Terry in horror.

'What have I done?' said Jiggs. 'I've shot down the man whose job it was to bomb Mr Cuthbert Drood, and who would have bombed him if he could have found the red lights that had been put there to mark the house. These guys have got other ways of killing besides automatics'

The police who jumped the railings of the square found a groaning man amidst the wreckage. They found also a hundred pound bomb, which was subsequently discovered to be packed with alanite.

They dragged the wounded man from the wreckage and he was sent in an ambulance to the nearest hospital – and Jiggs and Terry were in the ambulance.

'Not dead,' said Jiggs regretfully. 'That's too bad. But it wasn't such a bad shot, Terry – he was moving at a hundred miles an hour. Why, once when I was in Colorado I hit a duck – '

He boasted all the way to the hospital.

The wounded man gave no name. He had a bad wound where the bullet had ripped through his arm and a wound of less importance in the calf of his leg. He refused to give any name.

'You needn't worry about that,' said Jiggs. 'Stunts Amuta – that's right, ain't it, boy? You used to do trick flying, and ran an air line from Canada for Hymie Weiss, late but not lamented. You're a guy from Indiana.'

The man looked at him malevolently but said nothing.

'I've been trying to place you for the past ten minutes,' Jiggs went on, 'and lo, here you are! Stunts you're in bad. If you're the wise boy you'll come right across.'

'I've got nothing to say to you, Jiggs,' groaned the man.

'Maybe you'll like to say sump'n' before you pop,' said Jiggs significantly. 'And perhaps I didn't soak those bullets in the old garlic can.'

A look of terror came to the wounded man's face.

It was just about then that the surgeon ordered Jiggs out of the room.

'What's this garlic can stuff?' asked Terry when they were coming away from the hospital.

'Just to cheer him up,' said Jiggs remorselessly. 'These birds think that if a bullet's soaked in garlic it's poisoned. I had Stunts once – they call him Stunts because he's a pretty good airman and can do almost any fool thing with an aeroplane. I held him for first degree murder. He shot a night watchman, but he went into court with a file of alibis and a lawyer who cried all over the jury, and Stunts was honourably acquitted, shook hands with the jurymen and maybe dined with the judge. That's how it goes – or how it went in those days.'

The contents of the aeroplane had been taken to Scotland Yard. The bomb was already in the possession of the Ordnance Department. The contents of the airman's clothes lay on a table in the Chief Constable's room. There was a passport, issued by a South American state to Thomas Philipo, a travel agency ticket from Paris to Cadiz, and, in a suitcase found strapped to the plane, a complete change of clothing, and a pocket-book containing six thousand francs and three thousand pesetas, and travellers' cheques for two thousand pounds.

145

The home of the aeroplane had not been discovered. The number, which had been painted over, had been submitted to the Air Department, but the name given as the registered proprietor helped nobody. It was Jones.

'We can't charge him with anything,' said Terry, after the matter had been the subject of a short discussion between himself and the Chief Constable. 'We can't prove that he intended bombing the house, and the most we can do is to make a charge of being in unlawful possession of explosives without permission of the necessary authorities. He had two guns, and that would be another offence. But the Chief thinks it's hardly worthwhile charging him – the publicity would have a bad effect upon the morale of the people.'

'The only thing about this that's really interesting,' said Jiggs, 'is that it shows Green have marked Mr Drood down as their bird, and were out to sock him. No, there'll be no more attempts tonight – Kerky will have heard all about the plane being brought down, and he'll lie low because that's the first of his crowd that has fallen into the hands of the police. And while I remember it, Terry – you'd better send half a dozen men up to the hospital to look after Stunts.'

'I've spoken to Wembury about that, but he's in rather a dilemma. If he can't charge this man he can't put him under guard. The Home Office people are against any action.'

Jiggs nodded.

'Kerky will be waiting to see what you're going to do. If he thinks there's any likelihood of a charge he'll have Stunts out of that hospital before you can say "knife".'

All the evening the police had been searching for the car from which Kerky Smith had been machine-gunned, but without success. Kerky's handsome limousine had been riddled and his wounded chauffeur was on the danger list.

The Home Office had formed a small Public Safety Committee, which was in permanent session. One of the first matters that came up for consideration was whether Kerky Smith should be handed deportation papers and put on board the first ship sailing for the

United States. Here Jiggs was consulted, and his advice was emphatically against such a step.

'Kerky's quite ready to leave and if you decide to put him out of the country he'll go to Paris – and you can't stop him. No, let Kerky stay here. He'll cancel out in time. And nothing's going to happen in this blackmail racket for a week. The Blues and the Greens have got their own differences to settle, and until they find a working arrangement they're going to work out their own damnation!'

Jiggs had an uncanny knowledge of gangster methods, and the events which followed were almost as he predicted.

There came to London a week of most amazing happenings, so unbelievable that the Londoner, reading his morning newspaper, might well have rubbed his eyes and believed he was in another world.

On the morning following the attack on Kerky's car a policeman patrolling Seven Sisters Road, a fairly busy thoroughfare and one of the main arteries of London traffic, found a man lying in the front garden of one of the better-class houses. He had been shot three times, and was quite dead. The divisional surgeon who was summoned gave it as his opinion that the man had been killed elsewhere and dumped in the garden.

Almost simultaneously three sewermen, working on one of the main storm sewers in the north of London, heard two loud splashes, and, going in that direction, found the bodies of two men huddled in four feet of storm water which was running through the sewer at the time. Looking up, they were just in time to see a manhole on the street above being replaced. The men had been shot and bludgeoned. There were no papers in their pockets, but on the tab of the coat of one of them was printed the name of a tailor – Hemm, of Cincinatti.

Terry viewed the bodies in the mortuary in he early morning. One of those quiet, grey faces was strangely familiar. Photographs had been taken a few hours before and with the prints of these he called on Leslie and arrived just as she had finished breakfast.

'I wonder if you can help me, and if you can bear seeing the photograph of a man who was shot last night?'

She made a little grimace, but took the picture, and he saw a look of recognition in her eyes.

'Who is he?' he asked.

'One of the new servants I saw at Mr Tanner's when I called there two days ago to take back some books which Mr Decadon lent me.'

Until then Terry had been under the impression that the new staff in Berkeley Square had arrived before she left. As it happened, it was only by accident that she was able to help him.

'That's who I thought it was,' he said.

She shuddered.

'Isn't it ghastly, all this business! And Mr Smith was shot at yesterday!'

'I shouldn't have any sleepness nights over that,' said Terry.

He took the photographs to Berkeley Square, and Eddie Tanner identified the men without hesitation.

'They were both servants here,' he said. 'They went out early last night. When I found this morning that they hadn't returned I intended discharging them. Where were they found?'

Terry told him, and Mr Tanner listened in silence.

'I'm sorry. They were good men, and very willing servants. But I rather think they were both of foreign origin, and probably had some feud with their compatriots. When are you going to stop this gang war?'

'When are *you* going to stop it?' asked Terry bluntly.

Eddie smiled.

'I'm afraid Jiggs has given you an altogether wrong impression about me,' he said.

As Terry was leaving:

'I won't walk with you to the door because there's a gentleman with a machine-gun trained on my front door. You don't know it, but I do. And if you ask me where he is, I shall reply very politely that I can't tell you. I'll have the door opened very wide for you so that they can see who you are. It would be lamentable if they made a mistake.'

Terry heard him laughing as he walked up the passage and out into the square. It was an uncanny feeling to know that somewhere within a stone's throw a murderer, with his finger on the trigger of a Savage machine-gun, was covering you. He glanced round quickly and marked a dozen places where the assassin might be concealed. Amongst the foliage of the central garden, in an empty house immediately opposite, on one of the three roofs.

Persistence was his only hope. He called the local police station and had the good luck to find the divisional inspector.

'Somewhere in Berkeley Square is a man with a machine-gun,' he said. 'Get all the men you can, search every empty house, the roofs and the central garden. I don't suppose you'll catch him, but we'll take a chance. Report to me at the Yard.'

Soon after noon that day a man crossing the street at the juncture of Piccadilly and Park Lane was seen to stagger and fall. The policeman on point duty ran up to him, and found him bleeding from the head. He was rushed to a nearby hospital but was dead before he was put on the table. Nobody had heard the shot, but it was apparent that he had been killed by a rifle bullet aimed from some height above the ground. Again his clothing yielded no clue as to his identity. He had been a sallow faced man with dark, curly hair. The surgeon said he was of Jewish origin, but of Levantine stock. He had a small gold watch of an expensive American make. About his neck, and concealed under his shirt, was a thin gold chain from which was suspended a tiny platinum and gold crucifix. He had in his pocket nearly fifty pounds in English money and three hundred-dollar bills in a flat leather case, which yielded no further information about himself except that he was a member of a Chicago athletic club. There was no name on the card, but the number which was stamped on the right hand corner would probably help to identify him.

Jiggs went down and saw him, but shook his head.

'Don't know him,' he said. 'Did you find anything else?'

'A bunch of keys,' said the inspector who had conducted the search. 'One of 'em's an hotel key – the Banner Temperance Hotel in Gower Street.'

The manager of this hostelry was brought to the hospital and recognised the dead man as Henry Doe, a quiet inoffensive man with a very pleasant manner, who had been staying in the hotel for seven weeks.

'John Doe, of course, is a legal fiction,' said Terry.

'Even in the United States he's a legal fiction,' agreed Jiggs. 'The only thing that worries me is, was he Green or Blue? So far, Green has scored heavily.'

The next happening was a little more sensational. Two men were sitting in a small restaurant off Shaftesbury Avenue, when two others entered and sat down at the same table. Evidently they were not expected by the men who had originally booked the places, but no protest was made. The proprietor of the restaurant, a Sicilian, recognised them only as compatriots. He did not know them, and had not seen them before. Wine was ordered, a large bottle of Chianti, and four glasses filled.

The two men had ordered dinner, but had asked the head waiter to put back the meal. One of them rose and went to the proprietor, and asked if there was a private room they could have for half an hour, as they wished to discuss business. As it happened, there was a room available, and Mr Garcia took them upstairs, switched on the lights, and brought in an extra chair. He suggested that they should dine, but they only asked that the wine should be brought up to them, and this request was complied with.

They spoke in English: he was perfectly certain of that; not once did he hear either Italian or the Sicilian patois. Half an hour passed, and Garcia, who was rather pressed for space that night, his clientele being a little more than he could accommodate, went upstairs to ask the party if they would have their dinner there and free the table they had engaged. He knocked at the door, there was no answer, and he opened it and walked in. For a moment he stood paralysed. Two of the men lay with their heads on the table, which was smothered with blood. The wine glasses stood intact; they had been filled and emptied. There was no sign of the other two.

Mr Garcia's first inclination, as he told the police with great candour, was to scream. He remembered, however, that he was a businessman with a shop full of diners, and he went downstairs, called the head waiter and explained the situation. They summoned the police, whilst Mr Garcia explored all possible avenues of escape. There was one, an obvious one. At the foot of the stairs a door led to a little yard at the back of the restaurant, and thence to the street was a matter of opening and closing another door.

Terry was out. Jiggs was in the inspector's room, dozing at the desk, and arrived at Shaftesbury Avenue a few minutes later.

'Just an ordinary Sicilian killing,' he said. 'The glass of wine first, the amiable sentiment, and then – bingo! You heard no shots, Mr Garcia?'

'No, sir, I will swear – '

'You needn't swear. You've got a pretty noisy restaurant, and they were two floors up. You'd recognise these other fellows again?'

Garcia spread out his arms.

'How could I? I did not even recognise these poor when who are killed. They were just customers; I hardly looked at them.'

That was a fairly plausible statement. Jiggs, however, knew the Sicilian character. There would be no betrayal by the murderers' compatriot, and it was quite possible that he had not taken very much notice of his guests. He could only say they were clean shaven and dark, and that one of them wore a black hat. The description was a little inadequate.

Terry heard about the murders when he came back to the Yard from a fruitless journey into the country to see a suspicious looking aeroplane and interrogate its owner and pilot.

'The bickering proceeds normally,' said Jiggs, 'and in accordance with the ancient rule of the game, which is: the killer gets killed.'

Just before midnight there was a new excitement. Two cars came flying down Piccadilly, took the wrong side of the Circus, dashed through the traffic into Coventry Street and immediately opposite the Corner House a man sitting by the driver of the second car opened fire with a machine-gun. The fire was immediately answered from the car in front. Both machines swung round into Leicester Square, and the air shook with the rattle of the explosions. The Empire Theatre was discharging its last audience. There was a wild scattering of people to safety.

The machines flew through St. Martin's Place, across Trafalgar Square and down Northumberland Avenue on to the Embankment. They turned towards the City. Suddenly the leading car swerved, crashed into a lamp standard and burst into flames. The second car sped on, but a witness saw the gunner by the driver's side spray the wreckage with a final burst of fire. Passing motorists stopped and tried to extinguish the flames. A city policeman dashed up, dragged open the almost red-hot door, and sought to pull out the figures he saw heaped on the floor. At first he was unsuccessful, but a patent extinguisher put out the fire and they dragged the smoking figures on to the sidewalk.

There were three men in the rear of the car, and evidently they had been killed before the fire had started. The driver was still breathing when they got him out. It was subsequently discovered that he had been hit seven times.

'Very pretty,' said the Assistant Commissioner of the City Police as he viewed the ghastly corpses. 'What are Scotland Yard going to do about it?'

'Scotland Yard,' said an exasperated officer from that institution, 'will take any lessons that the City can teach.'

Between the city and the Metropolitan area, each with its own police force, there was a certain rivalry.

'In the meantime,' said the officer (it was Stalbridge, afterwards chief inspector), 'I would like to remind you, sir, that this shooting took place in the City boundaries, ad we shall be happy to leave the matter in your hands.'

'That,' said the Assistant Commissioner awfully, 'is rather impertinent, Inspector.'

'I'm sorry, sir,' said the Inspector, who was not sorry at all.

Very early the next morning Kerky Smith put through a call to Berkeley Square.

'That you, Eddie? Wondering whether you'd like to come along to eat?'

'Baked meats by any chance?' asked Eddie, but the Biblical allusion was lost on Kerky, who had no extensive knowledge of literature.

'How's that? Anything you like, Eddie. Peaches from the Queen of Sheba's garden, caviar out of the cellars of the Kremlin, eh? Come on, you old horse.'

'I'll think about it,' said Eddie.

Half an hour later he was ushered into Kerky's private room. Mr Smith was alone; the table was laid for two.

'Coffee or tea? They're both poisoned,' he said pleasantly. 'You oughta brought your chemist! I knew a guy in Chicago who got a big stock of liquor in – he was a high up man in the City Hall. In those days you used to send a sample of your hooch to the chemist, who told you whether it was straight stuff or just alky. This guy never sent any of his booze to be tested for fear the chemist said it wasn't fit to drink and he'd have wasted his money.'

'And he's still alive?' said Eddie amused.

'Sure he's still alive! You can't kill a guy like that. And talkin' of killin', Eddie' – he poured out the coffee with a steady hand – 'there's been a lot of wastage goin' on right here in London, and it's got to stop.'

'I guess the police will stop it,' said Eddie Tanner, picking two pieces of sugar from the bowl and dropping them with a plop into his black coffee.

'I guess so,' said Kerky. 'I had a funny dream last night, Eddie – dreamt these birds who were sending round green and blue notices had a hook-up, sixty and forty, and sent out one notice – in red.'

'I don't know sixty and forty,' said Eddie. 'They're my unlucky numbers. I'm a member of a fifty-fifty club, and if I could trust the low-down hoodlums who said fifty-fifty loudly enough I might see red with any man.'

Kerky smiled broadly.

'Would you like a kipper, Eddie? There's too many bones in 'em. Gosh, it'd be awful to choke to death – now wouldn't it? What you say to me goes, Eddie. It's red from now on. Who's your aide? I hear poor Tomasino was found in a rain sewer – too bad!'

Eddie smiled.

153

'I heard that the guy who dropped him there was burnt up in a car last night – too bad!'

Kerky Smith reached his long hand across the table. Eddie took it. There was a hard, significant shake, and Kerky went back to the news of the day.

'Been reading about your uncle in the morning paper. That poor old guy! This paper says he had a lot of business interests in America – wonder how many people know he financed the Weiss crowd and put up the money for that parade of choppers when they nearly got Al down in Cicero?'

'He was an enterprising old gentleman,' agreed Eddie.

'Ain't that right?' said Kerky. 'Elijah Decadon! He put more liquor into the United States than any man livin' or dead. God rest him!'

Eddie was looking at him thoughtfully.

'Why bring that up?' he asked.

'We-ell,' drawled Kerky, 'I was just wondering how these blue and green fellers were going to divide.'

'Where the profits started when the old man was shot up? Nothing doing, Kerky. We draw a red line and start a new set of books. Is that right by you?'

Kerky nodded.

'I had to bring forward the idea, Eddie,' he said apologetically.

And so the newest and the unholiest alliance was cemented, and the little man who printed the notices – he was a very respectable printer, who had a small plant of his own in the basement which nobody knew anything about – put away his stock of green ink, and another member of the printing trade, who had a small plant in Croydon, put away his stock of blue ink, and thenceforward all notices were printed in red. And the notices themselves were revised to include the best features of both, and there might have been a smooth and harmonious partnership but for one disturbing factor – Miss Leslie Ranger.

# 23

Leslie had come back to the flat that morning feeling rather jubilant, for she had interviewed the venerable head of a small financial organisation, and had received the half promise of a secretaryship carrying the enormous salary of £700 a year.

As she opened the door she saw the letter that had been pushed under, and wondered why the messenger had failed to notice the letterbox. She recognised the handwriting the moment she saw it: it was from Eddie Tanner.

*Will you come along and see me this morning at about 11.30? I think I have a good job for you.*

She was relieved at the thought that she had already found a position, for, although she liked him, there was something about him which made her just a little uncomfortable, and she realised that part of that discomfort was fear. Yet he had been kind to an unbelievable extent. She did not realise how kind till later. His attitude had been considerate and deferential; never once had he offended her. And when he had promised her fifty thousand pounds he had meant it.

She had turned the matter over in her mind, and wondered in what way, and on what excuse, she could refuse such a tremendous reward for a service which really she had not performed. It was unthinkable that she could take the money; yet, being human, the prospect of possessing such a fortune sometimes left her breathless. She could have telephoned and told him about the Dorries, but that would be a little discourteous, and she went immediately to Berkeley Square to interview him.

Her finger was hardly on the bell-push before the door opened. The man in livery, who greeted her with a smile, was a stranger to her, but evidently she was known to him.

'Mr Tanner will see you at once, Miss Ranger,' he said.

She followed him along the familiar hall to her own little room. Evidently Eddie had taken possession of this as his sanctum.

'Come along in, Miss Ranger.' He pushed a chair up to the desk. 'And sit down. Now tell me all your news.'

'I'm glad you asked me to tell you first, because I think I've got a situation,' she said. 'At Dorries – it's one of the oldest firms in the City.'

He smiled.

'Old, but decayed. Yes, I know Dorries. It used to be swell – had branches all over India. Somebody told me they'd been refinanced. That might be quite a good job.'

He was looking at her oddly.

'That needn't interfere with the job I'm going to offer you, Miss Ranger.

He was standing by the desk, his fingers beating a noiseless tattoo on the walnut edge.

'Did you ever think of matrimony?'

She was so astonished at the question that she could not answer.

'That's a foolish question, isn't it? But have you ever thought of it in connection with me? I could give you a swell time.'

She found speech at last.

'You're not proposing to me, are you, Mr Tanner?'

'You can say "Eddie" if you like – it doesn't commit you to anything, and it sounds more friendly. Terry Weston told you that the first time he met you, didn't he – to call him Terry?'

She did not remember having told him. How did he know?

'It doesn't matter how I know.' He smiled at her astonishment. 'I'm a thought reader. I like you, and that's something better than being red hot in love with you. I can give you the grandest time.'

She shook her head.

'No?' he queried. He was not hurt, did not even seem disappointed. 'You don't feel that way, eh?... I'm sorry.' He flashed a big smile at her. 'That was the job,' he said, with a glint of humour in his eyes.

'I'm terribly sorry,' she stammered. 'It is a great honour – '

He shook his head.

'It's no honour, believe me. I've been married three times' – she gasped at his cool admission – 'and I can tell you that it's no honour for any woman to marry me.'

He paced up and down the room, his hands in his pockets.

'If you'd said yes, it would have been because you knew I could give you a swell position, not because you love me. I know when a woman loves me. It's only happened once. Three weeks after I married her she was certified insane – had illusions. I was one of 'em! After I got my divorce she recovered, married again and got three children, and she's President of the Women's Anti-Booze League – she's been drawing alimony out of booze for years and knows it.'

Leslie was staring at him.

'Were you a – what do they call it? – bootlegger?'

He nodded.

'So was the old man, Elijah – and how!' he laughed. It was the first time she had heard him laugh with any heartiness. 'It's your fate... I'm sorry.'

'Mr Decadon a bootlegger?'

He nodded.

'Elijah shipped more bad liquor into the United States than any subject of the king. He owned the first two speakeasies there were in Chicago, financed Dean O'Banion, and spent a million bucks trying to put Scarface to sleep. You didn't know that. And he did it all from London. He only paid about three visits to Chicago in his life. I was his vice-regent in the Windy City, and I can't tell you the number of times dear Uncle Elijah tried to double cross me. Why do you think I stayed here when I was in London? Why do you think he took the trouble to make a flat for me on the roof'

'Who killed him?' she asked suddenly, her grave eyes focused on his.

He was not in the least embarrassed.

'He killed himself,' he said coolly. 'Don't you ever shed any soft tears for Elijah – he was hard-boiled!'

She found it difficult to ask the question that was on her lips, but presently she summoned up courage.

'You're not in…there's no need for you to be…bootlegging, now?'

He was amused.

'Sure there isn't. No, I'm going to be an English country gentleman, take out naturalisation papers, buy an estate and just settle down.'

She shook her head.

'You couldn't settle down.'

He looked at her admiringly.

'You've said it!' He jerked out his hand. 'Sorry we can't make a deal, but I respect you for it. I think you're a fool, but I still respect you. I won't go with you to the door, for reasons that I can't explain to you. Alberto will get you a taxi – he's a braver man than I am!'

She wondered what this cryptic remark meant.

When she saw Terry later in the morning – he came with an engineer to make a survey and sketch of the aeroplane crash – she did not tell him either of Eddie's offer or of her visit to Berkeley Square. He was elated at her other news.

'Dorries? I don't know it, but I've heard of it. It's a pretty good firm, and a whacking big salary. You're in luck! How did you hear of it?'

'It may have come through the agency. I had a wire asking me to call. It's a sleepy little place in Austin Friars. There's a tiny bank attached to it and an issuing house. I start tomorrow.'

At nine o'clock she took possession of her new domain. Dorries had a history stretching back for two hundred years. They had been bankers, export agents, tea planters, and had fingers in almost every commercial pie that was stirred and baked south of Karachi and east of Bombay.

Her oak-panelled office was hung with portraits of the great Dorries of the past. When she was first shown to her desk she thought a mistake had been made.

'It's quite right, Miss Ranger,' said the head clerk, 'Mr Dorrie gave instructions you were to have this office.'

'Is he here?' she asked.

'No, he's not here. In fact, he never comes here. He lives in Kent. Our business is not quite as brisk as it was, or, I'm afraid, as important. When I was a boy Dorries was one of the most important houses in the City…'

The head clerk, at the end of a long historical survey, admitted to being seventy, and when she told him with the greatest kindness that he didn't look it, he was pleased. Almost all the staff were over fifty, except three or four stenographers, who were also book keepers.

He spent an hour with her, explaining the character and nature of Dorries' operations, and she realised that the staff and the business were dying together. It was rather a depressing thought.

It was not even a limited company, she discovered, but a sort of complicated partnership in which all sorts of mysterious people had microscopic shares. Recently these had been eliminated, and the business was now the property of Mr Dorrie and Mr Pattern, who never came to the office.

'Of course, I don't know Mr Dorrie's business,' said the head clerk, 'or how much of the firm he controls. Mr Pattern has been a partner for six months. I understand he's an old gentleman who lives in Bradford.'

In the afternoon she had an interview with the bank manager, and discovered the startling fact that she was, to all intents and purposes, Dorries. She had power to sign cheques, to make and determine agreements, and was subject only to the indefinite control exercised by Mr Dorrie, who was unlikely to control anything or anybody for very much longer, and Mr Pattern.

'It's a pretty big responsibility for a young lady,' said the bank manager. 'There's eighty thousand pounds cash credit and nearly a hundred thousand pounds on deposit on account of your little banking business.'

In the afternoon, she met the staff, and was introduced to one of those who had been light heartedly described as a steongrapher, but who proved to be a young man, very silent and uncommunicative, who was the accountant. He had only been in the business for three months, and was cordially disliked by the head clerk and the other elderly members of the staff.

Leslie had not finished her first day's experience as the head of a City firm before she realised that the unpopular accountant was the only competent member of the staff. It was he who conducted the considerable import business, he who arranged credits, who made appointments with her, who was to keep her acquainted with the bank balance and advise her on all financial transactions.

Just as she was leaving that evening the head clerk asked for oan interview.

'There is one point on which I forgot to instruct you, Miss Ranger, and it is this: Mr Dorrie especially asked me to remind you that in no circumstances must you discuss the business of Dorries with any person outside the firm.'

She was a little nettled.

'That warning is quite unnecessary,' she said.

She spent a busy three days improving systems, speeding up office methods and generally moving into that category of unpopularity in which the accountant held a prominent position in the esteem of the staff. On the Saturday she had a letter from a firm of lawyers, informing her that Messrs Dorrie were so satisfied with the work she had performed that her salary had been raised to £2,000 a year.

As she was leaving the office the old head clerk came up to her, rubbing his hands.

'You've brought us good luck, Miss Ranger,' he said. 'We've had eighteen new accounts opened this week! They can laugh at Dorries as bankers, but we were in the business before some of these joint stock companies were ever heard of.'

It was true that nobody quite took Dorries seriously as bankers. There had been a time when the great Indian houses and the East India merchants had an account, and some of them were fairly substantial. But the competition of modern banks and the destructive efficiency of banking methods brought about such a shrinkage that the house carried less than fifty accounts, and Leslie calculated that one was dying every month, so that the accession of new business was very gratifying.

The old man's information was not news to her. She had initialled and approved each account that was opened, but she had not realised that the appearance of eighteen in one week was very unusual.

She kept faith with Mr Dorrie, and did not discuss the business with Terry, but that was only natural in her as a woman. Women executives do not discuss their employers' business, and, beyond that she was quite happy in her new employment, Terry did not even know that her salary had had such a surprising rise.

There had come a lull in the storm which was shaking London. One newspaper in a sardonic leader had summarised popular opinion when it said:

Two days have passed without a gang shooting. What has happened? Another week of this state of lawfulness, and we may expect to see the pound return to parity.

It was on the day this article appeared that Scotland Yard heard of the new red warning. One had been sent to a wealthy brewer, who was also a Member of Parliament, and – crowning audacity – the letter had been addressed to him at the House of Commons.

It was a challenge which could not be ignored. The Member had babbled of his experience to other Members, the notice was rushed across to Scotland Yard, and Jiggs put on his glasses and read the communication through letter by letter.

'It's a hook-up,' he said. 'I've been expecting it. The wording's practically the same as the Green, except that they've taken over Blue's telephone idea and dropped the light in the window. Is this senator, or whatever he is, a rich man?'

'He's a millionaire,' said Terry. 'He lives in a flat in Park Lane.'

Jiggs nodded slowly.

'Where is he now – in the House of Commons? Why, I'll give you my advice. Get an armoured car and rush him to the Tower of London.'

If this suggestion had been made a week before, Terry would have dismissed it as fantastic.

'I don't know how the Council will take that, but it's sane.'

'Sure it's sane,' said Jiggs. 'These guys have started business all over again, and here's a picturesque example. They know he's sent the letter over to police headquarters, and they've marked him down. It's going to be something spectacular, Terry boy.'

'I'll see the Council right away,' said Inspector Weston.

He was gone an hour. When he came back he made a gesture of defeat.

'The Cabinet think that the armoured car and Tower idea would be an advertisement of our inability to offer this man protection. They've agreed to a strong escort bringing him from the House to his home and back to the Commons in the morning, and they're policing his flat in Park Lane.'

Jiggs shook his head.

'They could get him coming or going, but I've an idea they won't do that.'

'The Home Secretary thinks that as they did not get Mr Cuthbert Drood – ' began Terry.

'Poppycock!' snarled Jiggs. 'They passed up on Cuthbert, not because they couldn't get him, but because the gang war started that night. They'll get your Mr Ripple-Durcott as sure as you're alive. Not tonight maybe, but in three days, and you can bet your sweet life that until they get him all the notices are going to be suspended. This is the test case of the Combined and Co-operated Society for the Extermination of Won't Pays.'

His prophecy proved to be accurate. Mr Ripple-Durcott was escorted to his home that evening by a strong body of plain clothes detectives. Motorcyclists rode on either side and before his car. There were so many police in his flat that he had some difficulty in getting into his bedroom. At least, that was Jiggs' version.

He came to the House of Commons the following afternoon. A great crowd had gathered in Whitehall to cheer him as he passed. Mr Ripple-Durcott was not displeased with his new-found popularity.

Ordinarily the House of Commons was not very much interested in him. He was a dull man who made dull speeches, and told interminable and pointless stories in the smoking room. But the events of the day had elevated him into a national figure.

'Can you tell me,' asked Jiggs, 'why they've put Tetley in charge of this man?'

Terry hesitated.

'Wembury's a pretty obstinate man, and you seem to have got his goat over something.'

Jiggs grinned.

'The natural antipathy of the near competent for the superlatively adequate,' he said magnificently. 'I'm sorry about that,' he went on in a changed tone. 'I like Wembury – he's swell. And I guess if I was running a department in Chicago and some lah-di-dah Englishman butted in, I'd feel that way too. But all the same, Terry, you've got to persuade the big man that this Inspector Tetley is poison! I've been doing a little private detective work, quite alien to my nature, and it seems that this guy has been on howdy terms with the Big Boy ever since he came to town, in fact while this racket was being organised. Can't you persuade Wembury – '

'At the moment, no.' Terry shook his head. 'He's getting rattled, and I must say I sympathise with him. And Tetley's a pretty persuasive fellow. The fact that he's not terribly well educated, and that he's worked his way up in spite of a lot of disadvantages, stands to his credit. On the other side of the ledger, he was suspected of being in on a particularly bad gambling-house scandal about five years ago. We could never prove anything, and he only got out of it by the skin of his teeth. Anyway, I can't believe that he'd connive at murder.'

'He's not conniving at murder,' said Jiggs quietly. 'He believes that he's taking money for keeping his eyes shut to something which doesn't really matter. It's queer how you can make yourself think just what you want if you've got a brain like Tetley's. And don't suppose that he isn't getting scared, because he is. After a while even obvious things become apparent even to the nitwit. But he's in it, Terry, and he can't get out of it. He's in it worse now, because he's beginning to realise how far he's gone. One of these days his conscience will start working and he'll fall apart, but if he ever gets that way he had better keep it to himself – that's all!'

Nothing happened on the second night. On the third a slight fog descended on London, and Jiggs knew the moment was at hand. It rolled up in great billows, and began to spread out more and more thickly.

There was a Member of the House of Commons named Quigley, a bowed old man with a shock of white hair and a little white moustache and goatee. He was not a well known man. His appearances in the House had been rare since the first session. At nine o'clock that night he came slowly up the stone steps, crossed the lobby and passed through the stone corridor to the inner lobby. The policeman on duty touched his hat and opened the door. He walked into the House, stood for a moment by the bar, fixing his eyeglasses. There was a debate in progress; one of those uninteresting measures dealing with land valuation was being drearily discussed. Mr Quigley took a seat on the almost empty Government benches, and somebody drew attention to the fact.

'Quigley's gone over to the Government,' he said.

Mr Quigley was a member of the Opposition. The front bench, where members of the Government sit was empty except for an under-secretary who was in charge of the debate. Suddenly Mr Quigley rose, walked towards the Speaker with tottering feet, and had reached the gangway, when he turned quickly. His arm shot out. Three times he fired, and then, gripping his gun, he leapt over the outstretched legs of the under-secretary, raced past the Speaker and through the door behind the chair.

It was all over in a second. A man who had been sitting on the front Opposition bench crumpled up and fell in a heap. A policeman saw the running Member and tried to intercept him, but went down with a bullet through his shoulder.

Evidently he knew the geography of the place: he must have studied a plan carefully. He turned into a passage and through a swing-door on to the terrace of the House. He did not hesitate. Counting the lamps from the bridge end of the terrace, he chose the fourth, and, leaping up on to the parapet, dived into the river. Actually no one saw his exit. When a crowd of attendants and police came on to the terrace he was gone. A policeman leaned over the parapet, saw a long launch heading for the centre of the river and challenged it. There was no answer. He pulled a revolver from his holster and fired twice. Almost instantly there came from the dark waters flickering lines of intermittent light and the stammer of a machine-gun. Bullets sprayed the parapet, smashed a few windows, but did no other damage.

By this time the boat was in mid stream. The watchers saw again the flickering of machine-gun fire and heard the rattle of it. In mid-stream was a police launch, and the battle was one sided. By the time reinforcements came the launch had disappeared.

Wembury came into Terry's room, looking white and drawn.

'Is he dead?' asked Terry.

The Chief Constable nodded.

'Yes, he's dead all right, and officially so are we. Where's your American friend?'

'He went out the moment the report came through,' said Terry.

'He wasn't very far wrong about his armoured car and the Tower,' said Wembury bitterly.

He fell into a chair and sat with his face in his hands.

'This is not my job,' he said. 'I'm not paid for it. God, how we used to laugh when we got the news through from Chicago that their police couldn't deal with their racketeers and gangsters! And now we know why. We're fighting guns with feather-dusters.'

He leaned back in his chair and sighed heavily.

'That launch of theirs must have crept along the wall. It was in the shadow all the time, and the Thames police people didn't see it. By the way, the sergeant in the police boat is badly hit. Who was it suggested that the Thames police should have machine-guns, and who turned down the idea? Jiggs suggested it; I murdered it.'

He looked up as the door opened.

'Hull, Jiggs!'

'Hullo, Chief!' Jiggs was very cheerful. 'Sorry,' he said.

Wembury nodded.

'I know. Human nature being what it is, you ought to be glad.'

Jiggs scowled at him.

'My human nature isn't like any other human nature,' he growled.

'What's the solution, Jiggs?'

Captain Allerman swung round a chair and sat astride it.

'I'll tell you what's the solution, Wembury,' he said, 'and it's the only solution. Send a couple of parties to pick up Eddie Tanner and Kerky Smith, and bring them to Scotland Yard.'

'And then?' asked Wembury when he paused.

'And then,' said Jiggs deliberately, 'when they try to escape, give 'em the works.'

Wembury stared at him.

'You mean shoot them?'

'If they tried to escape.'

'But suppose they didn't try to escape?'

A slow, devilish smile dawned on Jiggs Allerman's face.

'Chief, if you'll leave 'em to me, I'll undertake that they'll try to escape all right!'

The Chief Constable shook his head.

'That's simply murder,' he said.

'What's happened tonight?' asked Jiggs. 'What's been happening all the week – just wrist slappin'? Murder? I don't know the word! It's murder to kill an unarmed citizen, but to put a real bad hoodlum into a squad car and shoot him on the way to the station – that's my idea of poetic justice.'

Again Wembury shok his head.

'It can't be done, Jiggs. We can deport these fellows – '

'Deport them!' sneered Jiggs. 'Over to Paris, France. And you couldn't deport Eddie Tanner, anyway. He claims to be American, but he's British-born. I've looked up his record so often that I could recite it at a Sunday school picnic. He was born right here in London. Though he's lived in America all his life he never took out papers on the other side. That's news to you.

'He's a swell feller, Eddie – I like him. There's something about him that's almost human – by which I mean he looks like a human being but isn't. You're not going to beat these birds by any gen'lemanly methods. I'll tell you something. Chief. In Sing Sing there's a class of privileged prisoners – they call 'em trusties. A trusty's allowed to go pretty well anywhere he likes – sometimes outside the prison – and they know he'll come back. But they've never made a trusty out of a hard-boiled gangster – did you know that? They've tried it and it failed. You can't put these birds on their honour. After they've committed their second murder they kinda lose the taste for it – honour, I'm talking about, nor murder.'

He walked to the window and looked out on to the foggy Embankment.

'There are quite a few people outside taking a peek at Scotland Yard, and I guess they're wondering what we're going to do about it. And the crowds outside the Houses of Parliament are bigger than any I've seen.'

The phone rang and the chief took it up.

'For me, I know.' He listened. 'Very good, sir... You fellows had better come over to the House with me. If there's a new Commissioner appointed, I'll put my resignation in his hands tonight. As it is, I'm going to tell the Home Secretary that he can dispose of me just as he wishes.'

The crowd outside the House of Commons was so dense that even the mounted police found it difficult to work their way through the packed masses. Between the railway station and the House is an underground passage. Curiously enough, this had been very heavily policed that night, for it had been the Chief Constable's theory that if any attempt was made to enter the House it would be by this approach.

They were taken into the big room of the Prime Minister. Half the Cabinet were present, and Jiggs picked out a tall, white haired man who looked the most worried, and guessed that this was the Home Secretary.

There were no recriminations. These statesmen realised just what was the problem that had to be solved.

'There's no question of accepting your resignation, Mr Wembury,' said the Home Secretary promptly when the Chief Constable made his offer. 'You're doing as well as you can with the weapons you have.'

Jiggs was introduced, and the haggard looking Prime Minister scrutinised him.

'What are we going to do, Captain Allerman? You know these people, you're acquainted with the methods employed to deal with them – what is your suggestion?'

Jiggs did not speak for a moment. He sat by the table, drumming his fingers on the polished surface. Presently he lifted his head.

'Any suggestion I make, gentlemen, will sound immodest. The first is that I be given absolute control of the Metropolitan police force for a month. The second is that you suspend all your laws which protect criminals – these fairplay methods of yours are going to get you in worse than you're in already. I suggest you scrap every rule you've laid down for Scotland Yard; that you suspend the Habeas Corpus Act, and give us an indemnity in advance for any illegal act – that is to say, for any act which is against your law – that may be committed in the course of that month. If you'll do this, I'll put these two gangs just where they belong.'

'In prison?'

Jiggs shook his head.

'In hell,' he said.

It was perhaps unfortunate that he used this extravagant illustration. The Home Secretary was a very earnest Non-conformist, who took his religion seriously.

'That, of course is...' He paused.

'Fantastical,' suggested Jiggs. 'I'm getting quite used to the word. It's the one you pull when any hard-sense suggestion is made to you.'

'In the first place,' said the Home Secretary stiffly, 'we could not give you complete control of the police. That, as I say, is – um – impossible. I'm not sure that it isn't against the Constitution.'

Jiggs nodded.

'She's a new one to me.'

'And to suspend all the laws because a party of assassins and blackmailers are terrorising London is equally absurd. You must give us a more practical suggestion than that.'

Jiggs shook his head.

'There ain't any,' he said. 'But, failing that, I'll give you the advice you want. Strengthen your police force, give a certain percentage of your officers revolvers – and it may be advisable to train 'em in the way of using them – deport all suspicious foreigners, and what else? Why, you can do as you did tonight – close the public galleries in the House of Commons, without realising that if you close the public galleries, there's only one way a man can get in, and that is as a Member.'

'I suggested that possibility – it was one of those fantastic ideas of mine! Mr Secretary, you're up against exactly the same stone wall that every police department in the United States is up against. Organised crime, carried out by criminals who regard murder as a normal method. Only you haven't got hoodlums and amateurs working this racket. I reckon there are nearly two hundred gunmen in London, and they're all experts. For months their dives and bolt-holes have been got ready for them. This racket has been planned for years – that's what you've got to consider. It was any odds that when the gangs came to London they'd come good and plenty, and that only the big timers – I'll interpret that, gentlemen: it means the more important armies – would be employed. I'll tell you something that you don't know. There isn't one of those gunmen, aides, legs, watch-out men, killers, who is pulling down less than five hundred bucks a week. In your depreciated currency that's about a hundred and forty pounds.

There's over two million dollars expenses in this racket, and that's coming back pretty quickly. It will come back in a flood after tonight.'

'Do you know who is behind this?' asked the Secretary.

'I know, and you know, Mr Secretary. I've already sent in the names in my official report. One is an American, one is an Englishman. There's no evidence against either. You can turn one of 'em out of the country at twenty four hours' notice, but the racket is going on, and going strong, whether he's in this country or in Paris.'

The meeting adjourned with no more than the conventional resolution adopted. An order went out from Scotland Yard that the uniformed police should be armed. One suggestion of Jiggs' alone was adopted; the establishment of an aeroplane patrol day and night over London and the creation of signal stations.

'I can't see how that will serve us,' said the Home Secretary.

'No, sir,' said the patient Jiggs. 'I don't see how you can.'

It was an excellent scheme. The watchers of the skies would keep close touch with the ground. They could follow in the daytime the movements of any escaping car, could trail it to its destination, and give information to the ground police if the occupants of the car dispersed. Incidentally, it would prevent a repetition of an air raid upon any certain house, if the Green section of the gang attempted to repeat the adventure which ended so disastrously in Cavendish Square.

'And that's that, boy!' said Jiggs when they were out in the street again and pushing their way through the thinning crowd towards the embankment. 'There's a dozen guns in this crowd, but they couldn't get away with it. That's the one thing they hate – crowds. The one thing they're afraid of is being lynched – you didn't know that? I've had real tough babies on their knees to me in a police station, begging me to be put in a cell where the crowd couldn't get 'em. What a grand film this would make! But the Censor would never pass it. It's against public interest to interfere with the illusion of the proletariat – that's a helluva good word I picked up listenin' to a soap box orator at Hyde Park Corner last Sunday night.'

Just as they were turning into the Yard the Chief Constable, who had remained silent throughout the journey turned to Terry Weston.

'I'd like you to see Tetley. I've told him to report to my office, but I'll have him sent in to you. You can take whatever steps you like. I want to know by tomorrow morning what precautions he took, and how this man was able to get on to the terrace of the House of Commons.'

Terry put through an inquiry about the policeman who had been wounded in the House, and learned with satisfaction that the man was making good progress. He rang the bell for a messenger.

Inspector Tetley was looking a hundred years old. Those jaunty, pin-pointed moustaches of his drooped dismally. The man was frightened; he was on the point of breaking, or Jiggs did not recognise the signs.

Tetley looked at Jiggs and then at his immediate chief.

'I'd rather see you alone, Mr Weston. I don't think that strangers – '

'This isn't the moment to consider your fine feelings, Mr Tetley. Captain Allerman is part of our organisation. Now will you explain how this thing happened tonight, and why the exits were left, not exactly unguarded, but without sufficient guards?'

'I did my best, sir,' whined Tetley. 'I had men in all the corridors, and I can't understand why the officer who was supposed to be on duty on the Terrace – '

'Well, if you can't understand it I will explain,' said Terry sternly. 'He was not on duty because he hadn't been instructed.'

Tetley did not contest this.

'We all make mistakes. I've had a very worrying time, Mr Weston, and tonight I had a headache so bad that I didn't know whether I was on my head or my heels.'

He looked appealingly at Jiggs, but could find no sympathy written in that rugged face. Tetley began to enumerate rapidly the disposition of his men.

'I saw the murderer come into the House,' he went on, 'and I was deceived. Why, even the attendants thought they knew him. I

171

was talking to some Members afterwards, and one of them said that when the old gentleman sat down on the bench – '

'We won't have any reminiscences at the moment. You'll report to this office at twelve o'clock tomorrow and bring with you your bank passbook,' said Terry brusquely. 'Also your wife's bank account – that which she has in her own name at the Edgware Road branch of the Northern and Southern Bank, and that which she has in her maiden name at the Dyers Bank in Bradford.'

He saw the man's jaw drop.

'You will also bring me exact particulars of the contents of Box 8497 at the Fetter Lane Safe Deposit. When you go there to ascertain, you will find an officer waiting for you and he will render you every assistance that you may demand.'

Tetley went out, a broken man.

'The queer thing is,' said Jiggs wonderingly, 'that I didn't speak a word!'

# 24

Mr Kerky Smith had had a very late night. He and his wife had been dancing at one of the most fashionable of the nightclubs. His deferential valet was never deferential when they were quite alone. He came and woke his employer.

'Kerk,' he said, 'that copper's on the wire.'

Kerky got up, glared at the interrupter of his dreams.

'What copper?' he asked sourly. And then, quickly: 'Tetley?'

'He calls himself Colonel Brunton – that's Tetley, ain't it?'

Kerky went out into the sitting room and took up the receiver.

'I've got to see you, Mr Smith. It's most urgent. Can I come up to the hotel?'

'No, sir, you can't come up to the hotel,' said Kerky. 'I've told you that before. I'll have a man pick you up somewhere.'

'I'm being watched,' said the agitated voice of Tetley. 'I didn't realise it till last night, when the Chief Inspector – '

'Maybe I'm not being watched, eh?' snarled Smith. 'I'll see you after I'm shaved – I'll be shaved in half an hour.'

He went to his favourite barber's in Soho, allowed himself to be lathered, and then the obliging barber plugged in a portable telephone and went out, shutting the door behind him.

Inspector Tetley was no farther away from him than on the first floor, and he was alone in a soundproof cabinet. Kerky listened to the recital of the man's woes and fears, heard in detail the interview of the night before, and –

'I'm resigning,' said Tetley energetically. It was the vigour of a frightened man, looking for avenues of escape. 'I think I'll go abroad. I'm all in. If that American comes after me he'll get everything out of me. He didn't say a word last night. There's about a couple of thousand due to me, Kerky – if you don't mind me calling you by your Christian name.'

'It isn't my Christian name, and I don't like it,' snapped Kerky Smith. 'OK' his voice was suddenly cheerful. 'Be on the Inner Circle, right opposite the Zoo, at ten o'clock to tonight, and I'll send one of my boys along with the money. But get there without anybody seeing you.'

He pressed a little bell that was within reach, and, when the barber came back, handed him the receiver.

'This soap's drying on my face,' he said irritably.

# 25

Cora Smith had had a peculiar upbringing. She was a little over fourteen when she first became acquainted with gang life, and since that age she had been of it and sometimes in it. All her life she had heard millions talked about as if they were pennies. Sometimes they were mythical millions, sometimes they were hundreds of thousands that looked like millions, and had been gained at the risk of life and liberty.

She had always been well cared for, always been expensively dressed, and had accumulated jewellery with the nonchalance of a small boy collecting marbles.

She had made two incursions into the field of matrimony before she met Kerky, and during her married life, and before, the atmosphere in which she moved knew neither pity nor remorse. Violent death was one of the commonplaces of existence. She had met slightly amusing fellows, who had made love to her one day and were under a merciful tarpaulin in the county mortuary the next. She had not been shocked for so long that she forgot she could ever be shocked.

Her philosophy was a simple one: it was to look beautiful in the eyes of the man who footed the bills, and to be faithful to him so long as he didn't double cross her. After that, faith had no meaning.

She was very fond of Kerky. None of her husbands had excited so much interest in her shallow little brain and the red marble which she called a heart. To her, only one mysterious crisis was possible: the loss of her man, whether by death or through the machinations of somebody more attractive to him. In her wildest dreams she could not imagine any woman more attractive than herself; but she knew enough of men to know that they sometimes had peculiar fancies.

If a swift bullet took her man there were no complications; finish was written to the chapter of their joint life and she made herself attractive for some other man. There was generally a vague sort of waiting list, and a tacit agreement that if she passed on it would be in a certain direction.

She did not worry very much about Kerky's break with her being brought about by a swift bullet. This, however, was another matter. She brooded about Leslie, and, when she was alone, fell into sour rages; and from brooding she came to planning. She searched for historical precedents and found plenty. There was that girl who went about with Harry the Pollak and slashed his secret girl with a razor. But that was no good: it was common, just the sort of thing that a nigger might have done. A more practical example was Sarah Vagenti, who took her rival by the hair of her head as she sat at dinner with Sarah's man and pumped three nickel shots into her. It took a whole lot of holy men and sob-sister stuff to save Sarah from the chair. Virtuous mothers of families in a thousand and one frame-houses in the State of Missouri grimly consigned her to death. Sarah was still in a Federal penitentiary.

Then there was the epic case of Looey Stein… Cora thought this over, and was filled with a splendid resolve.

'Why don't you go down to the country, kid?' Kerky asked her one day. 'What's the good of me buying you houses? Why, you've only been there once!'

She smiled at him graciously.

'You certainly think with your mind, Kerk,' she said. 'I was layin' in bed this mornin' wondering whether I oughtn't to go down and see that little dump.'

'Why don't you go down for a day or two? Take your maid, get some women in to clean up. I'll send you down a swell cook.'

She shook her head.

'Why, I don't think so,' she said.

The little house Kerky had bought her the previous summer was a riverside cottage between Maidenhead and Cookham. It had been rebuilt, and had in it a perfect household equipment. She had fallen in love with it the first time she saw the place, had fallen out of love after her second visit.

'I was reading today,' she said untruthfully, 'about Looey Stein. Say, she was a swell hater! The woman who put that Baltimore kid on the spot.'

Kerky shook his head disapprovingly.

'There's a big sign on that racket, Cora – "Women keep out!" '

He looked at her keenly through narrowed eyes.

'You're not thinkin' of doublin' for that game are you?'

'Don't be crazy,' she said.

If he had been indifferent she might have forgotten the nebulous project that was forming in her mind, but he had been keenly interested and concerned.

Leslie went out to lunch as much for exercise as for nourishment. She was going back to her office, and had turned out of Broad Street into Austin Friars, when she heard a shrill voice hail her by name.

'Miss Ranger!'

She looked round. A little coupé had pulled up with a jerk by the sidewalk and a woman got out. Mrs Kerky Smith was so radiantly lovely a figure in the drab setting of Broad Street that City clerks, going about their lawful occasions, forgot their business and turned to gape at her. But it was the kind of loveliness which it invariably embarrassed Leslie to see. This pretty woman was too exquisite, too much like the perfect magazine cover, to blend into the greys and browns of everyday life.

'Why, look who's here!' Cora Smith was all too genial. 'Won't you come along and lunch with me! It's too bad: Kerky's going over to Paris, France, on business, and I was wondering whether you and me – you and I couldn't get better acquainted. Where's your place of business?'

She looked round.

'Somewhere about here,' smiled Leslie. 'I'm terribly sorry, Mrs Smith, but I'm very busy.'

'What time are you through?'

Leslie told her five o'clock.

'Wouldn't you like to come along for a drive?' Cora almost pleaded. 'Say, I'm that lonely I could swap stories with a bellhop!'

Leslie was sorry for her, but not so sorry that she would have cared to spend a very long time in her company. Still...

She walked back with the woman, saw her get into her little coupé and drive off. It was a handsome and expensive machine. Cora Kerky Smith could have driven no other.

It was true that Kerky Smith had intended going to Paris, France, but he had changed his mind.

'You going out?' He looked at his watch. 'Half past four, kid. You'd better take someone along with you. Where are you going?'

'I'm taking that girl out – Leslie something.'

'Leslie Ranger?' He frowned at her. 'What's the big idea?'

'I thought I ought to get to know her, Kerky.' She wailed when she was feeling plaintive.

'That's OK not a bad idea. Phone me around six,' he said. 'Maybe you'll get her to talk about that guy at the Yard, but don't you talk, kid.'

She looked at him in amusement.

Leslie enjoyed the drive. It was rather a fine afternoon, and London was full of horrors. Every newspaper bill shouted 'Murder!' 'Outrage!' 'Gangs!' as the car flashed past, so that when Cora suggested a trip to her little country house, Leslie agreed. They stopped in Slough and bought sandwiches. Cora remembered afterwards that the girl might have telephoned somebody to say whom she was with. Kerky wouldn't make a mistake like that; nor would her classic exemplar.

It was dusk when the car turned into the long lane which would bring them, so Cora told her, to her house. The long lane had a longer lane branching off to the left. It ran between the hedges of two unkempt meadows. Then, with almost dramatic suddenness, it came to the charming bungalow, standing between high privet hedges. Leslie got down and opened the gates. The coupé half circled the house and stopped under a glass-roofed porch.

'I can't stay very long,' Leslie said.

'Just look in,' pleaded Cora.

She opened the door of the kitchen. There was a smell of mustiness peculiar to a closed house. As they walked into the drawing room the first thing Leslie saw was a canary cage, and, at the bottom, a pitiful little yellow shape.

'O, gee! Look at that!' said Cora. 'I forgot to leave him any seed.'

No expression of regret or of pity. Leslie stared at her. She could hardly look at the tiny songster that had died of starvation and thirst.

'I can't stand birds singing around the house. Kerky thought I'd like him. He paid twenty five bucks for him – "bucks" means "dollars".'

'So I understand,' said Leslie coldly.

'Go upstairs!'

There was something in the woman's tone that made Leslie look at her. She was standing very taut, her eyes wide open, blazing with excitement. In her hand was a small automatic.

'You heard what I said – go upstairs!'

Leslie felt a queer sinking feeling within her; her knees trembled.

'Don't be stupid,' she said. 'It's time we went home.'

Her voice sounded strange.

'Go right upstairs when I tell you!'

There was a passion in the voice of this lovely, doll-like creature that struck the girl dumb. Without a word she walked into the passage, up the stairs, and on to the first landing.

'Go into that room on the left.'

Leslie obeyed. The room was in darkness; it had been shuttered against storm. Cora turned on the light. It was obviously a servant's bedroom: it had a plain, iron bedstead and a chair. Leading out was a tiny bathroom.

'I'm going to tell you sump'n'. I damn nearly died for your sake – did you know that? I'll bet you didn't! That feller of yours, Eddie Tanner...do you know what he said to Kerky? He'd cut off my head

and send it home in a strawberry basket – and he'd 'a' done it! I know
Eddie… I was married to him…for three years. And because of you!'

'Of me?' said Leslie. 'That's ridiculous!'

'Ridiculous, eh? You got a notice, didn't you, asking for five
hundred? And you took it to the police, and they put the choppers on
you. That's how Eddie bought 'em off – picked me up on the street
and shut me into a little room, and if the choppers had got you he'd
have killed me.'

Leslie was looking at her in amazement. Incredible and humanly
impossible as the story sounded, she knew it was true.

'I owe you something for that, and I owe you something for
vamping Kerky. And you needn't tell me you didn't – I know what
women are…'

She told Leslie what women were, and did not mince her words.

Leslie belonged to this world, lived in it, and was not easily
shocked. She was not even shocked now, though it almost hurt her to
hear a woman speak as Cora Smith was speaking.

'I'm letting *you* stay locked up for a while, same as I was. Maybe if
I'm feeling good tomorrow I'll come down and let you out, but if I'm
feeling bad…'

She looked at Leslie. Her face had suddenly gone old, and she was
breathing rapidly.

'Well, maybe I will,' she said at last.

She opened her bag and took out two pairs of American handcuffs.
She had seen them a few days before at a toy store in Oxford Street
when she was shopping, and had bought them for the novelty. She had
shown them to Kerky, and he was not at all impressed.

'Throw 'em in the ashcan, will you? The worst things you can
bring in a house for luck,' he had told her.

Holding her pistol with one hand, she snapped one of the bracelets
over the girl's wrists, fastened the second pair of handcuffs to the first,
and gripped that round an iron pipe from the bathroom.

'You can't open those without a key,' she said. 'See how you like
it, kid.'

She drove back to town, and the nearer she got to London the more uneasy she became. For this was an end to her adventure that she had not foreseen. She had been so concerned in planning the first part that she had had no definite idea as to its conclusion. And Kerky...'

She had reached the end of the Great West Road, stopped her car, and was half inclined to go back and get the girl. When she released her tomorrow she'd squeal, and Kerky would raise hell, and maybe all Kerky's great racket would be sunk.

Cora was terrified. Now there was only one solution, and her little head reeled with a newly discovered horror.

She went to the telephone and called her husband, and when his anxious voice demanded, with florid trimmings, where she was and what she had been doing, her nerve failed her again.

'Kerky,' she faltered, 'I thought of going back...into the country...'

'You come right home. Where are you? I'll get one of the cars to pick you up, you...'

She didn't mind his abuse: it gave her some relief.

'Yes, Kerky,' she said meekly, and left her prisoner to the darkness.

When she came into the sitting room Kerky Smith's face was as black as gloom.

'Where have you been?'

He took in all the details of her dress with one sweeping glance.

'And where's your bag?'

She gasped, and staggered back. She had left the bag in the house; and there was something in that bag which nobody ought to see.

'Lord Kerky! What's the idea of barking at me? I didn't take the bag out – it's in my drawer. Do you want it?'

If he had been less worried he would have seen through the lie.

'No, I don't want it. Sit down here. Somebody's been in these rooms today, searchin' 'em, while I was out. Do you remember that little book I gave you the other day and told you to put in the safe deposit?'

She nodded dumbly.

'You put it there, did you?'

She nodded again. She dared not speak.

He heaved a deep sigh.

'That's OK, Cora. I was a fool to give it to you, anyway, knowing what a dumb girl you are.'

He got up from the chair and began to pace the room. The tension in his face relaxed. He was smiling when he asked:

'What about a show tonight, kid? "Legs and Lovelies," eh?'

'Fine, Kerk!' she said.

Her voice was steady, her active mind working as fast as it had ever worked. What would happen if she told Kerky that she had forgotten to put the book into the safe deposit, and that at that moment it was in her bag, in the house where she had left Leslie Ranger?

Leslie had seen the bag, had found it difficult to keep her eyes from it or to avoid drawing the woman's attention to what she was leaving behind. It lay on the chair in the servant's bedroom, more than six feet from where the girl was chained to the pipe.

She heard the door slam and the noise of the car as it went out to the lane. From where she stood she saw the reflected gleam of its lights when Cora switched them on.

The keys would be there. They had been tied to the handcuffs with little red tapes, and Cora had broken them and dropped them back into the bag. The chair was too far away for her to reach. She let the handcuff that was about the pipe slip down as near to the floor as she could, then, lying down, she stretched herself out on the tips of her toes and just touched one of the rungs of the chair. Another inch... she could not reach it.

There was a broom in a corner of the tiny bathroom. She could just reach it. Sliding the broom along the floor, she hooked the end of it to one leg of the chair and pulled gently. To her horror, the chair caught some projection in the floor and overturned. The bag was now barely within reach of the broom and her body combined. She made another desperate effort, stretched herself prone on the floor, and, gripping the handle of the broom in her feet manoeuvred it clumsily, but reached the other side of the bag and drew it towards her. She lost it four times before finally this jewelled little satchel came within reach of her trembling hands.

She opened it. There were the keys – four of them, two threaded on each tape. In a second she was free. All the time she had been listening, expecting to hear the car return, but there was no sound. She emptied the contents of the bag on to the table. The little automatic she put aside with a grimace.

There was a small red leather book. It was a curious book, for it was enclosed in two tiny chains which were linked together where they crossed, and were fastened on the top edge of the book with a large, thin lock, in appearance rather like a bloated half-crown. She found fifty pounds in notes and the etceteras she might expect to find in a woman's bag: lipstick, jewelled powder-box, gold pencil, and a few silver coins.

She replaced the contents in the bag. She would find some satisfaction in calling at the hotel in the morning and restoring the property to its owner.

At first Leslie had been terribly frightened, but it was the indignity of the experience which jolted her. It was some time before she got out of the house. Most of the doors were double-bolted. Eventually she forced a window of the drawing room. Very dusty, hot and tired, she tramped up the two long lanes. She met nobody, nor was she likely to until she reached the main Bourne End road. Even here there was nobody to whom she could tell her plight or ask assistance. There was very little assistance she needed, except a quick conveyance to London. She might have phoned Terry… She laughed at the thought.

By the time she came to the Bath road she had almost recovered her equanimity. There was a garage nearby, and she went in to hire a car. She had fifty pounds of Cora's and the least that malignant lady could do was to pay her expenses. The garage keeper shook his head.

'I'm sorry, miss. We've got a car you could have, but I haven't got a chauffeur. If you care to drive one yourself – '

Leslie leapt at the idea. She wanted to be alone. The drive to London would steady her nerves completely. She offered to make a substantial deposit, gave him her card, but that seemed to satisfy him.

She had to open her own bag to get the card, and the garage man was amused.

'Carrying two bags, miss – you're lucky!'

'I'm lucky to have this.' Leslie shook Mrs Smith's bag grimly.

The car was a two seater, a smooth running English car of a make she knew and could handle. Just before she left she pointed to the clock on the dashboard.

'Ten o'clock,' she said. 'I never knew a car clock that was in order.'

The garage man chuckled.

'That's in order miss, and, what's more, it's exactly ten o'clock.'

She could not believe that she had been nearly three hours in that beastly house.

The man was attentive, gave her all she needed – all except petrol. She realised this when she was halfway down the Colnbrook bypass and the car, after one or two convulsive hiccoughs, stopped. Usually the bypass has a continuous flow of traffic. Tonight only two cars passed in five minutes, and both ignored her signal. There was a gateway nearby. She took off the brake and allowed the car to run back down the sharp declivity on which it had halted, guiding it across the path into the field. She was scared that the battery was giving out too, for the lights were flickering. She switched them out, and waited till some slow moving machine came along that would stop and supply her with the petrol she required.

Then she saw a car come over the crest of the hill. It was moving swiftly, and slowed within three yards of where she stood. Then she saw it was a light van, and was stepping forward to ask for assistance, when she heard:

'You're not going to do a thing like this? For God's sake!'

The voice was almost a scream. Shuddering, she drew back. Where had she heard that voice before… It was associated with traffic and cars massed in the street…

Inspector Tetley, the man with the pointed moustaches! And then she heard him scream. It was the scream of one in terror of death.

# 26

Inspector Tetley was at his place nearly opposite the Zoo when the car drew up to the kerb. It was not, he saw, an ordinary car, but a light van, bearing on its side the name of a firm of grocers.

'Get up, will you, Mr Tetley, inside? There's a couple of chairs there,' said the voice.

He climbed up to the side of the driver and stepped back into the darkness. He saw the glow of two cigars.

'Sit right down, Inspector.'

A flap dropped behind him; the car moved on.

'Kerky couldn't come along tonight. He asked me to see you,' said the pleasant voice. 'How are things at Scotland Yard?'

Tetley did not wish to discuss Scotland yard at that moment, and with a man who might be, for all he knew, a police trap. He knew he was under suspicion, that he had been shadowed by that department of Scotland Yard which every crooked detective hates.

'We've got to take you well out of town before we give you this money, Mr Tetley,' the voice continued. (The second man never spoke throughout the whole journey until they struck the Great West Road, and he smoked all the time filling the close interior of the van with choking fumes.)

There was little conversation until then. Mr Tetley sat back in the comfortable armchair which had been placed in the back of the van, and wondered what could be more secret than this dark interior.

He was dealing with a class he did not know very well: his employers he was waiting the first opportunity to betray. He had his formula for such a situation. They would tell about the money they had paid him, but they could not produce credible proof. That was the formula before Terry had made his fatal pronouncement about the bank at Bradford. After that nothing much mattered except to squeeze a little extra bonus out of these foreigners.

He liked Kerky, he was swell. It was a word Mr Tetley was beginning to use, with a sense that he had learnt a new language. He tried it on one of his companions.

'Kerky's a swell fellow,' he said.

'Yeah,' said the man, 'swell.'

Mr Tetley lit a cigarette. By the light of it he saw his two companions: broad faced, clean shaven men wearing spotlessly white collars. One had a yellow tie with little green horseshoes on it; the other had a purple tie – eminently respectable men.

'Of course, I never knew anything about these shootings, and I haven't inquired into it too closely. I suppose there must have been some reason for it. Naturally, from my point of view it's very reprehensible…'

They let him talk, and he talked. Then the man who was driving drew aside the tarpaulin curtain and said something. Glancing out through the opening, Tetley saw that they were passing the little hostelry at the end of the Colnbrook bypass.

'Where are we going?' he asked.

'That's entirely a matter for you,' said one calmly. 'Tetley, you've gone yeller. Say, anybody who goes yeller is bad, but a copper who goes yeller is just plain dirt.'

There was a threat in the voice, something very ominous. Listening, Tetley heard the jacket of an automatic pulled back.

'What's the idea?' His voice was squeaky with fear.

'Keep quiet, will you! We're going to give you the works, that's what, Tetley. We're going to show the world just what yeller cops get when they fall apart.'

'You're not going to kill me?' he screamed.

The car slowed; somebody gripped him by the collar and dragged him out. Ordinarily he would have made a fight for it, but he was paralysed with the terrific horror of it.

The shrinking Leslie heard his first babbling protest...heard him scream. There were two shots, fired very deliberately. She saw something droop and fall with a thud on the sidewalk.

'Let's go,' said a voice, and the car moved on.

If its lights had not been dimmed they must have seen her, clinging to the gate in a frenzy of fear, with such a fierce grip that her hands bore the marks of the wire. She must not faint...she must just get right. She forced herself to look at the still figure on the grass covered sidewalk, Tetley... If only a car would come! She looked round: the lights of the little van that had brought the baggage of destruction had grown so dim that she could not distinguish them.

Then into view swung two great white lights. They came from the direction of the Bath road, and the car was moving slowly. She stepped into the middle of the road and held out both her arms, and, as the car stopped, dropped into the roadway almost under its wheels, in a dead faint.

She had not lost consciousness for more than a minute, for somebody was carrying her to the verge of the road when she opened her eyes.

'What's wrong? My God, it's Miss Ranger!'

There was no need to ask who the owner of that voice was. Jiggs was staring down at her.

'What's the matter? Where have you been?'

'In the country,' she said, and laughed weakly.

'We've been searching for you.'

He forced the neck of a little bottle against her lips. She swallowed and coughed. Jiggs, in his moments of recreation, favoured a particularly strong Bourbon.

'That'll do you no harm.'

Then she remembered, stared round and pointed. He could not see what she was pointing to, for the lights of his machine missed the heap on the sidewalk.

'What is it?' he asked, and, when she whispered: 'Tetley?' 'Can you stand?'

He lifted her up and propped her against the gatepost. From the gloom he called sharply to somebody else in the car – a police chauffeur, it proved to be – and the two men went forward.

'Get a policeman and an ambulance,' said Jiggs. 'I wondered how long it would be before this happened.'

'Is it Mr Tetley?' she asked with a shudder when he walked back to her.

Jiggs nodded.

'Yes, they put him on the spot. Would you believe it!'

She told him her own trouble. She wanted to get off this ghastly subject of death and murder, which was part of England's everyday life.

'Your car stalled on you?'

He went to his own machine, brought out a can of petrol and poured it into her tank.

'All right,' he said to the chauffeur as he was mounting his car. 'I'll take Miss Ranger to the police station and leave her there.'

She shook her head.

'I'll wait here. I really am not terribly worried.'

It was eerie, waiting in the darkness after the police car had gone, with that inert bundle of clothes only a few paces from her. Cars passed, unknowing of the tragedy. They stood together, Jiggs and the girl, their elbows resting on the gate, two idlers with apparently no interest in one another.

'We've been looking for you,' he said again. 'When Terry heard you'd been picked up in a car and driven away from your office he went crazy. The curious thing is that nobody seems to have seen you go, or who was driving you. Who was it?'

'Mrs Smith.'

'Not Cora!' he said in amazement.

'Yes, Cora.'

There was something in her tone which was very informative.

'Has she been trying to put one over on you?'

'I'll tell you later,' she said.

'Cora, eh?'

There was another long silence, and presently the lights of a car appeared over the bridge.

'There's our fellow…and here's the ambulance. Do ambulances have green lights? Yes, they do. I'll have to let the squad car take you back to town. If I were you I'd leave this flivver of yours where it stalled. I'll get the garage to collect it in the morning – anyway, it's their property. I'll have to stay behind and see what his poor devil can tell us.'

'Is he dead?' she asked.

'He'd be superhuman if he wasn't. I had one of my men put on the spot in exactly the same way and for exactly the same cause. It was way back in 'twenty seven, or it may have been 'twenty six. Anyway, it was BS.'

'What's BS?' she was forced to ask.

'Before the slump,' said Jiggs. 'Here they are.'

The ambulance brought a doctor. It had, as it happened, been waiting at the police station to furnish details of an accident that had occurred on the Bath road.

Three uniformed policemen got out of the squad car, and ambulance and squad car turned and focused their lights on what had started that day as a detective inspector of police. When the ambulance had gone:

'Come along young lady.'

Jiggs helped her into the car.

'You phoned to Inspector Weston?' he asked the driver.

'Yes, sir. He said he was very relieved.'

'That's about you,' said Jiggs, 'and not about Tetley.'

She was shocked.

'How callous you are, Captain Allerman!'

He smiled in the darkness.

'I'm going to be callous all my life about dead crooks,' he said. 'The moment I find myself getting sentimental over killers and legs, I'm going to quit being a policeman and join the nearest newspaper as a sob sister. You can't afford not to be callous about dirt, Miss Ranger. A dead crook's not finished – never forget that. His work's going on and on. Tetley's allowed his own pals to be killed, and maybe because of him we'll get a dozen other fellows put out of life before the week ends. So I shed no tears and hang no crêpe on my head. To me a dead murderer's no better than a live one, and when I start thinking he is, you don't know how sorry I'll be for myself!'

# 27

Cora sat through the interval after the first act without speaking a word.

'What's the matter with you?' asked Kerky.

She shook her head. Then, just as the curtain was going up for the second act of the play, she grasped his arm convulsively.

'Come outside, Kerky,' she said.

He followed her out into the vestibule, which was now empty.

'Remember that book, Kerky?' She could hardly bring herself to say the words; every syllable was an effort.

'Yeah.' He was prepared for what was coming.

'I didn't put it in the deposit. I meant to, but I didn't. It was in my bag...and I've lost my bag. I know where it is – I left it behind.'

Ultimately she told him of her crazy act of vengeance.

'I was mad with her...'

'Never mind about that,' he said quietly. 'Go back to the hotel, Cora.'

He snapped his fingers absent mindedly. A man who was watching him went away from the entrance of the theatre and came back in a few minutes with his car. He swung himself up by the side of the driver, and Kerky got in.

'West. Make for Slough and Maidenhead. Turn sharp right over the bridge.'

He pushed open the sliding window and sat back.

Dumb – that was all that was the matter with Cora, just dumb. He felt no bitterness, no resentment, just a little regret that he had to send her back home; for he was very proud of her, she was the gem of his collection, and he liked to think that he was envied by men.

But she wasn't as dumb as he. That was a cinch. Why keep an unmistakable record of the monies received from this new racket? Why put in black and white the rough draft of a gentlemen's agreement between himself and Eddie? Comparatively, Cora was intelligent. The girl chained to the wall would take a whole lot of explaining away. It brought him into the limelight, and that was a monstrous thing to do. If he could get there before somebody found her, he'd get himself out. He'd heard about this crazy escapade, and the moment Cora had told him… She hadn't spoken until they were in the theatre, and here was he in evening dress to prove it… He would apologise, offer her adequate compensation, possibly take her to Scotland Yard if she was obdurate.

He smoked half a cigarette and threw it away. As they flashed down the bypass he saw unmistakably an ambulance and a police car. He whistled softly; everything was going wrong tonight. Why in hell did they come this way, when they had the whole of London? He breathed heavily through his nose. Albuquerque Smith was not particularly happy with life as he found it.

He came to the house at last, saw the open window, and had a little shock. The key was still in the backdoor lock, and another dangling… That was Cora's way.

As he went into the house, he switched on the lights. He ran up the stairs, through the servant's room into the bathroom. There were the handcuffs, still fastened to the iron pipe. One of them was loose; the key was in that too. But there was no bag – of course there was no bag! This girl must have seen Cora put the keys in it. He searched every room, and then came out to the waiting car.

'I think we'll go home, James,' he said with a grin.

It was his gesture to Fate.

When he reached the hotel and went up to his room he found Cora lying on the bed just as he had left her, fully dressed, her head in her arms. He patted her gently on her bare shoulder.

'Stop that, baby,' he said. 'What's lost is lost.'

192

She turned round quickly and stared at him in dismay.

'Didn't you find the bag?'

He shook his head.

'I guess she took it with her as a souvenir.'

He took off his dress coat, collar and tie, and slipped on a dressing gown. There was just a chance. He reached for the phone and dialled Leslie Ranger's number, and, when he heard her voice:

'Thank God you're back! My fool wife told me about this ridiculous, crazy thing she'd done – I drove straight away down to the house to release you.'

She was a little staggered, but there was such sincerity in his tone that she believed him.

'I've only just got in,' she said. And then: 'Mr Smith... I have your wife's handbag.'

'Is that so?' he said softly. 'Perhaps you wouldn't mind if I came round and collected it?'

'I'll bring it in the morning,' she said.

'Say, Miss Ranger, you'd be doing me the greatest favour if you'd let me come round and apologise personally.'

It was a long time before she answered, and when she said, 'Yes, if you'll come right away,' he could have yelled at her responsiveness, if he had been a man who allowed his emotions full play. But he was not that kind of man.

He went back to his room, changed hastily and went out, not telling Cora where he was going. The elevator was up when he reached the flats, and he had to wait a minute until it came down. That minute was almost an eternity.

'Is Miss Ranger in?'

'Yes, sir, she's been in some little time.'

'Anybody with her?'

'No, sir, she's alone.'

'My name's Kerky Smith. You needn't mind telling anybody who asks whether I called.'

'I know your name, sir,' said the attendant.

'Sure you know my name,' Kerky Smith smiled. 'Your name's Appleton, detective sergeant, N Division, and you've been here three weeks.'

The elevator man was taken aback.

'I don't know where you got that idea from.'

'I heard it on the radio,' said Kerky Smith with great good humour.

When the door was opened he stood for a second outside. Not until Leslie invited him in did he follow, at a respectful distance. The bag was on the table; he picked it up and opened it. There was the book with the chain. The rest didn't matter. He was grateful, but…

A little dumb, this girl; not so dumb as Cora, but dumb. She could have called up Terry…she must have known a book with a chain cover meant something.

He crossed the pavement quickly to his car. His guard leapt up by the side of the driver.

'Jacky' – Kerky was speaking through the drawn glass screen which separated driver and passenger – 'that's a smart girl.'

'Sure she's smart,' said Jacky without turning his head.

'She could give us a lot of trouble, and I've got a hunch she will.'

'Yeah, that goes for me too,' said the guard. 'I don't like clever girls, I like 'em dumb.'

He turned over something in his mind.

'There'll be a squeal,' replied Kerky. 'Ain't there always?'

'I'm thinking of…' Jacky jerked his head. It was not in the direction of Berkeley Square, but Kerky knew whom he was talking about. He had forgotten Eddie. It would be very interesting to see what Eddie would do if Miss Leslie Ranger met with an accident one day.

At the same time, Kerky was not quite sure. The girl had given him back the book – that wasn't so clever. By the time he had reached the hotel he had almost decided to allow Leslie Ranger to live.

He found Cora exactly where he had left her, and threw the bag down by the side of her head. She heard the thud and looked round, recognised her bag with a little scream and opened it.

'Where's the book?' she asked tremulously.

'In my pocket.'

He took it out. The chain-mesh cover was his own idea, and he was rather proud of it. He had had a dozen little notebooks in that protective chainwork. This one he had bought in London.

'This goes in the safe deposit tomorrow, Cora. I'll put it in myself – if I don't burn it.'

That night he had a bad dream. He was standing in a steel pen before a judge, who was wearing a curious looking wig, and Terry was on the witness stand and had an open red book in his hand, from which he was reading most damning extracts. Kerky woke up in a sweat, got out of bed and put on the light. He passed his hand under his pillow and found the book where he had left it, immediately under his automatic. With a key he took from his pocket he unlocked the steel mesh, took the book into the dining room. The fire which had been burning when he went to bed still glowed. He threw the book in, opened a steel scuttle, and, taking out some kindling wood, threw it on top. Then he lit up the wood with paper, and sat watching until there was nothing in the grate but the red glow of the fire, momentarily rekindled to life, and the ashes of wood and paper.

'That's the best safe deposit,' he said, and, going back to bed, fell into a dreamless slumber.

Eddie Tanner came unannounced to breakfast. He came alone, without guard, passed the invisible cordon which surrounded Kerky, and walked into the sitting room with so firm a step that Kerky knew there was trouble.

'Before you start, kid, it wasn't my idea. Sit down and eat.'

'Whose idea was it?'

'It was altogether Cora's. Come in, kid, and tell Eddie you've been a bad girl.'

She came in in her *négligée*, beautiful to see. Eddie, who had seen her many times in the same attire, could not have rhapsodised even had he been called upon to do so.

'What did you do to Leslie yesterday?' he demanded.

She looked at Kerky and he nodded. Stumblingly, sulkily, and making as good a case for herself as she could, she told him. Eddie's face was a mask.

'You had a narrow escape, kid,' he said, quite pleasantly, 'and this is where we drop all interest in Miss Ranger. I've said it.'

'Dropped your interest, Eddie?'

He nodded.

'You know what you've been doing, don't you, Kerky – you and Cora? Pushing her right into Scotland Yard. She's got more brains than you and Cora combined. You won't ever believe that, but I'm telling you. And you're pushing her into the police business.'

'She can be pushed out,' said Kerky.

'Who'll do it?'

There was a challenge and a threat here. Eddie Tanner was not smiling. He was not pretending to be indifferent.

'Who's going to do the pushing out? Let's have his name, and he'll be deader than Tetley, and she knows how dead he was, because she saw him killed.'

The automatic smile came off Kerky's face.

'Says who?'

'I say it. She saw him spotted. She was standing by her car in a field when your guns put him out. Jiggs found her there. Does that make you laugh?'

It did not seem to amuse Mr Smith.

'If those boys had seen her there – '

'One of them would have been dead, probably two,' said Eddie. 'She had a gun – Cora's.'

'Where'd you get all this?' demanded Kerky with sudden fury. 'Standin' in with the police or sump'n', Eddie?'

Eddie's hand was in his pocket when he came into the room; it was there still. Kerky had almost forgotten this when he dropped his hand on to his thigh.

'Let us have a quiet morning, Kerky,' said Eddie softly. 'You're so near having nothing to think about – you don't know! I'm out of this racket.'

The devil came from Kerky's face and he beamed.

'The influence of a good woman, Eddie, same as in the pictures?'

'Something like that,' said Eddie. 'I'm out of it right now. Quick killings and quick movings are my motto.'

'Leaving me to hold the baby?'

'There isn't a baby to hold.'

'Now listen, Eddie, and don't get mad. You're fuller of news than a small town front page. Where did you get it?'

'Don't ask fool questions. I've been tipped off. I'm telling you, there's only one word that any sensible man can read in this situation, and that word is – slide!'

'Like hell I will!' said the other scornfully. 'You quit – you know your business. You've quit before, and I guess you'll go on quitting all your life.'

Eddie went quickly to the door. His companion thought for a moment that he had heard somebody outside, and this view was supported by the quickness with which he jerked open the door. In another second he had gone. Kerky could only stare at the door.

Cora had gone back to the bedroom. He went after her and stood looking at her for a time.

'Sally,' he said (when he called her Sally there was something doing), 'the *Leviathan* leaves at midnight. I'm going to phone making reservations for you. Have your maid pack your duds. You can drive to Southampton.'

'Listen – ' she began indignantly.

'I don't want to listen in case I hear you,' he said. 'Just do all the listening for once, will you?'

'You trying to get rid of me?'

'If I were trying to get rid of you, kid, I know fifty seven varieties of ways, and none of 'em sending you back to the USA in a swell suite. Wait in New York till you hear from me. Don't ask me a lot of fool questions – do as you're told.'

Just before she left she came in to see him, and she was perfectly calm and self possessed. He kissed her unemotionally, made her count

197

her money to see how much she had, and walked with her to the door, his arm around her.

'Listen, Kerky, when I'm in New York do you mind if I go around with Mike Harrigan, that boy who's working with Elstein?'

He grinned.

'Laying down a new carpet in the new home, are you?'

'Say, listen, Kerky – you know I wouldn't do any harm.'

'I know Mike wouldn't, if there was a cent in a dollar's chance of my coming west. All right, kid, run around, but don't flirt.'

From the window of his sitting room he watched the car go away from the front of the hotel, saw a little hand waving a handkerchief, and waved back, though he knew she could not see him.

'Swell kid, that,' he said, addressing the air, 'but dumb – gee, how dumb!'

There was a girl from Dallas, Texas, who had quite an elaborately furnished flat in Half Moon Street, and who lived without any apparent means of existence. Kerky got on the phone to her.

'Come round, will you, kid? I'm feeling kinda lonely.'

At midnight Cora put a telephone call through from the ship. Everything was lovely. The cabin was lovely, the sitting room was marvellous, the flowers were also marvellous. Kerky listened, his reserves of patience nearly used up.

'That's all right, kid. Have a swell time,' he said, and hung up the receiver with relief.

There were so many better things to do than to listen a lot of blah from a woman who had never had one original idea in her life.

# 28

The firm of Dorries was flourishing. Thirty two accounts, and heavy ones, had been opened in fourteen days. Leslie had to see the general manager of the bank with which they did business.

'You're doing remarkably well, young lady,' said that grizzled veteran of finance. 'Dorries have never had such a credit. Do you know what it amounts to?'

'I was staggered to find it was three quarters of a million,' said Leslie, 'and I'm getting a little scared. I know next to nothing about banking, and I can't understand why Mr Dorrie should have given me this responsible position.'

He looked at her shrewdly.

'I shouldn't think he'd made much of a mistake,' he said.

Leslie was clever, and had had a good business training, but there were departments of Dorries that took her quite out of her depth. Always it was the taciturn accountant who put her right again.

She neither saw nor heard from Dorrie or his partner, but one day at lunch she was talking to a girl who held an important position in a financial house, and when she returned to the office she sent for the accountant.

'Is it true that a month before I came Dorries were insolvent and were on the point of suspending payment, Mr Morris?'

He nodded.

'That's certainly true. They were refinanced. Mr Dorrie took in a new partner – well, as a matter of fact, he sold the business, and he himself has only a very slight interest in the firm.'

She shook her head.

'It bewilders me,' she said. 'Why are we becoming so suddenly prosperous? Why are people trusting us as agents to make huge shipments from abroad – there was one this morning. I saw the bill of lading for four thousand packages of cutlery. Do we sell cutlery?'

He smiled.

'No, Miss Ranger, but we are agents for people who sell cutlery. I expect you'll find a whole lot of orders which are difficult for you to understand, but you'll get into it.'

Always he told her, when she was puzzled, that she would 'get into it.'

If she had had a chief to whom she could go, if she had been assistant to somebody...but she was dazed to find that she was the virtual head of the business. She signed 'cheques for enormous amounts, arranged credits with American banking houses for sums which took her breath away; and all the time, day by day, money was pouring in.

With the actual receipt of cash she had no business or concern. She initialled day books, examined and approved statements, and for the first time she realised how valuable it was to be connected even with an insolvent firm that had created the machinery of exchange.

'What on earth do you do?' asked Terry.

It was the morning after her ugly adventure on the Colnbrook bypass.

'I do everything in this business except understand it,' she said ruefully.

He mentioned this to Jiggs.

'That sort of thing's always been a mystery to me, Terry, and always will remain so. High finance don't mean a darn thing in my young life. So far as I can understand, it means borrowing money from one feller and lending it to another, and making a rake-off between the rates of interest. But how it's done and who invented it, and how the fellers who do it escape conviction, why, that doesn't belong to my understanding either.'

On the previous afternoon, before the death of Tetley, the Government had decided to arrest and deport Kerky Smith, and it was on Jiggs' earnest pleading that they changed their plan.

'Don't put him out, keep him in. Shake this fellow's confidence, and we shake his organisation.'

Proof was almost immediately forthcoming that his view was an accurate one.

Kerky Smith was reading the morning newspapers in his sitting room. The waiter had just removed his breakfast things, and Kerky was at peace with the world. He had that sense of superiority which is the comfort of every general. Eddie Tanner was the cause of a certain uneasiness, but not much. Eddie had got cold feet, and was quitting just when the harvest was being gathered and the corn was at its ripest.

His valet came in from the bedroom.

'Kerky,' he said softly.

Smith looked up.

'The police raided your barber's this morning, took charge of all the phones and arrested Dinky. They've been tapping the wires for a week.'

Kerky screwed up his mouth as though he were going to whistle, but didn't.

'How do you know?'

'I got the wire,' said the other.

'I didn't think they knew the place,' said Kerky.

'They can't be dumb all the time,' said the other, and added: 'They found the safe.'

'There was nothing in it,' said Kerky quickly.

The valet shook his head.

'No, sir, it was cleared yesterday, but they knew it was there, and they've been questioning Dinky – how many letters he'd posted to America lately.'

'Who did the grilling?'

EDGAR WALLACE

'Jiggs. He had all the police out – all these London coppers – and him and Dinky had a session in that soundproof room...you know Jiggs.'

'I know Jiggs,' said the other between his teeth, 'and I know Dinky – he won't squeal.'

'Maybe,' said the valet.

He went noiselessly back into the bedroom.

Here was a serious situation. Dinky was one of the three treasurers of the organisation, paymaster, and a most ingenious bookkeeper. The little bookmaker's office upstairs had very lucky clients. Dinky sent packages of French and American currency to their American bankers by every mail. Men who called in to be shaved or have their hair trimmed went out much wealthier than they were when they arrived.

There was a tobacconist's in Kilburn where the same thing happened, except that the cellars went into a back room to inspect cigars, and came out satisfied.

'It was that shooting that started it,' said Kerky when the valet came in again. 'I'll have sump'n' to say to Eddie one of these days.'

'Is this the day you take advice?' asked the valet.

'Every day's that kind of day,' said Kerky.

'Well, leave him alone,' warned the man. 'Eddie's got a swell brain.'

'I'll take a look at it,' said Kerky.

'Guns fire both ways,' said the valet, and Kerky scowled up at him.

'What the hell's the matter with you today?'

'Noth'n'. Only I guess you're crazy to think that Scotland Yard doesn't mean anything. Nobody's so dumb they can't whistle.'

Kerky smiled.

'Have you got nothing to do but pull wisecracks?'

'I'm only sayin',' said the other carelessly.

A few minutes later Kerky, reading, heard the door open, and without looking up:

'Well?'

'Hullo, Kerky!' said a plaintive voice.

He sprang to his feet. It was Cora – Cora, to whom he had sent a mechanically affectionate radio message that morning.

202

'They took me off the boat, Kerky, just before it sailed. Two fellers come on, and a woman, and I had to pack and come ashore.'

'Police?' asked Kerky.

She nodded.

'Why didn't you phone?'

'I did. They gave me a phone, but I guess they were kidding to me. I got a message back that you were out.'

'What time was this?'

'Two o'clock this morning,' she said.

Kerky said nothing. He certainly was not out at two o'clock that morning.

'Why didn't they let you go? What did they say?'

'They said my passport wasn't in order.'

He was silent for a long time.

'All right, go into your room and take your hat off. I'll talk to you later. Don't come in till I send for you.'

She was hardly out of the room before he put through a call to an address in Half Moon Street, and, when it was answered:

'That date's off – Cora's back.'

He replaced the receiver very deliberately. If they wouldn't let Cora out of the country what chance had he got of leaving in a normal and legitimate way? They couldn't hold him if he wanted to go. He'd be in Paris in two hours in the aeroplane which waited day and night to take him. It was worrying. It was more than this, it was threatening. He was glad now that he had burnt the book. Suppose they raided and searched in the middle of the night…that would not have been amusing.

Jiggs, eh? He would attend to Jiggs. That guy had been a nightmare to him for years. Once he had thought he had him straightened, but you couldn't straighten Jiggs. He was one of those crazy people who didn't care about money. He had plenty. A grateful banker, who had once been kidnapped and held to ransom, and rescued at a particularly horrifying moment, had not only given Jiggs a large sum, but he invested it wisely and had sold his stock at the top. All the world knew Jiggs had this money. It had been presented to him at a public banquet, and Jiggs in response had made the worst and the most ungracious speech that has ever been made on such an occasion.

He would attend to Jiggs. It would be the last act of his before he quit – the peak of his accomplishment.

Troubles came in a rush that morning. His valet, who was a link between Kerky and the organisation, came with really serious news. 'The other fellows' had refused to 'cut.' Fifty-fifty had been the arrangement on all transactions. It was true that this had not been faithfully observed by Kerky and his treasurer, but a very large sum had come in from a man who held an important position in the City, so important that when the police came to know his name, which they did eventually, they gasped. That a man of his character should have meekly submitted to the blackmail was unthinkable. But headquarters had many shocks in the days when the gangs dominated London.

A demand for a share had gone forward; it had been curtly refused, on the ground that the Green section had made its demand before the amalgamation. Through the subterranean channel Kerky sent a message to Eddie Tanner. They met that morning in the widest open space of Hyde Park. Without guns, was the agreement, but both men carried an automatic under the armpit.

'One of these aides of yours is making a bit of trouble,' said Kerky.

'So they tell me.'

'Make it right, will you, Eddie? You're a square shooter, and this thing's got to be carried out on the level.'

'You've been holding up on me, Kerky,' said Tanner. 'Maybe you don't know it.'

'Why, Eddie!' said the other reproachfully.

Tanner smiled, named three cases in rapid succession, and Kerky knew he was speaking no more than the truth.

'You can take the lot from now on, Kerky. I'm out of it. I thought it was the grandest racket that had ever been put over, ad maybe it is. But I'm through.'

'Sure you're through!' sneered the other. 'You weren't so sure of Elijah's money – '

'Let's not talk about it, shall we, Kerky?... So long!'

He turned and walked off. Kerky could have shot him, but he knew other eyes, those of his henchmen, were watching from a distance. Both of them were under police observation, but that didn't matter. Eddie's guns were in the park, and all the time he had been speaking he had felt himself covered. There was no other way ...

When he got back to his hotel he found the radiant Cora looking a little agitated.

'Where's Jacky?' he asked. 'I want to see him. You go to your room.'

'Jacky's gone,' she said. 'Oh, Kerky, they came and took him... That...Jiggs.'

'Arrested?' Kerky blinked at her.

She nodded.

'Is that so?'

They could have arrested Jacky, they could have arrested his barber-treasurer, and he would not have been worried – but Jiggs.

In a sense the two chieftains of his organisation had gone, and they were in bad hands. Kerky was quick to recognise a desperate situation when he saw it. Within half an hour the two men had been replaced.

There was another worrying factor. London, which had at first been shocked, then dazed, was now raging. There was an electric something in the air which Kerky, sensitive to impressions, could feel.

He took his lunch in his room, sent a message to the secret airport where his plane was waiting, and, going downstairs, interviewed the head waiter.

'I'm giving a big dinner here next Wednesday,' he said. 'There'll be fifty covers, and I want you to get me a menu for a prince!'

The head waiter wriggled his satisfaction.

Kerky drove openly to Bond Street, did some ostentatious shopping, and the detectives who watched him reported to the lean, rugged faced American in his little office at Scotland Yard.

'Fine,' said Jiggs, and gave an order.

When Kerky returned to the hotel it was within half an hour of lunchtime. Cora was not in her room, and he rang the bell.

'Where's Mrs Smith' he demanded of the floor waiter who came.

'She's gone, sir. Two gentlemen came for her and took her away...
I think they were police. Captain Allerman was with them.'

Very nearly the best lawyer in London called at Scotland Yard for
information. It was politely refused. A canvass of the police stations
revealed the presence of neither Cora nor Jacky.

That afternoon there was delivered at No. 10 Downing Street, a
notice printed in red, of a familiar character. It demanded no money,
but an indemnity for all who had taken part in 'recent disturbances,' a
free pardon, and facilities for all concerned to leave England within
seven days.

'Kerky's on the run,' said Jiggs when he read the communication.

He rested his head in his hands for a while, then looked up.

'What's the Prime Minister doing right away? What public
engagements has he got?'

'He's opening a new technical college on the Thames
Embankment.'

'Is that inside the City or out?' asked Jiggs quickly.

'It's inside the City limits.'

'Just inside the City limits. I see the grand idea,' said Jiggs.

'The Chief Constable wants the Prime Minister to cancel the
engagement.'

'Cancel nothing,' said Jiggs. 'Let him go through with it – nothing
will happen to him, believe me!'

Terry smiled ruefully.

'I wish we could be as sure,' he said.

All London knew of the threat to the Prime Minister. All London
seemed to concentrate upon the Embankment that day. Every
available police officer was required, not only to control the crowd,
but to form the guard which Scotland Yard considered necessary.

Downing Street and part of Whitehall were closed from the
moment the threat was received. From early morning it seemed that
every train that emptied itself in the central area carried nothing but
uniformed men.

Jiggs spent an hour at his window in Scotland Yard watching
the amazing scene. Westminster Bridge was black with people. By

ten o'clock all traffic across that bridge and Blackfriars was suspended. The Strand and the approaches to Trafalgar Square were cut off by police orders.

The congestion in other parts of Central London was indescribable. Leslie Ranger took an hour and a half to reach her office, and arrived there to find the old head clerk in a state of gloomy agitation.

'Those accounts have been closed, miss – thirty two of them, and they're all drawing their money in American currency.'

She stared at him.

'What does that mean?' she asked.

Mr Morris, the suave accountant, was in no sense agitated.

'It's quite a usual thing. These accounts are carried on behalf of a number of gentlemen who are forming a syndicate. They've decided to put all their capital into the company – that is to say, into one account. They've merely asked us for their cash balance, which is not at all unusual.' He smiled again. 'If we hadn't got the money, Miss Ranger, it would be a serious thing, but fortunately we have. I'll go round to the bank and negotiate the exchange.'

He brought it to her just before lunch: a huge leather bag which she put away in the steel safe let into a wall of her room.

'Does this mean Dorries is broke again?' she asked in dismay.

He shook his head.

'No, Dorries is perfectly solvent. There's a sum of fifty thousand to the company's credit. It only means that we've lost a few customers who are in reality one customer, and there are certain orders from abroad which we have to cancel on behalf of clients; but you needn't feel perturbed about it, Miss Ranger.'

He looked her straight in the eye.

'There's a balance of forty nine thousand pounds, to be exact. The rent of the premises is paid, and there's a sufficient sum to pay all the staff a year's wages in a special account.' And then: 'You're not going down to see the Prime Minister open the technical college?'

She shook her head.

'Do you think anything will happen to him?'

'I shouldn't think so. But one never knows, with the condition London is in at the moment, what may happen. But there seem to be enough police in the West End to deal with any disturbance.'

The ceremony was to take place at two o'clock. At five minutes to two Leslie was in her office, scribbling the draft of a letter she was sending to an insurance company. The accountant's office was next to hers, and there was a communicating door. She had paused to find a right word, when she heard a sharp crack, as though the accountant had pulled down his window rather violently. She listened; and then, for no particular reason, she opened the door.

'Is anything –' she began, and stopped, frozen with horror.

The accountant sprawled across his desk. His white blotting pad was red. And over him stood Kerky Smith.

There was another man in the room, a little man with dark, piercing eyes. He stood near the door which led to the outer office.

'Don't scream, young lady.'

He jerked his head to his companion.

'Get out.'

The little man went noiselessly.

'Don't scream,' said Kerky Smith again, and came towards her.

She backed into her office, and he followed, closing the door.

'You've got a bag in that safe. Just let me have it, will you?'

She was incapable of speech, and could only shake her head.

'You'll be a wise kid if you don't give me trouble, Miss Ranger. Eddie's been banking here, hasn't he? I wondered what made him buy this bum business – wanted a hide-away for the dough. Well, he's got it.'

'Mr Tanner has nothing to do with this business,' she began, and he grinned.

'He's Dorries – and how! Open that safe, or give me the key.'

She shook her head. She stood with her back to the drawer of the desk where the keys were.

'If you scream I'll croak you…don't want to kill a woman if I can possibly help it, though Eddie would have snuffed out Cora like that!'

He snapped his disengaged fingers. 'Eddie's quit, but he's not going to quit with this.' He waved his hand to the safe.

The door of the outer office opened and closed violently. Eddie Tanner was there, his face red. There was a gun in his hand. With a quick jerk of his arm Kerky pulled the girl towards him. His arm went round her, shoulder to shoulder, so that she covered him; and as he did so he fired twice.

Eddie Tanner stumbled down on his knees, and the gun dropped from his hand. Flinging the girl from him, Kerky jerked open the drawer, and in another few seconds the safe was open and the bag in his hand. He was halfway to the door, when he heard three shots fired, and doubled back.

'I want you, Kerky.'

It was Jiggs. The two guns exploded together. From the accountant's room three men came running in. One caught Kerky as he staggered; the other two fired together.

Leslie crouched in a corner, watching the duel with terrified eyes. Jiggs was firing with both hands. Two men sprawled on the carpet. Kerky alone remained erect. His gun had jammed; he pulled another. As it came up, the two shots sounded like one.

'Got you,' said Jiggs.

Albuquerque Smith reeled against the wall, clutched at the sill and slid down to the floor.

'For luck,' said Jiggs, and fired again…

Three surgeons were busy with Captain Jiggs Allerman far into the night, and such was the vitality of the man that on the third day he was sitting up in bed, a jubilant, chortling wreck of a man, though there were two bullets in his body that had not yet been extracted.

'I ain't going to die, believe me! The day Alburquerque could kill Chicago is so far ahead in the calendar that you'd lose your eyesight looking for it. Sure I knew Dorries was a front. Eddie bought it because he wanted a safe cache for his money. He put in your young lady because he trusted her. The accountant was his treasurer, and one of the best gunmen that ever sidestepped the chair. He could do more with a sawn-off shotgun than any other man could do with a rod. I've been watching Dorries for a long time, ever since Miss Ranger went there, and I knew the day was coming when Kerky would go after that money.

'Double crossing was so natural to him that if he went straight he would die. I'll hand it to Kerky: that letter to the Prime Minister was an inspiration. He knew he'd get not only all the Metropolitan police, but all the City coppers concentrated in one area, and leave himself free to deal with Austin Friars. He'd have got away so easy, too, if Eddie hadn't been so soft and come streaking down to the City. Poor old Eddie, he's got his. I liked Eddie, he was a swell guy. He never shot a man in the back all his born days. Seen his will, Terry? I guess it will interest you…no, I haven't seen it, but I can guess it.'

He caught Leslie's eye and winked.

'Swell guy, Eddie,' he said again. 'He wasn't in the racket for money, but just because he was a natural born enemy of law, order, progress, and a quiet life. Killed his uncle? Sure he killed his uncle. I took a crack at him once myself when he was in Chicago. I'll tell you about it one of these days.'

'Why was he trying to get out of it?' asked Terry. 'Was he scared?'

Jiggs shook his head, winced, and defiantly shook his head again.

'You couldn't scare Eddie.'

This time he avoided Leslie's eyes.

'I guess that guy fell in love. That sounds unnatural, but he did. It might happen to anybody.'

An anxious nurse bent over him.

'You mustn't talk any more, Captain Allerman,' she said.

He scowled up at her.

'Not talk any more?' he growled. 'What's the matter with me – dead or sump'n'?'

# EDGAR WALLACE

## BIG FOOT

Footprints and a dead woman bring together Superintendent Minton and the amateur sleuth Mr Cardew. Who is the man in the shrubbery? Who is the singer of the haunting Moorish tune? Why is Hannah Shaw so determined to go to Pawsy, 'a dog lonely place' she had previously detested? Death lurks in the dark and someone must solve the mystery before BIG FOOT strikes again, in a yet more fiendish manner.

## BONES IN LONDON

The new Managing Director of Schemes Ltd has an elegant London office and a theatrically dressed assistant – however Bones, as he is better known, is bored. Luckily there is a slump in the shipping market and it is not long before Joe and Fred Pole pay Bones a visit. They are totally unprepared for Bones' unnerving style of doing business, unprepared for his unique style of innocent and endearing mischief.

# EDGAR WALLACE

## BONES OF THE RIVER

'Taking the little paper from the pigeon's leg, Hamilton saw it was from Sanders and marked URGENT. *Send Bones instantly to Lujamalababa... Arrest and bring to head-quarters the witch doctor.*'

It is a time when the world's most powerful nations are vying for colonial honour, a time of trading steamers and tribal chiefs. In the mysterious African territories administered by Commissioner Sanders, Bones persistently manages to create his own unique style of innocent and endearing mischief.

## THE DAFFODIL MYSTERY

When Mr Thomas Lyne, poet, poseur and owner of Lyne's Emporium insults a cashier, Odette Rider, she resigns. Having summoned detective Jack Tarling to investigate another employee, Mr Milburgh, Lyne now changes his plans. Tarling and his Chinese companion refuse to become involved. They pay a visit to Odette's flat. In the hall Tarling meets Sam, convicted felon and protégé of Lyne. Next morning Tarling discovers a body. The hands are crossed on the breast, adorned with a handful of daffodils.

# EDGAR WALLACE

## THE JOKER

While the millionaire Stratford Harlow is in Princetown, not only does he meet with his lawyer Mr Ellenbury but he gets his first glimpse of the beautiful Aileen Rivers, niece of the actor and convicted felon Arthur Ingle. When Aileen is involved in a car accident on the Thames Embankment, the driver is James Carlton of Scotland Yard. Later that evening Carlton gets a call. It is Aileen. She needs help.

## THE SQUARE EMERALD

'Suicide on the left,' says Chief Inspector Coldwell pleasantly, as he and Leslie Maughan stride along the Thames Embankment during a brutally cold night. A gaunt figure is sprawled across the parapet. But Coldwell soon discovers that Peter Dawlish, fresh out of prison for forgery, is not considering suicide but murder. Coldwell suspects Druze as the intended victim. Maughan disagrees. If Druze dies, she says, 'It will be because he does not love children!'

## OTHER TITLES BY EDGAR WALLACE AVAILABLE DIRECT
## FROM HOUSE OF STRATUS

| Quantity | | £ | $(US) | $(CAN) | € |
|---|---|---|---|---|---|
| | THE ADMIRABLE CARFEW | 6.99 | 11.50 | 15.99 | 11.50 |
| | THE ANGEL OF TERROR | 6.99 | 11.50 | 15.99 | 11.50 |
| | THE AVENGER | 6.99 | 11.50 | 15.99 | 11.50 |
| | BARBARA ON HER OWN | 6.99 | 11.50 | 15.99 | 11.50 |
| | BIG FOOT | 6.99 | 11.50 | 15.99 | 11.50 |
| | THE BLACK ABBOT | 6.99 | 11.50 | 15.99 | 11.50 |
| | BONES | 6.99 | 11.50 | 15.99 | 11.50 |
| | BONES IN LONDON | 6.99 | 11.50 | 15.99 | 11.50 |
| | BONES OF THE RIVER | 6.99 | 11.50 | 15.99 | 11.50 |
| | THE CLUE OF THE NEW PIN | 6.99 | 11.50 | 15.99 | 11.50 |
| | THE CLUE OF THE SILVER KEY | 6.99 | 11.50 | 15.99 | 11.50 |
| | THE CLUE OF THE TWISTED CANDLE | 6.99 | 11.50 | 15.99 | 11.50 |
| | THE COAT OF ARMS | 6.99 | 11.50 | 15.99 | 11.50 |
| | THE COUNCIL OF JUSTICE | 6.99 | 11.50 | 15.99 | 11.50 |
| | THE CRIMSON CIRCLE | 6.99 | 11.50 | 15.99 | 11.50 |
| | THE DAFFODIL MYSTERY | 6.99 | 11.50 | 15.99 | 11.50 |
| | THE DARK EYES OF LONDON | 6.99 | 11.50 | 15.99 | 11.50 |
| | THE DAUGHTERS OF THE NIGHT | 6.99 | 11.50 | 15.99 | 11.50 |
| | A DEBT DISCHARGED | 6.99 | 11.50 | 15.99 | 11.50 |
| | THE DEVIL MAN | 6.99 | 11.50 | 15.99 | 11.50 |
| | THE DOOR WITH SEVEN LOCKS | 6.99 | 11.50 | 15.99 | 11.50 |
| | THE DUKE IN THE SUBURBS | 6.99 | 11.50 | 15.99 | 11.50 |
| | THE FACE IN THE NIGHT | 6.99 | 11.50 | 15.99 | 11.50 |
| | THE FEATHERED SERPENT | 6.99 | 11.50 | 15.99 | 11.50 |
| | THE FLYING SQUAD | 6.99 | 11.50 | 15.99 | 11.50 |
| | THE FORGER | 6.99 | 11.50 | 15.99 | 11.50 |
| | THE FOUR JUST MEN | 6.99 | 11.50 | 15.99 | 11.50 |
| | FOUR SQUARE JANE | 6.99 | 11.50 | 15.99 | 11.50 |

ALL HOUSE OF STRATUS BOOKS ARE AVAILABLE FROM GOOD BOOKSHOPS
OR DIRECT FROM THE PUBLISHER:

Internet:   www.houseofstratus.com including author interviews, reviews, features.

Email:   sales@houseofstratus.com please quote author, title and credit card details.

# OTHER TITLES BY EDGAR WALLACE AVAILABLE DIRECT
## FROM HOUSE OF STRATUS

| Quantity | | £ | $(US) | $(CAN) | € |
|---|---|---|---|---|---|
| | THE FOURTH PLAGUE | 6.99 | 11.50 | 15.99 | 11.50 |
| | THE FRIGHTENED LADY | 6.99 | 11.50 | 15.99 | 11.50 |
| | GOOD EVANS | 6.99 | 11.50 | 15.99 | 11.50 |
| | THE HAND OF POWER | 6.99 | 11.50 | 15.99 | 11.50 |
| | THE IRON GRIP | 6.99 | 11.50 | 15.99 | 11.50 |
| | THE JOKER | 6.99 | 11.50 | 15.99 | 11.50 |
| | THE JUST MEN OF CORDOVA | 6.99 | 11.50 | 15.99 | 11.50 |
| | THE KEEPERS OF THE KING'S PEACE | 6.99 | 11.50 | 15.99 | 11.50 |
| | THE LAW OF THE FOUR JUST MEN | 6.99 | 11.50 | 15.99 | 11.50 |
| | THE LONE HOUSE MYSTERY | 6.99 | 11.50 | 15.99 | 11.50 |
| | THE MAN WHO BOUGHT LONDON | 6.99 | 11.50 | 15.99 | 11.50 |
| | THE MAN WHO KNEW | 6.99 | 11.50 | 15.99 | 11.50 |
| | THE MAN WHO WAS NOBODY | 6.99 | 11.50 | 15.99 | 11.50 |
| | THE MIND OF MR J G REEDER | 6.99 | 11.50 | 15.99 | 11.50 |
| | MORE EDUCATED EVANS | 6.99 | 11.50 | 15.99 | 11.50 |
| | MR J G REEDER RETURNS | 6.99 | 11.50 | 15.99 | 11.50 |
| | MR JUSTICE MAXELL | 6.99 | 11.50 | 15.99 | 11.50 |
| | RED ACES | 6.99 | 11.50 | 15.99 | 11.50 |
| | ROOM 13 | 6.99 | 11.50 | 15.99 | 11.50 |
| | SANDERS | 6.99 | 11.50 | 15.99 | 11.50 |
| | SANDERS OF THE RIVER | 6.99 | 11.50 | 15.99 | 11.50 |
| | THE SINISTER MAN | 6.99 | 11.50 | 15.99 | 11.50 |
| | THE SQUARE EMERALD | 6.99 | 11.50 | 15.99 | 11.50 |
| | THE THREE JUST MEN | 6.99 | 11.50 | 15.99 | 11.50 |
| | THE THREE OAK MYSTERY | 6.99 | 11.50 | 15.99 | 11.50 |
| | THE TRAITOR'S GATE | 6.99 | 11.50 | 15.99 | 11.50 |
| | WHEN THE WORLD STOPPED | 6.99 | 11.50 | 15.99 | 11.50 |

**Hotline:** UK ONLY: 0800 169 1780, please quote author, title and credit card details.
INTERNATIONAL: +44 (0) 20 7494 6400, please quote author, title and
credit card details.

**Send to:** **House of Stratus Sales Department**
**24c Old Burlington Street**
**London**
**W1X 1RL**
**UK**

Please allow for postage costs charged per order plus an amount per book as set out in the tables below:

| | £(Sterling) | $(US) | $(CAN) | €(Euros) |
|---|---|---|---|---|
| **Cost per order** | | | | |
| UK | 2.00 | 3.00 | 4.50 | 3.30 |
| Europe | 3.00 | 4.50 | 6.75 | 5.00 |
| North America | 3.00 | 4.50 | 6.75 | 5.00 |
| Rest of World | 3.00 | 4.50 | 6.75 | 5.00 |
| **Additional cost per book** | | | | |
| UK | 0.50 | 0.75 | 1.15 | 0.85 |
| Europe | 1.00 | 1.50 | 2.30 | 1.70 |
| North America | 2.00 | 3.00 | 4.60 | 3.40 |
| Rest of World | 2.50 | 3.75 | 5.75 | 4.25 |

PLEASE SEND CHEQUE, POSTAL ORDER (STERLING ONLY), EUROCHEQUE, OR INTERNATIONAL MONEY ORDER (PLEASE CIRCLE METHOD OF PAYMENT YOU WISH TO USE)
MAKE PAYABLE TO: STRATUS HOLDINGS plc

Cost of book(s): —————————— Example: 3 x books at £6.99 each: £20.97

Cost of order: —————————— Example: £2.00 (Delivery to UK address)

Additional cost per book: —————— Example: 3 x £0.50: £1.50

Order total including postage: ———— Example: £24.47

Please tick currency you wish to use and add total amount of order:

☐ £ (Sterling)　　☐ $ (US)　　☐ $ (CAN)　　☐ € (EUROS)

VISA, MASTERCARD, SWITCH, AMEX, SOLO, JCB:

☐☐☐☐☐☐☐☐☐☐☐☐☐☐☐☐☐☐☐

**Issue number (Switch only):**

☐☐☐

**Start Date:**　　　　　　**Expiry Date:**

☐☐/☐☐　　　　　☐☐/☐☐

**Signature:** ————————————

**NAME:** ————————————————

**ADDRESS:** ————————————————

————————————————

**POSTCODE:** —————————

Please allow 28 days for delivery.

Prices subject to change without notice.
Please tick box if you do not wish to receive any additional information. ☐

House of Stratus publishes many other titles in this genre; please check our website (**www.houseofstratus.com**) for more details.